DREAMERS
OFTEN LIE

DREAMERS
OFTEN LIE

JACQUELINE
WEST

DIAL BOOKS

DIAL BOOKS
An imprint of Penguin Random House LLC
375 Hudson Street
New York, NY 10014

Library of Congress Cataloging-in-Publication Data
Names: West, Jacqueline, date, author.
Title: Dreamers often lie / Jacqueline West.
Description: New York, NY : Dial Books, [2016] | Summary: "After waking up in the hospital, Jaye returns to school to discover a mysteriously familiar boy in her class and the trappings of Shakespeare's plays all around her" — Provided by publisher.
Identifiers: LCCN 2015031235 | ISBN 9780803738638 (hardback)
Subjects: | CYAC: Love—Fiction. | Brain damage—Fiction. | Theater—Fiction. | Shakespeare, William, 1564–1616—Fiction. | BISAC: JUVENILE FICTION / Love & Romance. | JUVENILE FICTION / Social Issues / Depression & Mental Illness. | JUVENILE FICTION / Performing Arts / Theater.
Classification: LCC PZ7.W51776 Dr 2016 | DDC [Fic]—dc23
LC record available at http://lccn.loc.gov/2015031235

Printed in the United States of America

10   9   8   7   6   5   4   3   2   1

Design by Jennifer Kelly
Text set in Walbaum MT Std

For Ryan

ROMEO: I dreamt a dream tonight.

MERCUTIO: And so did I.

ROMEO: Well, what was yours?

MERCUTIO: That dreamers often lie.

—*Romeo and Juliet*, ACT I, SCENE IV

PROLOGUE

There was blood on the snow.

White, with a smattering of red. Like petals.

One petal was stuck to my lips. I could feel it dissolving with my breath, its rusty sweetness coating my tongue.

My cheek hurt. Everything hurt.

And the sun was too bright. It seared through my eyelids, making my whole skull clench. I tried to turn my face away, but I couldn't. I tested my fingers, my feet. Nothing moved. Maybe it was the cold, or the tight-packed snow, or that I felt only halfway inside of myself, like my body was a costume I hadn't finished putting on. I just kept still, watching as the roses bloomed through the whiteness around me, their red petals growing larger.

I don't know how long I'd been lying there when someone lifted my hand.

I squinted up.

Flares of sun erased his edges. I could make out a pair of pale eyes. Tangled black hair. The brightness made my head pound.

What's going on? I tried to ask. *How did we get here? Why is half of my face on fire?* But all that came out was a groan.

"She speaks!" His voice was deep and warm. "Oh, speak again, bright angel!"

No one with blue eyes and tousled black hair had ever called me an angel.

Wait—I knew that line. Was this a play? Were we rehearsing something?

He was still holding my hand.

I blinked up at him as he raised my hand to his lips and kissed the back of my wrist.

That's nice, I thought. *Old-fashioned. A little dramatic. But nice.* And there was something familiar about it. We must have practiced this before.

The world went diamond-bright and silent. My cue. What was my line? I scrambled after the thread of it. *Stay— Stay—* Something about hands. Something about light.

My arm settled back into the snow.

Too late. He was already gone.

Scene over.

The smell of roses grew stronger. The ground sagged, the whiteness sinking until the hole around me was so deep that it took a whole crowd to hoist me out.

Jaye, said a new voice. *Stay with me.*

Lots of hands lifted me. Lots of hands laid me down.

The place where they put me was thin and hard and narrow. It rattled as they rushed it over the snow. What scene was this? What was I supposed to do now?

A metal door slammed.

The white sun switched off and a red light switched on. It spun like a spoon in a glass full of blood.

Jaye. Come on, Jaye. Stay with me.

A knot of people twisted around me, faces looming closer, disappearing. The ground beneath me roared. Something in my head roared with it.

Hang on, Jaye. Stay with me.

But the cold had snipped and sliced at me until there was nothing left to feel it.

The petals rained over me, red and weightless.

I closed my eyes.

They buried me.

CHAPTER 1

My eyes started to open without my permission.

I fought to keep them shut. The second I opened them, I'd be sucked up into the tooth-brushing, clothes-finding rush to school, searching for my algebra textbook, remembering the assignment I'd skipped when I got caught up in the Hitchcock marathon on AMC. By the time I staggered downstairs, everyone else would be dressed, flushed and glowing from their early-morning runs and showers, and I'd still have pillow creases on my face and a flat spot in my hair.

I tried to wriggle down into my rumpled purple quilt.

But this morning, the quilt was tucked with weird severity across my chest. And someone—probably Mom—had already come into my room and opened the thick velvet curtains I'd made with scraps from the costume shop.

Mom must have turned on the lights too, which meant I'd *really* overslept. The glow that fell over me wasn't the chilly blue of dawn. It wasn't even the paler blue that meant I'd already hit snooze twice. This light was yellow and electric and ugly, and it was prying at my eyelids like a butter knife.

I flung out a hand and groped for the alarm.

But the alarm hadn't buzzed.

And my arm didn't move.

I opened my eyes.

This was definitely not my bedroom.

This room was spotless. Its tile floor gleamed. Its windows sparkled behind half-closed blinds. The walls were bare. No theater posters, no doodles, no collages of ticket stubs and quotes from Ibsen and Tennessee Williams. The sheets around me were as clean as printer paper. Everything was coated with that ugly yellow light.

That light. And that smell.

I knew that smell.

Liquid soap. Rubbing alcohol. Bodies.

Bodies that leaked and sweated and bled things that should have been kept sealed inside.

The hospital smell.

My throat constricted.

In the usual nightmare, I'd be running through the maze of hospital halls, veering around corners, looking desperately for the right room. Sometimes, just as I spotted the door, a blockade of nurses would appear and tell me that only family was allowed inside, and when I said I *was* family, no one would believe me. Sometimes I never found the door at all. I always woke from these dreams with my legs cramped and tired, my heart pounding.

But this time, I was the one in the bed.

This time, the needle was in my arm. The machines beeped along to my own pulse.

This was wrong. This made no sense.

Might as well sink deeper and start again.

The darkness lashed out. It wound around me, tightening, pulling. I felt the bed tilt, my head rising, feet falling, until I slid straight out of the sheets into something covered in prickly upholstery.

When I looked up again, a long, empty stage stretched in front of me. Its red velvet curtains were bleached by the beam of a spotlight.

Yes.

Yes.

This was where I was meant to be. In the high school auditorium, waiting for rehearsal to start.

The panic of the dream flowed out of me. Happiness gushed into its place, bringing everything else with it. The sight of the cast list. *TITANIA, the FAIRY QUEEN—Jaye Stuart* printed there in big black letters, and still I had to read it six times to believe it. The sensation of the battered paperback script in my hands, all my gorgeous lines highlighted in ribbons of green ink.

I bounced in the creaky seat.

Where was everybody?

Tom and Nikki almost always beat me to the auditorium. By the time I got here, they'd be deep in some project, sketching makeup designs, arguing over the pronunciation of the word *zounds*. Crew members came even earlier, opening the curtains, flipping on the work lights. But now there was no one.

I craned around. Behind me, rows of empty seats dwindled upward into shadows. Except for that single burning spotlight, the entire house was dark. I was about to get up for a better look around when there was a soft creak to my left.

I turned, expecting to see Nikki or Tom. Maybe Anders or Hannah. Some other friend. *Not Pierce Caplan,* I told myself, before the beating in my chest could get too hopeful. *Don't even think about Pierce Caplan.*

But the person in the next seat wasn't anyone I knew.

I recognized him anyway.

He had sunken cheeks, and a sharp, stubbly jaw. His hair looked like it had been through several nights of bad sleep. He was dressed all in black, so every part of him but his head and his hands seemed to seep into the surrounding dimness. There was a prop human skull in his lap.

He stared straight at me.

"Hello," I said slowly.

"Hello." Hamlet's voice was low and polite. "Are you here for the play?"

"For rehearsal? Yes. But we're doing *A Midsummer*

Night's Dream." I glanced down at the yellowish skull. "I think you're waiting for the wrong show."

He shook his head. "I'm only here to watch."

"Oh." I pulled my eyes away from the skull. "Well, we're just getting started, so there won't be much to see. Unless you really love high school drama." I smiled. "The offstage kind, I mean."

Hamlet didn't smile back. "How so?"

"The usual stupidness. Someone likes someone who doesn't like them back. Somebody gets a part that somebody else wanted. A bunch of the senior girls are mad that a junior—meaning me—gets to play Titania. A bunch of the theater kids are mad that a guy who's never done a play before gets to be Oberon . . ."

"But you are not mad."

"Me?" I turned to face him head-on. Hamlet's eyes were like cracked ice. "Not really. No."

"No." Now Hamlet began to smile. It was a knowing, lopsided smile. It made the skin of my arms prickle. "Why should Titania cross her Oberon?"

I've honed a giant repertoire of expressions in my bedroom mirror. *Morose. Effervescent. Smitten. Terrified.* I can leap from one end of the spectrum to the other, pull off layers of strange combinations. It's like having a thousand disguises that I can take with me anywhere. Now I smoothed my face into my innocent/nonchalant expression, the expression that said I didn't care that Pierce

Caplan—perfect, golden, untouchable Pierce—was playing my husband in *A Midsummer Night's Dream.*

"We should really be getting started," I said. "I wonder where everybody is . . ."

I craned around to search the house again. I could still feel Hamlet's cracked-ice stare numbing my skin. I didn't think he had blinked yet.

"God has given you one face, and you make yourself another," he said at last, so softly that I wasn't sure I'd actually heard him. When I glanced back, he was spinning the skull in a slow circle in his lap.

I put a little more space between us.

Hamlet stiffened suddenly. "*Shh.* Listen."

"I don't hear anything."

He lifted the skull on one palm. Its features glinted in the semidarkness. "Do you know him?"

The skull's empty eye sockets stared back at me. The crest of its forehead was ridged and uneven, one large crack spidering over the bumps of bone. Its grinning teeth were slightly crooked, some edges worn flat, others tilted inward. Too much detail for a prop.

I swallowed hard. "No. I don't know him." The twinge in my neck crept up into my own skull, opening like the petals of a flower. I could feel it pulse behind my right eye.

"He wants to speak to you." Hamlet's face was serious. Almost tender. Like he was lifting a puppy or a full bowl of soup, he tilted the skull's gritted smile to my ear.

I forced myself not to jerk away.

"I don't hear anything," I said again, after a second. "Are you going to make it talk, like some creepy puppet?"

"*Listen*," Hamlet hissed. The skull's teeth brushed my earlobe. "He says, 'Remember me.'"

The pulse behind my eye thumped harder. "'Remember me'? What am I supposed to remember about Yorick?"

"Not Yorick." Hamlet frowned like this was obvious. "Your father."

My whole body went cold. I whirled toward him, making my voice stiff and clear as an icicle. *Katharine Hepburn. Maggie Smith.* "Don't talk to me anymore."

Hamlet leaned toward me again, his cracked-ice eyes wide. "I think I saw him yesternight."

"Stop it." I tried to stand up, but my body was fastened to the chair.

He pointed to the stage. "Look where it comes again!"

From behind the curtain, there came the hollow sound of footsteps.

The ache in my head froze. My heart shot up into my throat and stuck there.

The dusty velvet curtains twitched.

Another strangled heartbeat. Then the curtains parted, and a man stepped out onto the lip of the stage.

The dimness smudged his edges, and the spotlight gave him a blurry glow, but I'd seen enough portraits on scripts and books and classroom walls to recognize him. The

Renaissance-Elvis pompadour. The heavy-lidded eyes. The gold hoop earring.

In person, Shakespeare looked younger. Sharper. Every motion he made was pared down to fine lines, so he seemed to move with perfect precision, not a flicker of energy wasted.

His eyes were very dark. They speared through the spotlight, straight down into mine.

"Be as thou wast wont to be," he said, in a quiet, resonant voice. "See as thou wast wont to see."

"Jaye . . ." said another voice. "Jaye?"

The auditorium collapsed.

The armrests sagged under my elbows. The prickly upholstery flattened into cotton sheets. The ache in my head thawed, pounding back to life.

"Jaye? Are you still awake?"

A face floated above me. I blinked up at it, fighting against the flood of ugly yellow light, while the white ceiling and white walls and white floors rebuilt themselves, and the floating face crystalized into my sister.

Sadie looked a little like me, with all the good parts amplified and the bad parts erased. Her jaw was firm. Her nose was straight. She had a runner's long, slim body. Her hair was sleek and wavy and shimmery red-brown. I suppose at least my hair might have looked like hers, if I wasn't always dyeing it. But I needed the things that made me different from Sadie. Comparisons were a bad idea.

Sadie sat on the edge of the bed, wearing a thin green sweater and one of her million scarves. Its fringe brushed my arm as she leaned over me. "Are you okay?"

I didn't know what expression to put on. I recognized the room, in a hazy way. And Sadie had said "are you *still* awake." Terrified confusion didn't seem appropriate. I struggled for a blank face.

"My head hurts." My voice came out deep and raspy, like I'd been gargling with gravel.

"I know it hurts." Sadie leaned back again. "You've said so about eight thousand times."

"My cheek hurts too," I said, in my new, raspy voice. "Have I said *that* eight thousand times?"

"Seven thousand." Sadie's eyes narrowed slightly, and I knew she was doing that thing where she tries to pry beneath my outer layers, to see past what I'm showing her and peel me down to the truth. "Do you remember where you are?"

". . . The hospital."

Sadie waited. So did I.

As usual, she cracked first. "And what are you *doing* in the hospital?"

I traveled backward through the fragments. The auditorium, Hamlet, the cracked skull. A sparkling white field. Snow. A deep voice. Someone gently lifting my hand.

"I was . . ." I mumbled. "It's just—flashes."

Sadie gave a muted sigh. "We were skiing," she prompted.

"Skiing?" I blinked twice, but this time, the room didn't change. "You mean—you and Mom and *me?*"

"I know. Jaye Stuart participating in a sport?" Sadie shook her head. "Blue moons colliding. Snowballs piling up in hell."

It must have been the grogginess filling my body, because I almost broke the rule. "But we haven't gone skiing since—"

"I know." Sadie cut me off just in time. "Mom and I just thought it would be nice. Good memories. You know."

I had to fight to keep the disbelief off my face.

Good memories? Mom and Sadie shushing happily off on their skis. Me wobbling, stiff and terrified, on the learner's slope, whining about the cold, my sore ankles, the steepness of the hills. Dad's teasing smile turning embarrassed. Then tight. Then angry. I remembered one trip—I must have been eight or nine—when he grabbed me by the arm and shoved me down the incline while I screamed and cried and strangers stared at us. At the bottom of the bunny hill, Dad leaned close and hissed at me through clenched teeth, *"You're not even trying,"* before gliding away, leaving me alone. I'd spent the rest of that trip—and every ski trip afterward—waddling up and down the grounds near the lodge, trying to look like I had just finished a great run, or like I was just about to head out on another, practicing my lies for Dad. *I did the learner's slope four times,* I'd say, hoping my frostbitten cheeks would be enough evidence. *I tried. Really.*

"I hated those trips," I told Sadie.

"Well, there may have been bribery involved, but you'll have to ask Mom about that."

I scraped the memories away. "So, we were skiing. And then?"

"There was an accident." Now Sadie looked at my cheek instead of my eyes. "You hit a tree."

"And *that's* why I don't ski." My right cheek tingled. In fact, the entire right side of my face felt tender and hot, like it had when we were little and Sadie accidentally bashed me in the eye with a Little League bat. I raised a hand to touch it, but taped tubes and needles jerked my arm back. "Wait." The sparkling whiteness and fog and bloody roses were piling up again. "I hit a tree?"

"You were unconscious for a while." Sadie rearranged one of the tubes I'd pulled out of place. "There's a fracture in your skull. But the doctors don't think it's too serious. There's no bleeding in your brain or anything."

The words—*skull, fracture, bleeding in the brain*—seemed to belong to someone else. Someplace else. They slithered out of my reach. I closed my eyes, hoping Sadie wouldn't see how lost I was.

Her voice had been so bland. So factual. So well-rehearsed.

"Sadie . . ." My throat burned. "Have you told me all of this before?"

"Have *I* told you?" There was a pause. Too long. "Yes. More than once."

I kept my eyes closed. "I don't remember."

"But this is the first time you've *asked* me if I've told you before," said Sadie. "That's probably a good sign."

"I don't remember any of it."

"The nurses say that's totally normal. They say people with head injuries do all kinds of things they don't remember afterward. Especially when they're on painkillers. Some of them hit people, some of them shout things, some pull the needles out of their arms and run out of their rooms in their little flapping hospital dresses." Sadie's voice changed, and I could tell that she was smiling. "I guess you sat up in bed the other day and recited Juliet's whole 'Wherefore art thou Romeo' speech at the top of your lungs."

"I did?" I opened my eyes. "I didn't even know I knew that speech."

Sadie's grin widened. "Apparently the entire wing could hear you."

I laughed. It was just a short laugh, but it made my chest throb like I'd been punched. It took a few seconds before I could speak again. "So . . . how did they say I was?"

"Oh my god." Sadie threw her head back. "You are *such* a drama queen."

Her words worked their way through the fog. *The other day, you sat up in bed . . .*

"Sadie," I began, "how long have I been in here?"

Sadie's smile vanished. She craned back slightly, like

she wanted to get out of my reach. "For the record, you've never asked me *that* before either." She straightened the tubes taped to my arm again, even though they didn't need straightening. She didn't look at me when she answered. "It's been six days."

". . . Six *days?*" Panic flash-froze my insides. "How— what have I been doing here for six days?"

"Resting," said Sadie flatly.

"But I can't—" My lungs had crystalized. The words came out with a wheeze. "*Six days?* I can't even remember them."

"That's because you've been *resting.*"

Oh my god. Six days. *Six days.* My thoughts ripped apart, flying in all directions. Some flew to my mother. *Where is she? Is she all right?* Some flew to the play. *What have I already missed? Has Mr. Hall given my role away? Has Pierce even noticed that I'm gone?* And some flew backward, to that hole in the snow, the whiteness filling up with blood-red roses. *Six days.* How could I not remember *any* of it? Would I forget all of this in another few minutes, and only remember to ask again on day twelve? Day twenty? Day four hundred?

"Oh my god, Sadie." I reached for the bed's plastic railing. "I have to get out of here."

"Nobody wants you here. Believe me."

"No." I tried to sit up. The bones of my spine seemed to have fused, and the best I could manage was to roll onto

my left elbow. The tubes in my other arm pulled. Somewhere nearby, a high-pitched alarm began to beep. "I need
to get out of here. Mom must be——"

"Jaye, hang on." Sadie darted around the bed and
gripped my shoulders. "You can't just——"

I writhed upright. My ribs dug through my chest like
spears. A tube in my elbow snapped free. The white walls.
The machines. The beeping. "I need to get out of here."

"Jaye, just let me get the nurse. It's going to be——"

"No," I said, in my most forceful voice, even though it
made my throat sting. I lurched sideways, managing to
swing one leg out of the bed. Sadie tried to push me back.
An alarm began to blare. "I'm getting out of here."

The door flew open. A nurse in blue scrubs strode toward
the bed.

Our mother hurried after her.

Something had happened to her face. Mom usually
looks a decade younger than she is—she always has that
yoga glow, and her face and voice are like raw silk, smooth
and soft, with a little natural waver in the fiber. But now
she looked twenty years older. I could tell she hadn't been
eating. She hadn't washed her hair in days, either. Tight
lines curved around her mouth, like wires cutting into the
skin.

I'd seen her this way once before.

She had to get out of here too.

"Mom——" The nurse pushed me back onto the bed, repeating my name. I tried to shove her hands away. "Mom, I'm fine. I just need to get out." I fought back the desperation. "Make them let me out."

Mom grabbed Sadie's arm. "What happened?" I heard her whisper.

"She was asking how long she'd been here, and when I told her—"

"No. Mom, I'm all right. I swear." The walls. The smell. The beeping and wheezing machines clustered around Dad's narrow white bed. My head was going to explode. "Let's get out of here. *Please.*"

"Jaye . . ." The nurse adjusted something in my arm. "Hang on, Jaye. Just stay with me . . ."

The room smeared. Shadows climbed the walls like fast-growing vines.

"Jaye, can you hear me?"

In the row of vinyl chairs beneath the window, William Shakespeare sat, staring back at me.

His eyes were deep blue. A slip of yellow light glittered on his hoop earring. Keeping his eyes on me, he placed one finger against his lips.

And then the room turned inside out.

CHAPTER 2

I was early to auditions for *A Midsummer Night's Dream*.

I'm usually late for everything. Family dinners. Classes. Detentions for being late to those classes. But I was not going to be late for this.

After the final bell on audition day, I stayed at school until the 5:00 start time, wandering the halls and mumbling to myself like a crazy person. Preparing a monologue from Shakespeare had seemed kind of like wearing the T-shirt of the band you're about to see, so I picked Roxanne's speech from *Cyrano de Bergerac* instead—the one where she tricks the friar into marrying her to the man she actually loves. I'd memorized it weeks ahead of time, etching the words onto my brain until they were almost like breathing. I'd practiced in the mirror. In the shower. In our echoing, cobwebby basement. Now I practiced a few last times as I paced around the nearly empty school halls.

At a quarter to five, I pushed through the scarred door that leads to the backstage hallway. No one had turned the stage lights on yet, so the air around me was dark and thick. I took a deep breath. The hallway always smells like house paint, sawdust, cold cream, and ancient clothes. It should be an ugly smell, but it's my favorite smell in the world. If there was a perfume that smelled like the backstage, I'd wear it. A burst of energy shot up through my legs, straightened my spine, zinged into my lungs. Mr. Hall calls it electrification. The feeling of being ready to step onstage and shine.

I strode through the dimness and threw open the greenroom door, letting out a blast of light. Then I almost jumped backward.

Pierce Caplan stood in the middle of the greenroom.

My first thought was that he must have gotten lost on the way to the gym. Or that maybe he was here as part of some team prank, stealing stage makeup or old prom dresses for a freshman hazing ritual. But he was holding the audition sign-in sheet and clipboard. A ballpoint pen was in his hand.

His back was to me. I got one good look at his T-shirt, the shape of his muscular shoulders, the waves of his dark blond hair. Everything about him was a disorienting mix of familiar and unfamiliar, like a house you've visited a thousand times, but that's now occupied by strangers.

He turned around.

Pierce didn't look surprised to see me. He didn't look happy, either. Or *un*happy. He just gave me a smooth half smile, said "Hey, Stuart," and turned back to the clipboard.

The electricity inside me blew out like a fuse. My head went dim. Roxanne's speech vanished. All that was left was the shape of Pierce's back. Dad's arm wrapped around his shoulders.

"Oh," I said, like a moron. "Hi."

Pierce's pen whispered across the sign-in sheet. He held the clipboard out to me.

"What are you doing here?" The words shot out before I could decide how to say them. They came with an edge. A little sharp, a little shaky.

Pierce's eyebrows went up. "Auditioning."

"But—why?" Still too sharp. "Don't you have—I don't know—whatever sport they play in winter? Hockey, or curling, or something?"

"Swim team," Pierce supplied. There was a tiny smile in the corner of his mouth—but maybe it was just left over from the earlier one. "I quit. Coach Black will be pissed when he finds out, but he'll just have to deal with it."

"So . . . what are you doing *here*?" I smoothed my voice. Firm. Cool. More like his. "You've never done any plays."

Pierce looked straight at me for a moment. His eyes were the hazel I remembered, but his jaw was squarer, and his chin was a different shape. I wanted to reach out and re-form them, like Play-Doh. And then I would wad his whole face into a ball and smash it down into its little yellow tub.

"Actually," he said, "I'm here because of you."

I felt the firmness waver. "Because of me?"

"Yeah. It's my last chance to get to do this. You know, before graduation, and going off to college. Being an adult with no time for fun stuff."

What was he talking about? Electric moths spiraled from my stomach up into my brain. I fought not to let them flicker across my face. Was this an apology? Was this the start of an explanation for the way he'd unsnarled himself from all of our lives?

I hardened my face again. "What does continuing to age have to do with me?"

"*Arsenic and Old Lace*," said Pierce.

Now I must have looked like someone had just yanked a hair out of my nose. I blinked at him. "What?"

"The play, last spring." His lips curved into a smile. "You were great."

I hadn't seen that smile—that full-on, genuine smile—in so long. Not aimed at me, anyway. The hardness started to melt. I even felt my cheeks go hot. *Damn it.* I looked down at the laces of my high black boots.

"Oh," I managed. "Thanks." So, he'd seen me dressed up as a batty old lady, complete with poodle wig and body pads. Oh god. I hoped he *knew* they were body pads.

"I thought, 'I've got to try that at least once in my life.'" Pierce went on. "So here I am."

"Oh," I said again. And then I couldn't think of anything else to say. Everything was either too big or too small.

"Well . . . break a leg," I finally blurted. "That's what us theater freaks say."

"Yeah. You too, Stuart."

He gave me another flicker of a smile. Then he brushed past me, close enough that I could smell the sharp minty-ness of his skin, and stepped out through the greenroom door.

"When the cast list was posted, and I saw that the two of us would be playing Titania and Oberon, it seemed like life was making some kind of giant joke." I cleared my gravelly throat. "That this guy who went from being my oldest friend to being some fashion-model stranger was going to be with me every day, pretending to be my husband . . . Ugh. He's like a walking knot of memories." I clenched my fist, and the needle in my arm twinged. "I hated him for a while. *Hated* him. He probably hated me too. I probably remind him of all the same things." I shrugged at the damp girl sitting at the foot of the hospital bed. "I mean, he tells me that he's doing it all because of me. But then, after they post the cast list—*nothing.* He doesn't even say 'congratulations,' or 'this is weird,' or 'this is great.' Nothing."

Ophelia rearranged the bouquet of tongue depressors in her lap. "I know how that goes," she said. "One minute he's flirting with you, the next minute he ignores you. He's one way when you're alone and another way when anyone else is listening. It's exhausting."

"Exactly."

Ophelia straightened a fold of her muddy skirt. "Hamlet

was always visiting me, giving me little gifts. I was sure he felt something. But . . . my father said . . ." Ophelia's face went suddenly blank. She sniffed at the tongue depressors, her eyes far away and glassy. "No, no . . ." she sang softly. "He is dead, go to thy deathbed. He never will come again."

She tucked a tongue depressor behind her ear. Her eyes flicked to me. She leaned closer, and I could smell river water, mud and rotting leaves and dead things, even through the hospital antiseptic.

"Don't let them know what you see." Her breath was dewy against my face. Then she sat back and picked through the tongue depressor bouquet again. "Here's a daisy," she announced. "I would give you some violets, but they withered all when our father died." She held out the wooden stick to me. "Jell-O?"

The room dissolved from gray to white. I closed my eyes, the ache in my head twisting tighter. When I opened them again, Sadie sat at the foot of my bed. She waved a small spoon in front of my face.

"Come on," she prompted. "It's *red* flavor. The hospital's signature dessert. Open up."

I parted my lips just enough for the spoon to slide in. My skull ached in places I'd never known could ache. Every movement I made cranked the pain higher.

Sadie shoveled in the Jell-O. Its sweetness made the roof of my mouth vibrate.

"Where did she go?" I mumbled through the mouthful.

"Mom? She's right outside, talking to the doctor."

"No. I mean . . ." I looked past my sister. The rest of the room was empty. There were no damp splotches on the white sheets. Ophelia's words trickled through me again. *Don't let them know what you see.*

Because they'll think you're insane, I filled in. *And they would be right. Because you're taking advice from* Ophelia.

"Sadie, is Mom okay?"

"Not really," said Sadie. "But she will be. When you are."

"Just—" I glanced at the closed door. "She looks bad. Please watch out for her."

Sadie nodded briskly. "I am. I promise." She carved another red scoop out of the cup. "You know," she said, in a brighter, falser tone, "one of my earliest memories is of feeding you." She lifted the bite toward my mouth. "I think I was three, so you must have been one and a half. You were in the high chair. I was feeding you pureed pears, and you had this slimy goop all over your face, but you were *so happy.* You would laugh each time you took a bite, like pear goop was the best thing in the world." She patted my chin with a napkin. "Still a drooler."

Behind her, the door swung open. A doctor in a white coat strode inside. Mom followed him like a small, sweat-suited shadow. Her gray eyes were bloodshot. Her hair still looked unwashed.

Before the door could swing shut again, a thin blond man dressed entirely in black slipped in after her.

Hamlet was back. Fantastic.

Mom and the doctor flanked my bed. They were already in the middle of a conversation. I didn't recognize the doctor, who was tall and bony, with thick eyebrows. I kept my eyes fixed on his face, but it was hard to focus on his words. Especially when Hamlet tiptoed around the bed and grinned at me over my sister's shoulder.

". . . As we've said, according to the most recent scan, the contusion looks relatively minor."

Mom nodded, her eyes coasting over my face. I wasn't sure she even saw me.

"Of course," the doctor went on, "in cases where consciousness seems unstable, we . . ."

Sadie slipped another bite of Jell-O into my mouth. Behind her, Hamlet raised the cracked yellow skull. Its bony forehead was wrapped in strips of white medical gauze.

I almost choked.

"Too much?" Sadie asked.

I shook my head.

". . . due to the impact to the frontal lobe," the doctor concluded.

Hamlet tapped the front of the skull helpfully. I glared at him.

"With this type of injury, it's just hard to tell," the doctor said, answering some question from Mom. "Effects on memory, personality, physical functions can vary widely . . ."

Hamlet made the skull nod at me. I closed my eyes.

26

I'd heard speeches like this one before. It had been two years, but the words were still as clear as memorized dialogue in my head. *Frontal lobe. Cranial hemorrhage. May not regain consciousness.* I wished I could swat the words out of the air like wasps, keep them from ever touching my mother again.

"Want any more?" Sadie asked.

Don't let them know what you see.

I opened my eyes. "Sure. Thanks."

I kept my gaze on my sister's hands, away from the dark figure behind her.

". . . especially with the severity of the headaches she seems to be experiencing. Then there's the bruised cartilage in the rib cage, although that seems to be causing her less pain already. And of course there's the scalp laceration. It's healing well, the staples are out, things are looking good. With time, it should fade to a faint scar."

I swallowed another spoonful. "When can I go home?"

Everyone's heads swiveled toward me. Hamlet tilted the skull inquisitively at the others.

Sadie's face was unreadable. The doctor looked at my mother. Mom's gaze skidded past my face and onto the pillow.

". . . Soon," said Mom at last.

The doctor patted my ankle. "We'd like to keep you under observation here just a bit longer."

"I understand." My throat still burned, and now it was

sticky with Jell-O, but I tried to put on my calmest, most mature voice. My Meryl Streep voice. "I've just missed so much school already. I want to get back to normal as soon as I can."

"That's what we want too." The doctor gave me a smile. "We just need to make sure you do it safely. And even after we release you, you'll have to keep taking it easy for a while. No activities. No screens. Minimal reading. Nothing that would tax your brain. It's dull, I know, but your brain needs time to repair itself."

"That means no school for a while," said Mom, in a voice like tissue paper.

The doctor turned from me to my mother. "She's really doing very well." He waited for her to nod. She didn't. "Any other questions?" he went on, looking around. "From any of you?"

"No." Mom had to clear her throat and repeat the word. "No. Thank you."

"I'll check on you again soon." The doctor gave us all another nod and smile before striding out of the room. The door clicked shut behind him. I realized that Hamlet had vanished too.

Mom stepped closer to the bed. She placed one hand on Sadie's shoulder. Then, tentatively, she reached out and put her other hand on my arm. She looked like someone walking across an icy street, holding on to both of us for balance.

Sadie stared down at my blankets.

Mom let out a long, quiet breath. One of her yoga breaths. Then she forced her eyes up to my face. "Would you like us to bring you anything from home? Any clothes, or bath stuff, or . . ."

"No, thanks. It's okay." I gave Mom a smile. "I just want to *go* home."

"You will." Her voice was carefully light. "Soon."

"I'm feeling fine. Honestly. I mean, my head aches, but it's not that bad. Really, Mom."

Mom gave a little nod. She chafed her hands together.

"It's just—you know—if I could be recovering out there instead of in here, I'd choose out there." The ache behind my eye let off a small explosion. I fought to keep from wincing. "Maybe I could do half days at school, or something. Or maybe I could just go to rehearsals at first, and keep up with everything else at home."

Mom gave another tiny nod. "We'll see."

"The doctor just said I'm doing really well, right? And I don't want to waste any more time." *Stay calm. Mature. Logical.* "I mean— I can catch up with everything else on my own, but the play is—" *STAY CALM.* "It's a one-time thing. This might be my only chance to play this role. Maybe *ever.* If I don't go back soon, Mr. Hall will have to give my part away."

Sadie gave a noisy sigh. Over her shoulder, I could see that Shakespeare had reappeared in his vinyl chair below the window.

Mom straightened slightly. "Jaye . . . the play is not the most important thing here."

Shakespeare's eyes were like magnets. I had to fight not to look at him. "It is to me."

"It's not more important than you getting better."

"But it's why I *need* to get better." Desperation was seeping into my voice. I squeezed it out again. "I mean, it's part of why. Please, Mom. I'm *fine*. I'll be careful. I just need to get out of here."

"Jaye . . ." Mom turned to Sadie for support, but Sadie was staring into the Jell-O's wobbly red depths, pointedly keeping still. Mom turned back to me with a sigh. "If the doctors think you're well enough, and if you're really feeling and acting like normal, then . . . Soon."

"Okay," I said. "Soon."

I could do that.

I could act normal. I could pretend to be the pain-free, ordinary, everyday Jaye. The one who belonged in the auditorium with Nikki and Tom and Pierce, running lines for *A Midsummer Night's Dream*. The one who couldn't see William Shakespeare leaning back in his hospital chair at this very second, picking a bit of lint off his tights. He gave me a knowing smile. I ripped my eyes away.

You can pretend everything's fine, I told myself, turning back to Mom. *Pretend you can handle all of this. Just like you've been doing for years.*

CHAPTER 3

Voices rippled through the dimness. One higher, one lower. Both unfamiliar. Coming from somewhere nearby. My eyelids were heavy, but I raised them just enough to let in a blurry sliver of light.

I was still in the hospital room.

It was night, or very early morning. The walls were gray mist. The reflection of moonlight on snow—or maybe just the haze of city streetlights—slipped around the edge of the blinds, and a thin band of electric light slid through the crack under the door.

In the dimness, I could see two figures standing beside my bed. One was tall and narrow. The other was small, with short, choppy hair. At first I thought the smaller one might be Nikki, but when it spoke, it didn't have her voice.

"Blood pressure?" the tall one murmured.

"One sixteen over seventy," said the small one.

The tall one leaned closer. High cheekbones. Pointed chin. "Bandage?" he asked. Tiny green lights, like fireflies, whirled above his head.

"Right here."

I felt a tug on the tender spot inside my elbow.

The other face moved nearer. I could see its sharp features, its messy hair full of leaves.

Something cool and damp rubbed my inner arm. Something else pattered down onto my face, sprinkling my half-shut eyelids.

Raindrops? I thought. *No. Petals.*

Oh, said my groggy brain. *Right.* A Midsummer Night's Dream. *Puck and Oberon. How did the love spell go? Flower of this purple dye, hit with Cupid's archery; when thou wakest, if he be by . . .*

The petals dissolved against my burning forehead. I felt each wet spot shrinking at the edges, tightening on my skin. What came next? *If he be by . . .* But the words were vanishing like the petals, going up in little puffs of flame.

Oberon's voice spoke again. ". . . No more than the weary vexation of a dream. Now, my Titania, wake you, my sweet queen."

Titania's line. What was it? The ache roared hotter. *Come on. They're all waiting. Everyone's waiting . . .*

A blast of yellow light fanned across the room.

I blinked.

A male nurse in blue scrubs was just gliding out the open door. Another nurse, a woman with short curly hair, tucked the sheets gently under my side.

"There she is," the nurse whispered. "Any pain?"

I shook my head. A lie.

"You've been getting some real sleep?"

I swallowed. Even my tongue felt scorched. "I think so. It's kind of hard to tell."

The nurse smiled. "Well, even if you're not completely out, just lying still and resting your brain will help."

"That's the problem." I closed my eyes halfway, blocking out the light from the open doorway. "My brain really doesn't want to rest."

"Remember your technique." The nurse gave the sheet a last tug. "Focus on that calming image, and clear your mind as well as you can."

Calming image. Calming image? What else had I forgotten?

Before I could start to panic, an empty stage with red velvet curtains settled down in the center of my mind.

I felt my bones loosen.

"Got it?" the nurse murmured.

I closed my eyes the rest of the way. "Got it."

"Good. Now, just rest." Her voice shrank as she backed away. "Press the button if you need anything."

There was a click from the door. The yellow glow disappeared. I could feel the darkness against my eyelids.

The empty stage waited.

I knew just how my footsteps would sound if I climbed up onto the black boards. I knew how those red velvet curtains would feel against my fingers: heavy and fur-soft on the outside, rough and rigid on the back. I gazed up at the imaginary stage in the imaginary theater in my head, and my breaths came easier. The fire in my skull was burning down.

It hadn't quite gone out when the curtains gave a ripple.

And then, again, there were voices.

First it was Oberon's. *Wake when some vile thing is near . . .* Beneath that, very softly, I could hear Hamlet muttering about dreams, and then another voice, another man's voice, repeating, *I dreamt a dream tonight,* again and again, until my head pounded along with the words. What play was that from? I couldn't remember.

Don't try, I told myself. *Empty stage.*

But the voices wouldn't stop. And now there were more. Oberon and Puck, and Hamlet, and Lady Macbeth joining in with her sleepwalking scene. The curtains rippled again, like someone on the other side was struggling to get out. I tried to hold them still.

Empty stage. Empty stage.

But the harder I tried, the stronger it got, until the folds of velvet split apart.

I braced myself for Shakespeare, like last time. But the person who stepped out onto the stage was someone younger. Someone in dark clothes. Someone with an angular jaw and tapering eyebrows. Pale eyes. Tangled black hair.

This time I recognized him. Maybe because the lighting

was better. Maybe because now he was onstage, where he belonged.

Romeo stepped over the lip of the stage and headed toward me. His legs were long and thin, but he moved smoothly. Almost gracefully. He wore a little half smile.

"It was you, wasn't it?" I asked sleepily. "In the snow."

He sat down in one of the chairs beside my bed, just far back enough that I couldn't see him, not even from the corner of my eye. But I could feel him there. Listening.

"You know . . . Oberon and Puck make sense," I said after a second. My voice was starting to slur. "I'm in their play. Shakespeare makes sense. I guess Hamlet and his stupid cracked skull make sense. But I haven't even read *Romeo and Juliet* in years."

Still no answer.

"Fine. Don't talk to me. I won't talk to you either." I turned my eyes up to the ceiling. "I don't need someone to walk in and find me calling an empty chair Romeo, anyway."

"No one's going to walk in," said a voice. Deep. Familiar. "It's the middle of the night."

"Look." I tried to point at the window, but my arm just gave a little flop against the blanket. "It's almost morning. You have to go."

"That's just the moon." The sheets crinkled softly as he leaned over the bed. "Let's talk. It's not day yet."

I closed my eyes. *Don't let them know what you see.*

"I get it," I said. Or I thought I said. My lips felt fuzzy, and my body was full of wet sand, and the mist was swirling closer. "That was a dream, and *this* is a dream, and Hamlet and Puck and Shakespeare and everything else. Because of this." I tried to point to my head. Another arm-flop. "But I *know* it. I'm not crazy." I managed to pull my hand out of his grasp. "I know it."

"Juliet," I thought I heard him say, before the darkness wrapped itself around me again. It coiled gently, turning me heavy and boneless, and it had just pulled me down to a place where there were no more words or faces or questions when my sister's voice reached in and dragged me back up.

"Jaye, you could *try* to help me out here. You don't make a great Barbie doll."

I looked down.

I had gotten out of bed. Partway out of it, at least. My back was braced against the mattress, and I could see my own bare feet on the white tile floor, very far away.

Sadie was crouched beside me, yanking a pair of khaki pants up my legs.

I smeared the confusion off my face. *Just pretend. Pretend this is the dressmaking scene from* Jezebel, *and you're Bette Davis.*

"Who picked out these clothes?" I asked as Sadie wrenched the waistband up under my hospital dress.

"Who do you think? I'm afraid to step inside your room,

let alone into your closet. Something made of black velvet and dust bunnies would swallow me."

Sadie untied the hospital gown. As she slid it over my arms, I noticed that the needles were gone. Fraying wads of cotton were held against my skin with strips of tape. I looked like an old couch leaking its stuffing.

Sadie held out a peachy-pink sweater. "Arms up."

"Oh my god. I haven't even seen that sweater since middle school."

"Let's hope it still fits, or you'll have to wear your hospital gown home. *Arms up.*"

Sadie pried the sweater over my head. Its fibers scraped a tender spot, making me suck in a breath.

Sadie grabbed my wrist before I could rub my sore forehead. "Hold still. We're not done yet." She pulled my arms down, tugging hurriedly at the sweater cuffs. "God, I can't wait to get out of here."

"*You* can't wait?" I stepped into the boots Sadie had positioned for me, wobbling a little. "I hate these places."

Sadie stared into my eyes. "Plus, you're feeling *much better*, right? Not just trying to escape?"

"Yes," I said defensively. "I'm feeling much better."

Mom stepped into the room. Her winter coat hung open over a zippered sweatshirt, and her hair looked frosty-wet, like she'd rushed out of the house right after a shower. "All set, ladies?" Her eyes flicked around the room, not lingering anywhere. "Ready to go home?"

I put on a smile that made my cheeks sting. "So ready."

They helped me into my winter coat. The long black wool felt scratchy and hot and unbelievably heavy, like I was wearing a brick wall. My boots weighed twenty pounds apiece. With Mom and Sadie holding me by either arm, we shuffled out of the white room. I was sure an alarm would go off when we stepped through the door, like the two of them were shoplifting me. Had I actually pulled it off? Did everyone believe me? It took all my concentration to put one foot in front of the other, to keep my spine straight, to keep my head from tumbling off my neck.

"Sorry I'm so slow." I had to stop moving for a second to get the words out. "It feels like I haven't walked in months."

Mom spun toward me, her face instantly worried. "But the nurses have been walking with you every day. You walked around this whole floor yesterday. Remember?"

"Oh. Yesterday. Yeah." I made my nod casual. "I just meant . . . I feel rusty. That's all."

Mom tightened her grip. "Tell us if we're going too fast. Or if this feels like too much for you right now, we could—"

"No. I'm fine. I'm slow, but I'm fine. Let's go."

The hallway walls were pale green. The floor was covered in misty gray tile. I could see our shadows coasting beneath us, like birds' reflections in icy water.

Other shadows fluttered behind us. I glanced over my

shoulder, expecting to see an impatient nurse or doctor stuck in our wake.

Instead, there were fairies.

Three of them. They had sparkly skin and pointed features and bare feet. All three of them beamed at me.

Then they started to sing, in little flutey fairy voices.

Over hill, over dale, thorough brush, thorough brier;

Over park, over pale, thorough flood, thorough fire,

I do wander everywhere, swifter than the moon's sphere . . .

I clenched my teeth and turned away. The fairies kept singing, skipping behind us, showering us with petals that apparently only I could feel.

Mom gave me another anxious look. "Is something wrong?"

"I just—I thought I forgot something. But I didn't." I tugged her hand with my arm. "Let's go."

We turned the corner into another, busier hall. Elevator doors pinged open and shut in the distance. Patients with walkers and rolling IV poles stared after us with tired eyes. I kept my head down, pretending I couldn't hear the harmonizing voices right behind us.

Sadie led the way into an elevator. When the metal doors closed, sealing us on one side and the fairies on the other, I realized I'd been holding my breath. Mom touched my shoulder, just once, delicately. Sadie kept glancing at my forehead, but whenever I turned to face her, she looked away.

We stepped out of the elevator into a lobby that looked like an empty greenhouse. Mom and Sadie guided me across the gleaming floor and out the main doors.

A surge of freezing air smashed against us. It pushed through the layers of my clothes, forcing the air back out of my lungs. How long had it been since I'd breathed outdoor air? I couldn't remember. The raw spot on my forehead zinged.

Mom and Sadie hustled me through the parking ramp toward our gray minivan. They buckled me into the middle row of seats, like I couldn't be trusted to fasten a seat belt myself. My breath made little puffs in the enclosed air.

Come on. I jiggled my feet as they slammed the doors. *Let's go let's go let's go.* Once I was away from this place, with its smells and tubes and misty walls, maybe everything else would be left behind too. Maybe my mind would follow my body back into its normal life.

Mom and Sadie stuffed my bags through the van's back hatch. I heard another thump of doors. And then one quiet, resonant voice—definitely not one of the fairies' voices—began to sing.

Over park, over pale . . .

I whirled around. The pain in my head kindled.

The seats behind me were empty.

When I turned back toward the windshield, the voice went on.

Thorough bush, thorough brier . . .

Mom settled into the front passenger seat, turning halfway around to keep one eye on me. Sadie plunked into the driver's seat. She fit the key in the ignition, and a blast of music filled the freezing air. It made my skull ring, but at least it drowned out the sound of Shakespeare's singing.

"Sadie," said Mom warningly.

Sadie turned the music down.

We bumped out of the lot into the city streets. I sank down, letting the thump of the music beat against the pulse in my head. *Empty stage.*

Empty stage.

CHAPTER 4

We'd lived in the same red brick house my entire life.

I knew every hole in the front porch screens. I knew the exact number of steps it took to get from my bed to the bathroom in the middle of the night. I could hit every light switch without looking. But as the minivan jostled up the snowy driveway, the house suddenly looked unreal to me. It seemed too small, or too thin, like we might step through its front door and find that it was just a façade, a flat wooden set with nothing on the other side.

Mom and Sadie helped me along the walkway. From the porch steps, I glanced back at the van. Empty. Nobody in a tunic and tights was following us up to the front door.

Thank you, I thought. Then I wondered who I was thanking.

Mom opened the door. There was our living room, just where it should have been. There was the worn gold couch draped with blankets. The cluttered end tables. The slate fireplace, its mantel clustered with dusty photographs.

"You sit down and take it easy." Mom peeled the coat

gently off of my shoulders. "I'll go heat the oven, and we'll have a nice, non-hospital-food dinner in about an hour."

I glanced at the old wooden wall clock. Five thirty-five. Rehearsal was probably just ending. "Can I invite Tom and Nikki over?"

"Jaye, what definition of 'taking it easy' involves inviting your friends over the second you get home?" Mom shoved my coat into the crowded closet. "No visitors. Not tonight." She passed me the cordless phone, which had been lying in a pile of papers on the coffee table. "You can have five minutes on the phone, and I'm timing you. Then you need to rest."

"What happened to *my* phone?"

"The doctors said no screens, remember? That means no texting, no e-mail, no photos. Not for a few more days, at least." Mom nodded at the receiver in my hand. "Your five minutes are dwindling."

Sadie had already settled down with a textbook and a stack of notes at the dining room table. I squeezed past her, into the sunroom. The room was narrow and chilly in winter, and its row of windows stared out at our snow-buried backyard, but at least I could shut its French doors behind me.

Nikki answered on the second ring.

"Ohmygod! How are you!" she shouted, without even saying hello. In the background, I heard another voice yell, "Jaye! JayeJayeJaye!"

"That was Tom," said Nikki. "So, how *are* you? How do you feel?"

My throat gave an unexpected clench. "I miss you two."

"We miss *you*," said Nikki. I heard Tom's more-distant echo: "We miss *you!*"

"I'm not allowed to leave the house or have people over yet, but I couldn't wait to talk to you."

"When are you coming back?" Tom's voice shouted into my ear.

"Monday, I think. Four more days. How are rehearsals going?"

Nikki's voice answered again. "Well, all the cheerleaders show up to watch now."

"Why?"

"Why do you think?"

"Give me a *P*!" Tom chanted in the background. "Give me an *I*!"

"Mr. Hall hasn't already given my part away, has he?"

"He's got the understudy learning it. One of those snotty show choir girls." Nikki's voice grew muffled. "What's her name?"

"Michaela," said Tom.

"Michaela," Nikki repeated. "Oh—and I was going to tell you, tonight—"

The French doors creaked open. "Time's up," said Mom, holding out her hand for the phone.

"Already?" I put on my least-obnoxious pleading face.

Mom's hand didn't move.

I sighed. "I have to go," I said into the phone. "But I'll see you soon."

"See you soon!" shouted Nikki.

"We love you!" shouted Tom, more distantly.

"How about a cup of herbal tea?" Mom offered, taking the receiver. "We've got peach, chamomile . . ."

"No, thanks. I'm just going to go up to my room for a while."

"No reading, remember."

"I remember."

"And no homework. No working on your lines."

"Mom, I *remember.*"

"Are you sure?" Her voice turned lightly teasing. "Do you need a chaperone? Because I can send your sister up there with you."

"Please don't."

"*Please* don't," echoed Sadie from the dining room. "Even mold would try to escape from her room."

Mom reached out and rubbed my upper arm. She'd touched me more in one day than I could remember her doing in the last full year. Her face was bright. "You know, I could show you a few yoga poses."

"But I'm not supposed to—"

"Nothing strenuous. There are some very simple sitting or reclining poses that could help you focus on your breathing. Calm your mind."

"Thanks, but I'm not feeling very yoga-ish right now."

"Okay." Mom's hand slid off of my arm. "Dinner in forty-five minutes."

She glided away into the kitchen.

I had to stop and rest twice on the way up the old wooden staircase. My heart thundered like I'd just run around the block, rushing more fuel to the ache in my head. My legs were bags of wet cement.

You're all right. I practiced slowing my breathing, even though it made my chest feel like it might explode. *You're fine. You're fine.*

But when I reached the upper hall, I stopped. I stood there on the worn beige carpet, paralyzed by the same sense I'd had in the driveway. That this was all just a plywood set. That the walls on either side of me were hollow, with each familiar door leading nowhere.

I reached out and touched the wall to my left. It felt solid. It was covered with the same framed family photos that had hung there all my life, a few more pictures joining the collage each year. Dad was in many of them. Really, they were the only Dad-things that hadn't disappeared. A month or two afterward, without anyone talking about it, his other things were just . . . gone. His clothes, his shoes, his toothbrush and soap and razor and vitamins and that kind of mineral water that nobody else liked. Just gone. I suppose it would have made a louder statement if all of the pictures had suddenly vanished too.

There was Mom and Dad's wedding portrait, both of them slimmer and younger and tanner and more gorgeous than should have been humanly possible. There was the picture of Dad on the finish line at the New York Marathon. There were snapshots of Sadie and me as babies, Sadie and me and Mom posing mid-hike on family trips, Sadie and Pierce and me with Dad and Patrick Caplan, Pierce's father, holding up rods that dangled with shimmering sunfish. In the center of the wall was a big photo of Dad with Pierce taken two and a half years ago, the fall of Pierce's sophomore year. In the photo, they're grinning. Dad's arm is around Pierce's shoulders. Pierce holds up a gold medal on a thick red ribbon.

I'd done this a thousand times. Standing in that spot. Staring at that picture. It was like pressing on a bruise: You push harder and harder, and suddenly the pain breaks, and it doesn't hurt at all anymore, because you've made it feel as bad as it possibly can.

Swaying a little, I headed into my own bedroom.

Mom—or maybe Sadie—had cleaned up while I was gone. The bed was made. Clothes I'd left on the floor had been stacked and folded. The scummy coffee cups that had sat on my bedside table for weeks had disappeared. Everything else looked just about right: the vases full of dusty dried roses, the stacks of plays and stage makeup books and biographies of Sarah Bernhardt and Katharine Hepburn, the collage of theater posters and programs and ticket stubs covering the walls. I'd painted those walls myself, three years ago. Dad hated the color. Midnight Plum. A purple so deep, it was almost black.

"Do you know how many coats of paint it'll take to get this room back to normal?" he'd said, turning in a circle in the middle of the carpet, his ropy arms folded across his chest.

It was still Midnight Plum.

I stumbled to the dressing table, plunking down onto the cushioned chair.

Mom and Sadie hadn't even tried to pick up over here. The tabletop was an explosion of tangled necklaces, scribbled notes, lost beads, splatters of nail polish. As I shut an open tube of mascara, I realized I hadn't put on makeup in days. No pencil in the eyebrows that didn't match my dyed hair. No concealer. Nothing. I grabbed the mascara and leaned forward.

That's how I saw my new face for the first time.

There had been a tiny bathroom in the corner of my hospital room. The toilet was flanked by metal railings. Soap and sanitizer and lotion dispensers hung like little plastic mailboxes beside the sink. There had been no mirror. It had always felt strange to look up from washing my hands and find only a blank wall looking back.

Now I knew why there hadn't been a mirror.

A wide, shaved strip ran from one side of my forehead up over my scalp. The exposed skin was so pale, it looked blue. Around the shaved strip, my purple-red hair was greasy and flat, and a scar, long and twisting and ridged like a centipede, wound its way through the shaved patch. I could see the tiny divots where the staples had been. Half-moon bruises hung under both my eyes. On one cheek, directly beneath the shaved patch, was a thin red line where something had gouged me. The rest of that side of my face looked like it had been scraped away by tree bark. I suppose it *had* been. Rashy splotches of fresh skin burned against the pasty background.

My mouth filled with something sour. My stomach started to twist. *Empty stage.* I closed my eyes. *Empty stage.*

Vaguely, I heard the front door creak, my mother's voice speaking. The sounds faded away without sinking in. I opened my eyes again. The face was still there. I brushed one finger over my scar and felt startled when the monster-girl in the mirror raised her hand too.

We were still sitting there, staring at each other, when I caught a glimmer of motion over monster-girl's shoulder.

I turned around.

Pierce Caplan stood in my bedroom door.

CHAPTER 5

I made a noise somewhere between a gasp and a honk. The very last sound Audrey Hepburn would ever make— that was the sound I made at that moment. I sounded like a congested walrus.

Pierce stayed in the doorway. He wore a thin winter jacket. Jeans. Nikes. Beads of melting snow hung in his hair. A soft gray scarf was looped around his neck, surrounding his perfect face like a frame.

"Hey," he said. "Sorry if I startled you."

Blushing made my whole face sting. I felt the scar tighten, the fresh skin on my cheek burn. "A little." I jerked my head to the right, trying to shake my oily hair over the worst parts, and felt the ache slam sideways. "So. Hello."

Pierce's eyes wandered away from me. They coasted around the room, taking in the walls, the books, the bed. "This is pretty different from the room I remember. Everything used to be pink."

"Yeah. A long time ago." I tugged at a hank of hair. Pierce went on gazing around my bedroom, and the itchy embarrassment that filled me started to harden into something like irritation. "A *really* long time ago."

Pierce leaned against the doorframe. "The rest of the house looks exactly the same, though." His eyes flicked back to me. "Sorry. How are you feeling? I should have asked that first."

My shield of hair swung back to its usual place. "Pretty disgusting."

"Well, you look . . ."

"Disgusting? Yes, I know."

"No. You look good. I mean—better than I thought you would."

"Oh." I turned the scarred side of my face away, tilting my chin into my chest. My eyes caught a flash of fuzzy pink. That's right. I was still wearing the ancient, peachy-pink sweater and khakis that my mother had picked out. Fantastic.

"Well, you don't need to just stand in the door," I said a bit grumpily. "You can come in."

Pierce stepped into the room. His jacket swung open over his snug WILSON HS TRACK T-shirt. I could smell the cold air on him, the minty scent of his soap. He looked around again. I was in the only chair. There was nowhere else to sit except for my bed. After a beat, Pierce lowered himself onto the very edge of the mattress.

"So, what are you doing here?" It came out like an accusation. "Sorry. I was just—"

"No. It's . . . it's weird for me to be back here too." He paused, looking like he'd caught himself saying something wrong. "But I've missed coming here. I don't want you to think . . ."

"I don't think," I said, when he didn't go on. "I don't think anything."

We were both quiet for a second.

Pierce lifted the folder he had pinned under one arm. "I brought you some stuff from Mr. Hall." He held it out to me. "An updated script with all the blocking written in. So you can catch up a little over the weekend."

The thought that I wasn't going to be doing any catching up over the weekend flashed through me, followed by a rush of anger, and then another rush of fear. But I just took the folder, keeping my face tilted awkwardly to the side. "He asked *you* to bring it to me?"

"I volunteered."

"Oh."

I searched my brain for something else to say. Pierce's nearness triggered a smear of memories, along with that hot prickling in my face and a buzzing in my stomach. It grew stronger each time I caught the scent of his skin.

Pierce didn't speak either. I wondered if he was remembering too, or if he was just counting the seconds before he could escape without looking like a jerk. But he didn't move.

We were still sitting there, watching each other from the corners of our eyes, when the nurse from *Romeo and*

Juliet burst out of my bedroom closet. She bustled toward Pierce, her long robes flapping.

"A *man*, young lady!" She held both hands over him like he was the grand prize on a game show. "Such a man as all the world—why, he's a man of *wax!*"

"Verona's summer hath not such a flower," another voice murmured, closer to my ear.

Shakespeare and his black tights were perched beside me on my dressing table.

"Nay, he's a flower, in faith," the nurse gushed. "A very flower!"

Pierce tilted his head. "Are you okay?"

I must have been staring into space like a hypnotized cat. I glanced to my right. Shakespeare smiled back at me. "Yeah. I'm fine."

"Here." Abruptly, Pierce was beside me, one sturdy arm sliding beneath mine, wrapping around my back. His other hand grasped my elbow. The folder fumbled in my fingers. He half boosted, half guided me across the floor and set me down on the bed, bracing me with his body. Against my side, he felt solid and warm and reassuringly real. "You don't look okay. Should I get your mom?"

"No," I said quickly. "Don't. I just felt dizzy for a second."

He didn't let go of me. "Are you sure?"

"Totally sure."

Across from me, the dressing table was Shakespeare-less once again. Juliet's nurse had vanished too.

The mattress bounced softly as Pierce got to his feet. "I guess I should let you rest."

"You don't need to—" I caught myself, but it was already too late. "I mean—you don't have to leave so fast. Mom's making dinner. You could stay."

Pierce shook his head in a way that actually looked disappointed. "I promised I'd be home for dinner. My parents are having people over."

"Oh."

"But ask me some other time. It would be good to catch up. With all of you, I mean."

"Yeah." I looked at his collar. "Some other time."

He backed toward the door. "I'll see you Monday, right?"

"Yes, you will. Thanks for the script."

In the doorway, Pierce paused. "Hey. I'm really, really glad you're all right."

I still couldn't quite meet his eyes. Or speak. I just nodded, shaping my lips into an almost-smile, staring at the button on his collar.

Pierce turned away. His steps thumped along the hall, down the stairs. I heard the murmur of Mom's voice intersecting with his again, the creak of a hinge, and then the front door thudding shut.

I dropped the folder onto the carpet.

My chest felt tight. The ache in my head pounded from side to side like clothes in an unbalanced washing machine.

I'd been so close to falling apart. In front of Pierce

Caplan. If there was anyone I *didn't* want to see me crumble into a pathetic, messy pile, it would be Pierce. In all the years I'd known him—basically my entire life—I'd never seen him fail at anything. He didn't spill things. He didn't trip on bumpy pathways. He never said or wore or did anything that was less than exactly right. Pierce was golden.

There was another footstep in the doorway.

Mom breezed into my room. She leaned back against the wall, smiling almost coyly. "So," she said, pointing the smile at me. "That's what Pierce Caplan looks like these days."

I made sure there was nothing coy in *my* voice. "Yes, it is."

Mom shook her head, still smiling, her gaze wandering past me toward the darkened window. "It's so funny to go from seeing him every day to maybe once or twice a year. He practically *lived* here when you were little."

"I know, Mom. I remember."

"He had his own toothbrush and towel and everything. It's like he's aged in fast-motion. He's gotten so tall and handsome, hasn't he?"

I looked at the tops of my socks. "Hmm."

Mom was quiet for so long that I thought she must have gone away. But when I glanced up, she was still standing there, leaning against the wall with her arms wrapped around herself. Her eyes were shiny with tears.

I hated it when Mom cried. She didn't do it often. That

she did it *ever* was bad enough. It made me feel like my spine had been split in half and pulled out through the soles of my feet.

"What?" I said. I sounded irritated. Angrier than I meant to.

"It's just nice to see you two together again," Mom whispered. "Lots of good memories." She pulled herself away from the wall. "Dinner will be out of the oven in twenty minutes."

I knew how I'd missed Pierce for the past two years. It was sharp at first, like a smaller, cleaner version of the wound Dad left, and then it grew increasingly dull, until what I felt wasn't missing him anymore, but resenting him for making me miss him in the first place. I hadn't thought much about what Mom might feel. We'd certainly never talked about it. Once that hideous winter was over, we'd never talked about *any* of it. The Caplans had been our best friends, and when they'd disappeared along with Dad, Mom had lost four people at once. I'd assumed it was the ugliness that distanced us. Everyone wanting to avoid the reminders, the conversations. But the way Mom looked now, smiling and teary, just because Pierce had spent a few minutes in our house again . . .

"Hey, Mom?"

She halted in the doorway.

"You didn't, like . . ." I slowed myself. *Watch your words.*

Neutral tone. "Did something happen between us and the Caplans?"

Mom blinked. Her tone was neutral too. "What do you mean?"

"Like—maybe—when you were dividing up the business afterward?"

"They bought us out. Which was just what we wanted."

"So there wasn't—with what happened—" I groped for the words. "We weren't going to sue them or something?"

Mom's eyebrows twitched, but she barely looked surprised. "Of course not," she said softly. "It was an accident. Everyone knew that." She tapped one fingertip on the doorframe. "Twenty minutes." Then she turned and glided out of view, revealing Sadie lurking in the hall behind her.

I sighed. "Well, you might as well come in. Eavesdropper."

Sadie sauntered across the room and flopped down onto the bed beside me. "I thought you loved an audience."

"Not right *now*. I didn't want anybody to see me *right now*. And they already have."

We both stared into the dressing table's wide mirror.

"We could get you a wig," Sadie suggested, after a second. "Or a cute hat."

"I'm not really a hat person."

"How about a helmet? We could paint 'I shouldn't have gone skiing without this' on the sides."

"How about just 'I shouldn't have gone skiing'? Of course, then I wouldn't have needed the helmet in the first place."

In the reflection, Sadie's face tightened.

"What?"

"Do you think Mom and I don't feel bad enough for making you go with us?" she demanded. "Do you think I don't feel terrible for even suggesting it in the first place?"

"No." I made my tone milder. "I know you feel bad."

For a beat, we studied our reflections. My tanned, shiny-haired sister. Softer, paler, shorter me, now with a giant zipper of scar tissue on my forehead.

Sadie shook her head. "I really thought you would have gotten over it by now."

"Over what?"

"The little-kid, drama-queen stuff. The way you'd pitch a fit any time we did something *you* didn't want to do."

I frowned. "What are you talking about?"

"Camping. Waterskiing. Hiking. Ski trips—"

I pulled away from her so that our arms no longer touched. "I was genuinely scared."

Sadie gave a skeptical head tilt.

"I was terrible at those things," I lunged on. "I thought I would get tangled in the tow rope and drown, or fall off a mountain, or crash into something . . ." I gestured to my head, my voice rising in false surprise. "And look!"

"Oh my *god.*" Sadie leaned away from me. "Ever heard of a self-fulfilling prophecy?"

The pain in my head was thumping like a giant drum now, but I wasn't going to back down. "It's proof that I *wasn't* just being dramatic. I knew, and you all still pushed me. That's why I hated it. And Dad——"

There. The word was out, dangling between us.

Keep going.

"Dad was so *mean* about it." My throat filled. My voice started to wobble. "I still remember all the . . ."

"Jaye." Sadie whirled toward me. "He was trying to *encourage* you. He was pushing you to try harder. To do your best. That's what he did to everybody."

I swallowed. "This was different."

"Jaye . . ." She let out a long, irritated sigh. A second later, she threw both arms around me, jostling my skull. I fought back a wince. "I'm sorry," she said. "I should be humoring you. You're supposed to stay super-quiet and calm, not have a meltdown an hour after getting home."

"I'm not having a meltdown." I snuffled. I glanced at the mirror again. Now the paler, smaller, injured one of us also had watery red eyes. "God. I look horrible."

Sadie squeezed my shoulder. "Remember what the nurses said about not looking at yourself until you feel back to normal."

"The nurses said that?"

"Several times."

I touched the ridge of the scar again. It felt rubbery and dead, almost like it had been made of putty and stage makeup. "It doesn't matter anyway. I'm going to go back to school and rehearsal, and then everybody *else* will look at me, and then Mr. Hall will replace me—"

"Replace you?"

"Have you ever seen a fairy queen with staples in her head?"

Sadie shrugged. "I've never seen a fairy queen. Maybe they all have staples in their heads." I snorted, but Sadie squeezed me tighter. "You'll heal. You already look much better."

"You mean I looked *worse?*"

"Well, in the hospital, when they first let us in to see you . . . Yeah, you looked worse." Sadie's voice was suddenly small. "Head wounds bleed a lot, you know."

"I know."

I could practically feel Sadie's thoughts seeping through her shoulder into mine. Our constantly-in-motion father lying so still in that narrow white bed. His bruised eyelids. The tube wedging his lips apart. The bandages wrapped around his head, where the blood from flying shards of glass seeped through, forming tiny pink blossoms in the white gauze.

"God," I whispered. "Mom must have been . . ."

"Yeah," said Sadie, when I didn't go on. "It was bad. At first."

"I'm so sorry."

"You don't have to be sorry." Sadie pushed a hank of my

hair into place. "Once you woke up, she got a lot better. It was just at first that it was really hard."

"I don't want her to have to feel like that again. Ever."

"Well—hopefully she won't," Sadie said. "You look *so much* better. Really." She gave my shoulders another squeeze. "Come on. Let's go eat."

She hauled me to my feet. Then she led me out of the room and down the stairs without letting go of my hand.

CHAPTER 6

If you sit by yourself in a dark room for long enough, you'll see ghosts.

We used to play this game at slumber parties: Find some dark closet or basement pantry and take turns hunched inside, waiting for the total blackness to form itself into impossible shapes. Then we'd lunge out, screaming.

It was a lot like brain rest.

For the next four days, I lay in my room, without music, with my velvet curtains shut, until morning blended into night and back into morning again. If I kept my eyes open, strange things started to appear on the ceiling. Cracks wriggled. Glow-in-the-dark stars moved. Shadows waved at me from the corner of my eye and disappeared when I turned to catch them. If I kept my eyes closed, the inside of my eyelids became the screen for movies played in fast-forward. Clips of school, classes, stupid things I'd said. A silly argument with Nikki over who'd heard of a certain band first. Pierce Caplan at one end of a half-empty hall, not even noticing me watching him from the other end.

But what my brain really wanted was to run lines for *A Midsummer Night's Dream.*

Staring at the bumps on my ceiling was a ridiculous waste of time, and even my subconscious knew it. I'd wake up with Titania's words in my head, or the fairies' lullaby playing over and over, and have to try to push them out again.

I *needed* to run my lines. I wasn't even sure how many of them had been left intact in my memory. If I didn't catch them soon, they would dissolve and seep away. And then there was the folder of notes from Mr. Hall. The folder I hadn't even opened.

The folder that Pierce had delivered.

Which, of course, brought me back to Pierce Caplan, Pierce and the tornado of questions and memories and stomach butterflies that came with him, and—

Empty stage. Empty stage.

Sometimes I hung on for a long time. I'd focus on the red velvet curtains and breathe in the dust and paint, and there would be no sound but the hum of anticipation coming from inside of me.

And then the voices behind the curtain would begin.

Michaela Dorfmann and the show choir girls whispering, my name sprinkled now and then into the hiss. Ayesha, the stage manager, calling for places. Titania giving her *Come sing me now to sleep* speech, and Hamlet's voice interrupting, *But in that sleep of death what dreams may come . . .* Mercutio from *Romeo and Juliet* rambling about the fairy queen Mab who brings dreams in her nut-shell chariot. Macbeth muttering, *Nature seems dead, and wicked dreams abuse the curtain'd sleep* . . .

And no matter how hard I tried to keep it still, the stage's red velvet curtain would start to twitch.

Terror prickled through me. Every time. I was frozen, imagining who was about to step through the seam: Shakespeare, or Romeo, or Hamlet, or someone else. Some*thing* else. Whatever gruesome image my brain decided to toss into the middle of my thoughts like a grenade. *Something wicked this way comes.*

Then the curtains would rip apart, and my eyes would fly open, and I'd jolt up in bed, feeling sloshy and sick, and I'd try to focus on a ticket stub or program taped to my wall—any little, insignificant thing that could drag my brain away.

On the third night home—at least I think it was the third—I closed my eyes with the stage peacefully empty in my mind. A few seconds passed before a voice startled me.

"Jaye?"

My eyes flicked open.

My bedroom ceiling still hung above me, scattered with burned-out plastic stars. Between me and the ceiling were two faces. Nikki's and Tom's.

I felt my whole body brighten. "Hey!" I hauled myself onto my elbows. "What are you two doing here? Did you sneak in?"

They didn't smile back.

"It happened again tonight," Tom whispered.

"What are you talking about?" I asked. A tiny twinge of worry started to worm in. "What happened?"

Nikki's eyes were wide. Almost frightened. "We knew you wouldn't believe us unless you saw it for yourself."

"With the things I've seen in the last couple of weeks, I'd believe pretty much anything." I glanced from Nikki to Tom. "Seriously. I don't know if it was the injury or the medication or just—"

"*Shh,*" hissed Tom. "Listen."

We all froze.

The house was heavy with middle-of-the-night quiet. Even the street outside was still.

"I don't hear anything," I whispered back.

But both Nikki and Tom had stiffened. They backed silently away from the bed. For the first time, I could see that they were dressed in full suits of leather and chainmail. Nikki had a sword tucked into her belt. Tom held a long staff with a hooked blade at the end.

"Crazy costumes, you guys," I whispered. "Why are you—"

This time Nikki cut me off. "Here it comes again!"

The two of them stared through my open bedroom door. I was sure the door had been shut when I'd lain down in bed, but now I could see straight into the hall, the walls silvery with moonlight from a distant window.

"It wants to speak to you," Tom breathed.

They whipped my blankets back. Cold air rushed over me.

"Hey!" I reached for the quilt, but Tom had already grabbed my arm.

Nikki shoved my feet over the side of the bed. "Hurry! Before it leaves again!"

With all four hands, they pushed me through my bedroom door.

I staggered into the hallway. My baggy T-shirt and flannel pants suddenly felt as substantial as cobwebs. The air was ice-colored. Shivering, I glanced in both directions, from the dark holes of the other doorways to the black cliff of the staircase.

Something flickered there, in the darkness. Slowly, it turned toward me, and I could see its messy blond hair and haggard face.

"I saw him," Hamlet murmured.

My skin cascaded with goose bumps. "Saw who?"

"He stood just there, as though he wanted to speak." Hamlet gestured down the stairs without taking his eyes off me. "He wants you to follow him."

I looked over my shoulder. Nikki and Tom were gone.

"Wait a second." I turned back toward the staircase. "Is this . . . is this supposed to be the opening scene of *Hamlet?* Like, Nikki and Tom were the castle guards, and they've just seen the ghost of your father . . ."

Hamlet didn't even seem to hear me. "We must follow it." He plunged suddenly down the stairs, glancing back to make sure I was following. "Come!"

The usually creaky steps were silent. I padded down into the living room, Hamlet gliding ahead of me like a shadow, my bare feet freezing against the floor. In the dimness, I could make out the two armchairs, the cluttered little tables, but everything had turned fuzzy, all the edges blurred by moonlight. When I looked up, I saw that the windows were dark.

Hamlet paused at the threshold of the dining room, listening to something I couldn't hear. Then he streaked into the kitchen. I hurried after him. The air seemed to be growing colder. My skin shriveled against my ribs.

Hamlet stopped in the middle of the kitchen floor, facing away from me. I followed his eyes. The door leading from the kitchen down into the garage hung open, letting in a gasp of icy, oily air. No wonder the house was freezing.

I reached out to close it, but Hamlet blocked me.

"The air bites shrewdly," he murmured. "It is very cold."

"Yeah. That's why I'm closing the door."

He stopped me from reaching for the doorknob again. "It comes!" Hamlet's cracked-ice eyes were stuck to something through that open doorway. "It wants to speak to you alone."

I inched forward, across the threshold. There was nothing beyond that door but chilly darkness. Not as far as I could see. But as I set my toes on the first cement step, I caught something else. A sound. A soft, repeating, rasping sound.

Hamlet hung back as I crept down the steps.

The cement floor was frigid. The scents of rust and gasoline and dirt and of something else—something sharper—twisted in the air. Our garage had no windows, and still, everything was suddenly lit with that fuzzy silver moonlight. The dingy walls. The stained workbench. And, right in front of me, the hulk of a strange black car.

It wasn't our car. It didn't belong here. But I knew exactly what it was.

The rasping sound came from the car's far side. It sounded almost like someone raking dry leaves. Like heavy, painful breathing.

The side of the car that faced the kitchen door looked perfectly ordinary. I edged around the trunk, my throat turning sour, my heart tightening. The car's other side slid into view.

It was destroyed. Just as I knew it would be. Metal panels crumpled inward. The front right corner folded up like a paper fan.

Something jingled against my toes.

I looked down. The garage floor was covered with broken glass from the car's windows, some of the fragments as fine and powdery as snow.

The front passenger-side door stood open.

A body hung in its cavity, knees on the floor, head hidden inside.

My stomach lurched.

I didn't want to see this. I didn't want to get any closer.

But the rasping sound dragged me.

I staggered forward until I could see that the body wasn't still. It was moving, rhythmically, back and forth, again and again. As it leaned back, I caught a flash of brown hair. A wide velvet collar.

I took another step.

Warmth seeped between my toes.

Something dark and thick was dripping through the open door. It splattered down onto the cement, pooling, spreading, its edge reaching for me.

The rasping stopped. Shakespeare turned and looked up at me, a red-stained rag in his hands. More stains, deep red against white, seeped up from the edges of his cuffs. He shook his head wonderingly. Tauntingly. "Who would have thought the old man to have had so much blood in him?"

For a beat, I was sure I was going to be sick. I lunged backward. My feet clinked through the glass as I charged around the wrecked car, up the stairs, back into the kitchen.

I slammed the door behind me.

Doubled over, heaving, I stumbled through the dining room. Hamlet had disappeared. I pounded up the staircase, along the silent hallway, and through the door of my own bedroom. I slammed that door too.

I flung myself onto the bed and switched on the reading lamp. I yanked the quilt over me, curled into a tight ball, and pressed my thundering head against my knees.

Breathe.

The shards of glass. The dark puddle. That awful rasping sound.

I dug my fingernails into my palms until pain lanced up my arms.

Empty stage. Empty stage. Empty stage.

But I couldn't clear this away. And if I was sleeping, I didn't wake up.

CHAPTER 7

Outside the high school, the morning was still dark. There wasn't even a hint of sunrise in the black sky, just the electric glow from the city beneath it. It might as well have been the middle of the night.

But inside, it was bright. And warm. And loud.

Sadie dragged me through the crowded hallways. "Excuse us," she blared, nudging a knot of underclassmen out of the way. "Coming through."

"Could you maybe try to sound less like a carnival barker?" I jerked my elbow away. "Everybody's staring at us."

"Everybody's staring at *you.*" Sadie grabbed my arm again. "And we're running late because *you* took twenty minutes rearranging your hair this morning, and Mrs. Taylor will blow a fuse if I'm tardy to AP History."

She took off, still holding my sleeve. I flopped after her like an untied shoelace.

Locker doors slammed around us. Fluorescent lights blazed. I kept my eyes on the floor and my mind on staying vertical, but I could still hear the whispers that buzzed us like mosquitos.

"Skiing accident . . ."

"Brain damage . . ."

"Guess she almost died . . ."

Just look at the floor, I told myself. *Look at the floor and keep walking.*

Two pairs of pointed boots strode across the edge of my vision. The boots led up to two pairs of tights, one green and one blue. The legs in the tights were knobby and muscular and clearly didn't belong to any teenage girls.

I couldn't help it. I looked up.

"But thou art not quickly moved to strike," said the guy in blue tights.

Beside him, the guy in green tights and tunic tossed his head. "A dog of the house of Montague moves me!"

They strutted past. In a blink, the crowd of moving bodies had swallowed them. My head throbbed.

Empty stage. Empty stage.

"Come on, Jaye." Sadie spun me back around. "God, you're going to make us both tardy."

Because Sadie was leading the way, and because it was the shortest route between the main doors and my locker, we veered into the hallway behind the old gym.

I usually avoided this route. And I usually avoided it because it meant passing the track and field office.

They'd left Dad's name plate on the door, right above

the name of his replacement. Somebody had gotten a sign engraved with one of Dad's inspirational quotes: *"Just do your best, and your best will keep getting better."—Coach Doug Stuart,* and hammered it up at the top. Then runners had started signing the door, leaving Sharpie signatures and messages and sketches, like it was one big yearbook page. Next to the door was a trophy case crammed with more Dad memorabilia. His face grinning out at us from a memorial plaque. Framed photos of him with his teams positioned between the sparkling trophies. Pierce was in several of the photos. Sadie was in some of them. There was no sign of me anywhere.

Sadie dragged me down the hall, both of us staring straight ahead.

When we finally reached my locker, she waited behind me, jiggling impatiently. I put my fingers on the combination lock. My mind was a cloudy blank. 20. 24? 25? I'd opened this lock eight thousand times. Why couldn't I remember? I let my hand move without thinking. 20 . . . 25 . . . It still took me three tries to get the combination right. The ache in my head plunged forward as I bent down to grab my textbooks.

"*Jaye!*"

A small, blue-haired fairy was barreling toward me.

I shot upright. My mouth went dry.

Of course Puck would have followed me here too.

I took a step back, straight into the locker doors.

Puck sprang past my sister and threw both skinny arms around me. The fairy's hair smelled familiar—like styling foam and cheap incense. She leaned back, beaming up at me, and I realized that she was wearing a very un-fairylike Bauhaus T-shirt.

"Oh my god. Nikki. I'm—" I managed to gasp before a pair of stripy arms shot around me and Tom was bouncing me up and down.

"Whoa. Take it easy, you two." Sadie's voice reached me through the barricade of Tom's shoulder. "Try not to knock the injured girl over if you can help it."

Tom released me. "Sorry! Sorrysorrysorry."

"Yeah, sorry!" Nikki grabbed both my hands and swung them back and forth, beaming manically. "It's just so good to finally *see* you!"

"You look amazing," added Tom.

"I look like something a serial killer stitched together."

Tom shook his head. "Amazing. Amazingly alive."

"Hey, party people," Sadie broke in. "I have to get up to the third floor. Can you two make sure she gets to anatomy?"

"Of course we can." Tom tucked me under one arm. "We'll be her bodyguards."

Sadie snorted. "That teddy bear who sells fabric softener would make a better bodyguard than you." She turned to me. "Jaye. Remember. Take it *easy*."

"Yes, Sadie. *I remember.*"

My sister gave me one more pointed look before rushing toward the nearest staircase.

"Can one of you walk in front of me so I can hide?" I pleaded as Tom steered me into the stream of students.

"Come on, Jaye Bird." Nikki threaded her arm through mine. "You might as well get used to the inconveniences of fame."

"Here's the red carpet." Tom swept one arm across the crowded hall. "You've just climbed out of your limousine, being careful not to flash the photographers . . ."

We worked our way through the junior hall, past the vending machines, toward the gym corridor. Two guys in lettermen jackets did an actual double take as we shuffled by. A clump of dance team girls looked up from their pastel vitamin water, their eyes hooking on me. One girl's pink glossed lip twisted in disgust.

"Everyone tries to catch a glimpse of the star's daring new facial piercing," said Tom loudly.

Just ahead of us, the gym doors burst open.

"Look out," Nikki warned. "Morning practice just ended."

I ducked against Tom's shoulder, bracing myself for a flood of sweaty basketball players.

Instead, a troupe of actors in medieval costumes trotted through the double doors. Hamlet strode in the center of the group. Against their patchwork brightness, his black clothes stood out like an ink stain. My knees locked.

"Speak the speech, I pray you, as I pronounced it to you, trippingly on the tongue . . ." Hamlet gave me a slow, deliberate smile as they all trundled past. "But if you mouth it, as many of our players do . . ."

"Jaye?"

I had come to a complete stop. My heart thumped against my larynx.

A few steps ahead of me, Nikki and Tom had stopped too. They watched me with worried little frowns.

"I . . ." I glanced down the hallway. Hamlet and the troupe of actors had disappeared. "I'm okay. Just . . . sometimes the headache doesn't let me do anything else."

"We were going too fast." Nikki swatted Tom's arm. "Come on. We'll go obnoxiously slow the rest of the way. Like old people in an art museum. I promise."

They grabbed my arms again, more gently this time.

A few seconds passed before Nikki asked, "So, are we going to dance night at Third Street this weekend?"

"Not allowed," I said gloomily.

Tom sighed. "And I don't have money for cover."

"What happened to your paper route money?" Nikki asked.

"*Shh.*" Tom glanced around, making sure no one had overheard. "The paperboy thing is my dirty little secret." He sighed again. "Jonah took it."

Nikki's eyebrows rose. "Your stepdad took your paper route money?"

"*Shh!* God, it sounds like a sitcom plot when you say it *that* way."

"Why did he take it?" I asked.

Tom shrugged. "He doesn't trust me."

"What does he think you're going to do?" Nikki demanded. "Buy eighteen bucks' worth of cocaine?"

"He thinks I'm going to go out to a club and get corrupted by the druggies and the gays and the girls with blue hair."

Nikki gave Tom an extra-sweet grin.

Nikki's hippie-drunk turned born-again Christian mom had provided Nikki with a series of stepdads: first another drunk-hippie type, then just a drunk, and then a surly evangelist who'd gotten her mother to turn her life around and upside down. Jonah was stepdad number one for Tom, but his marriage to Tom's mother seemed to be the only thing he'd ever stuck with.

Of the three of us, I had the most normal family. The most normal childhood. The most normal house, even with the presence of my father filling every room like some tanned, athletic ghost.

The smell of rubbing alcohol and vinegar grew stronger as we reached the anatomy labs. It was enough like the smell of the hospital that for a second I wanted to turn around and run home and bury myself in my rumpled purple blankets.

But then I remembered: Rehearsal. That's what all of this was for.

Just seven hours to go.

In the doorway, Nikki gave me one more hug. "See you at three!"

Tom blew me a kiss. The two of them raced off around the corner.

Keeping my head down, I threaded the half-empty rows of desks and took my place at the back, letting my bag thump to the floor. I slouched in the blue plastic seat. No matter how many times I rearranged my hair to fall over the scar, it kept flopping back to its usual position. The twenty extra minutes at the bathroom mirror that morning had been a total waste. Beneath the shaved spot, the ache rolled and kicked like a creature trying to hatch.

Across the aisle, someone sat down in a desk that was usually empty.

I angled my face away.

Still, from the corner of my eye, I could see that he was tall, with long legs and heavy black boots stretching out beneath the seat ahead of him. One dark-sleeved arm rested on the desktop. I tried to stop it, but my eye followed the arm up to his face.

Angular jaw. Dark, thick eyebrows that arched high and tapered down to neat points at the ends. Pale blue eyes. Tangled black hair.

Great. Romeo had followed me to anatomy class.

As though he'd felt my stare, he turned toward me.

I jerked my eyes away. Someone had scribbled *Ellison Bites* on the surface of my desk. I studied the scroll of the last *s*, ignoring the dark shape that was leaning farther and farther into my peripheral vision.

Be normal. For god's sake, just be normal.

"I think you dropped this." Romeo's voice was deep and soft. Just like I remembered.

I ignored it.

"Hey," he said, a little more loudly. "Is this yours?" One long-fingered hand waved a pill bottle in front of my face. I watched the letters AMITRIPTYLINE—JAYE STUART flash back and forth on its label. "I think it fell out of your bag."

"I can't see you," I hissed through my teeth.

Romeo lowered the pill bottle and craned closer. "What?"

"I can't *see you*." Two desks ahead of me, Kayla Vang turned around. I lowered my voice and tried to keep my lips from moving at all. "You're not really *here*."

Romeo's eyes traced the wound on my face, following it up and over my skull. "Okay," he said slowly. "Then I'll just leave these pills right here, on the edge of your desk."

The bottle landed with a soft click.

"God." I let out an exasperated breath. "Couldn't all of you leave me alone for just half of one day?"

"All of us?"

"You. Everybody in the hall. *All of you.*" I scraped my hair sideways again. "And since when does Romeo say 'okay'?"

The warning bell clanged, cutting off whatever he might have said back. My head rang. The room was filling. I kept my eyes pinned to *Ellison Bites* until all the other seats had been taken, and Mr. Ellison himself was sauntering to the front of the room, positioning his *There are no stupid questions, just plenty of stupid answers* mug on the podium.

The ache was getting worse. My cheeks were hot. The scraped skin beneath my right eye stung.

The second bell sounded, slamming through my brain with the force of a shot put.

Mr. Ellison's lips began to move, but his drone was drowned out by the pulse in my head. The pressure was building, tightening.

Then I heard my name.

"—Jaye Stuart." Mr. Ellison nodded at me. "We're glad to have you with us again, and that you've made such a quick recovery." He paused for a second, as if he expected the sleepy classroom to break out in applause. It didn't. "As we've been studying the bones of the skull, I think we've all taken an extra interest in your situation."

He paused again, obviously waiting for me to speak. Heads were swiveling toward me. I could feel the stares of my classmates clustering like flies around the scar.

"Oh," I said. "That's . . . nice."

"Would you be willing to tell us a bit about your experiences?" He gestured to the podium. "If you're feeling up to it, of course."

I clutched the edges of my desk. "Sure," I managed. Casual. Polite. "I'm up to it."

I forced myself to my feet. Blurry faces turned with me as I made my way up to the front of the room. *Empty stage. Empty stage.* But the stage wasn't empty. I was standing on it. I aimed my eyes over everyone's heads, just like I would do in the auditorium. Still, I could feel Romeo staring at me from the last row, his gaze like a cool, steady stream of air.

Just play the scene. You're a girl in a high school classroom, telling everyone about her recent injury. You're a little tired, and your head hurts. That's all.

I smoothed my forehead. Pitched my voice lower. *Your cue.*

"Okay. Um . . . Over winter break, my mother and my sister and I went skiing." I moved through the recitation, piecing together splinters of memory and fragments of what I'd been told. Beside me, I could see Mr. Ellison's doughy face light up when I got to the part about CAT scans and cerebral contusions.

"So it was a linear fracture, not a depressed fracture," he broke in. "That was lucky. Class, in a depressed fracture, the broken bone moves inward, which puts pressure on the brain. Or Jaye could have sustained a comminuted fracture, in which the bone would have broken into several smaller pieces, and those could lacerate the brain tissue. Very dangerous." He peered down at my scalp, leaning close enough that I could smell his coffee breath. "And they used staples instead of sutures to close the wound, correct? Would you mind bending forward so everyone can see?"

I'd heard that Mr. Ellison would swerve to hit small animals on his drive to school, so he could bring in the roadkill for dissection. At the moment, I completely believed it.

The room was waiting.

I bowed my head. A collective gasp went up from the class. I could hear them craning in their seats, desks creaking.

"And what is the name of the part of the skull that was fractured, class?"

"Frontal bone," the class chorused.

"Thank you, Jaye. You can take your seat."

I streaked back down the row. My face felt like it had been broiled. I sat down hard at my desk, making the chair's metal legs scream against the floor. Romeo's silhouette rippled in my peripheral vision. I leaned on my palm, cutting him off with a curtain of purplish hair.

"We've got both an old and a new student joining us today," I heard Mr. Ellison say through the watery thumping in my ears. "Rob Mason has just moved here from— where was it, Mr. Mason?"

"Portland," said a deep voice to my right.

Oh god.

There was more squeaking and shifting of desks. The class's attention swung away from me like a spotlight moving to another actor.

Oh my god.

"And you're a senior this year, correct?"

"Right."

The voice. I hadn't dreamed it.

But I had *recognized* it.

I peeked at him through the curtain of hair. He was staring straight ahead, not looking at me.

Oh god oh god oh god. I had actually called him *Romeo.*

"Welcome to winter in Minnesota," said Mr. Ellison dryly. "All right, everyone. Take out your books and open to page one fifty-seven . . ."

I wanted to sink down through the cold tile floor. I wanted to dissolve into tiny blushing bits. Most of all, more than anything, I wanted not to have said what I'd said. *Oh my GOD.* I narrowed my focus to the cap of the pill bottle. Only 6.75 hours until rehearsal. Forty-two more minutes until I could run away from Rob Whatever-His-Name-Actually-Was and pretend that this had never happened.

Here's what else had never happened: He had never picked up my hand and raised it to his lips. Even though I knew exactly what it would feel like if he did. Even if he reached across the aisle right now and—

Empty stage.

I left my eyes glued to the bottle cap, listening to the tick of the clock under Mr. Ellison's drone.

When the bell finally rang, I jumped up so fast, I almost knocked my desk over. The bottle of pills toppled off the edge and rolled across the floor. I swooped down and grabbed it, my head ringing, before the new kid could pick it up again. Still, his face intruded into my vision, his eyes blue and cool and irritatingly clear.

"Are you all right?" he asked, in that same familiar voice.

I didn't answer.

I swept the books off my desk, snatched the strap of my bag, and rushed up the aisle. By the time I got to the door, I was running.

CHAPTER 8

The auditorium was dark. Wonderfully, warmly, inside-of-your-own-eyelids dark. Mr. Costa had let me leave algebra early so that I wouldn't have to deal with the noisy crush of passing time. For a few minutes, I had the theater all to myself.

I hurried down the aisle, grabbing the backs of the nearest seats for balance. The red velvet curtains were open. Work lights glowed softly above the stage, revealing clusters of wire and canvas trees where strings of unplugged fairy lights dangled, glinting, from the branches.

I dropped my bag in the fourth row and climbed up the stage steps, holding my script in both hands. The boards thumped under my boots. The sound was deep and comforting, like the heartbeat of some huge, peaceful creature. I crossed to center stage. Spreading my arms, I tilted my head back, looking up at the rows and rows of lights, inhaling the scents of paint and makeup and sawdust.

The pressure in my skull started to fade. I was weightless. My head and ribs and hands dissolved, erasing all the bruises and scars, until I wasn't there at all anymore. All that was left was an empty shape, something someone else could fill.

All right. Your first entrance. Oberon and Puck are speaking, and Titania walks on and says . . .

What? My mind went terrifyingly blank.

Says what?

Says . . . "What, jealous Oberon? Fairies, skip hence . . ."

Yes. That's it.

Now just hold on to it. Just—

"Jaye!" a voice shouted.

The bell must have rung. Cast and crew members were pouring down the aisles. Still, it took several seconds before I realized that the voice had been speaking to *me*. Somebody hugged me, and somebody else spun me around. Anders and Hannah and Ayesha all grabbed me at once, and Nikki and Tom were talking—too fast—in my ears, and I was being dragged off to look at the rehearsal photos on somebody's phone, and I finally glanced up to see Pierce Caplan striding to the foot of the center aisle, his eyes fixed on me.

He smiled.

I felt my face smile back.

"Ensemble assemble!" Mr. Hall's ringing voice called from the edge of the stage. Everybody who wasn't already there scurried into place. "We're making up for lost time, so let's not waste any. No warm-ups today. We'll plunge right in." He clapped his long, pale hands. "Gather around, please!"

Somebody steered me into the tightening circle.

"First of all, our Titania is back!" Mr. Hall threw an arm around my shoulders. There were cheers. I felt myself blushing, my stomach full of warm electricity. "We're going to take it easy on her for a while, so we'll just start at the top of Act Two and see how far we can get. Ayesha, call for places, please."

The stage manager strode toward the wings.

Mr. Hall turned to me. "If you need a break at any time, just let me know," he said, in a softer tone. "This is why we have understudies. Don't push yourself. Understood?"

"Understood."

"Places!" Ayesha shouted from the wings.

Giving my shoulder a last pat, Mr. Hall bounded down into the house. The other actors scattered to their spots. I saw Pierce slipping between the narrow black curtains on the far side of the stage. I took my own place at stage left. The ache hovered around me like a clump of fog.

Now focus. Focus. "What, jealous Oberon? Fairies, skip hence . . ."

The stage lights shifted from gold to blue. Nikki and a freshman whose name I couldn't remember skipped on stage and started their scene. The lines cycled through my brain, setting off little flares of recognition.

I knew this scene. I knew this whole play. I'd been studying it for almost a year, ever since Mr. Hall announced that *A Midsummer Night's Dream* would be the spring production. The script in my hand felt comfortable and superfluous, an extra blanket on an already-warm bed.

You can do this.

My cue. I strode out onto the stage, the fairy entourage behind me. My mind bolted to that last walk down the hospital hall, the singing fairies tagging after me. I jerked it back.

Pierce waited at his mark. A beam of silver light made his profile glint like metal. He watched me step closer, wearing Oberon's regal smirk. "Ill met by moonlight, proud Titania."

I inhaled. Air and words combusted inside me. I felt filled with light. "What, jealous Oberon?" My voice was stronger than it had been in weeks. Stronger than I actually was. "Fairies, skip hence. I have forsworn his bed and company."

Pierce grabbed my wrist. "Tarry, rash wanton. Am I not thy lord?"

I whirled back to him. "Then I must be thy lady. But I know when thou hast stolen away from fairyland . . ." I blazed through the rest of that speech, a long, winding one about storms and seasons, the light inside of me big and bright enough to fill the room.

It was so good to be here. It was so good to be someone new.

"Do you amend it then; it lies in you." Pierce cupped my cheek with his left hand.

I met his eyes. He looked straight back into mine. This was as close as the fairy king would ever come to an apology.

Pierce's voice grew softer. "Why should Titania cross her Oberon?"

For a second, I felt Titania's hesitation. The easiness of giving in. Taking him as he was.

I took a breath. But before I could get out the next line, in the distance, over Pierce's shoulder, a dark figure stepped out of the wings.

It glided into the pool of stage light.

Dark tights. High forehead. Heavy-lidded blue eyes.

Shakespeare sauntered closer to us, his hands clasped behind his back.

Please, no. Not right now. Please please please.

For a long, heavy beat, I couldn't tell if time had stopped inside of me or outside of me. If I was really standing there, center stage, while Pierce touched my cheek and the entire cast and crew waited for my next line. If this was happening at all.

Maybe I would blink, and Shakespeare would be gone. Maybe I was asleep. Maybe I was still lying in that stiff white hospital bed, or in that red-flecked hole in the snow.

Shakespeare tilted his head. He looked at me with something that wasn't quite amusement. "O," he murmured, "what a noble mind is here o'erthrown!"

I felt the fog envelop me. It seeped through my skin, snuffing out the light. The ache started to pound again.

The silence around us was building. My cue. My line.

"And I . . ." I whispered, "most deject and wretched, now see that noble and most sovereign reason, like sweet bells jangled, out of tune and harsh . . ."

Shakespeare's lips moved with mine. ". . . Woe is me," we breathed together. "To have seen what I have seen, see what I see."

I shut my eyes. "Wait."

Pierce's hand drifted away from my face.

"Wait." I could feel the solid boards under my boots, hear the steady buzz of the lights above me. "That's not Titania."

"No," said Mr. Hall's voice, from somewhere that seemed very far away. "It's Ophelia."

I opened my eyes.

The other actors had frozen in their places, staring at me.

Mr. Hall stood at the lip of the stage. "Have you been studying *Hamlet*, Jaye?"

"No." I shook my head. "I . . . No."

Pierce had backed away. When I glanced at him, his eyes flicked from my face to the floor. Maybe trying to save me some embarrassment. Maybe embarrassed for me.

"I mean, I've read it, but . . ." Pain throbbed behind my right eye. "I'm sorry. I think—"

Mr. Hall cut in before I could finish. "Why don't you take a break for the rest of the scene?"

This wasn't really a question.

Murmurs broke out around us as Mr. Hall ushered me down the steps. "Are you all right?" he asked. "Should I be calling the nurse? Or your mother?"

"None of the above. I'm okay, really." Behind us, the whispers grew louder. "I just felt a little dizzy," I said in my stage voice, loud enough to be overheard. "It must have been the heat of the lights or something."

Mr. Hall folded his arms across his chest. "Are you absolutely sure?"

Behind him, I could see Pierce staring down at us. "Yes," I said. "I'm absolutely sure."

"If you feel any worse, let me know immediately." Mr. Hall waited until I'd lowered myself into a seat before whirling back toward the stage. "Michaela, you'll be taking over for now. Let's pick it up from Titania's entrance."

Michaela Dorfmann skipped out of the wings, not even bothering to hide her smile.

I sank down into the seat cushion. The fake velvet scraped the back of my neck. Around me, the auditorium grew hazy, an arrangement of clouds that might abruptly blow away.

The seat to my right gave a creak.

Shakespeare settled into the next chair. He gazed straight ahead, neatening the lace on his cuffs.

"Go away," I whispered.

He ignored me.

For a moment, we stared at the stage together, me grimacing, Shakespeare smiling slightly. Pierce and Michaela were playing out Oberon and Titania's argument. The fog inside my head swirled. Only Shakespeare's face lanced clearly through it.

"Why are you doing this to me?" I breathed through my teeth, as softly as I could. "You're ruining my life."

Shakespeare put on a sorrowful voice. "Alas, how is it with you, that you do bend your eye on vacancy, and with the incorporal air do hold discourse?"

"Shut up." I whipped to face him. His blue eyes were dark and calm. His mouth still wore that little smile. "You're not incorporeal. You're *too* corporeal. And I am not crazy. I know what's real and what isn't."

"Yes," said a supportive voice from my left. "When the wind is southerly, we know a hawk from a handsaw."

Hamlet had taken the seat on my other side.

I cupped my hands over my eyes. "Oh my god."

"You remember." Hamlet nudged my arm insistently. "You knew him. Didn't you?"

He kept on nudging until I dropped my hands. I was staring straight into the empty eye sockets of that stupid broken skull.

"He says, 'Remember me,'" Hamlet whispered, holding the skull closer. "'Remember—'"

"All right," I growled under my breath. "I don't know whether you're still here because of the injury, or whatever cocktail of painkillers and mood-balancers they gave me, or just my own messed-up brain, but I'm not going to let you do this to me. I'm not doing this to *myself*."

Shakespeare gazed at me for a long moment.

"Was your father dear to you?" he asked at last, his voice very soft. "Or are you like the painting of a sorrow, a face without a heart?"

I shot to my feet. My head thundered. My lungs burned against the fence of my ribs.

I caught myself just in time to keep from screaming at an empty theater seat, then raced to the end of the row, across the aisle, toward the stage door in the corner. Its hinges were silent, and I slipped through it into the darkness.

CHAPTER 9

The door thumped shut behind me.

Across the threshold, a short flight of stairs angled up toward the backstage door, its steps lit by the red haze of two exit signs.

I sat down in the middle of the flight and I buried my face in my arms. The ache in my head was too big for my skull. If I didn't keep completely still, it would shatter.

Was your father dear to you? The words echoed with the pulse in my head. *Was your father dear to you? Was your father dear to you?*

How did he know just how to destroy me?

I pressed my thumbs into my temples.

Of course he knew. He was inside my head. He knew everything I knew.

He knew that when somebody dies, everybody else bands together and re-creates them. They take out the flaws, erase the bad stories, crunch the memories that don't match into tight, dark corners. In a few days—a few hours, sometimes—all that's left is the perfect version, and no one can ever mention the flawed, mixed-up, *real* version again. That's the rule.

I pushed harder.

The problem is, if you can't talk about it anymore, how do you even know if that version was real in the first place? Maybe everyone else's version—the wonderful, kind, funny, flawless version—is the truth. Maybe you were the only one who couldn't see it. Maybe you were the only one who didn't *get* to see it. Because either everyone is lying, or you, all by yourself, are wrong.

I was running out of air.

Empty stage. I counted my breaths. In and out. One, two. Three, four. The darkness inside my arms grew quieter.

No one else knew. No one needed to know. If I was only a painting of a sorrow, I was a really good one.

Empty stage. Empty—

Somewhere nearby, a deep voice said, "M?"

My head shot up.

It was too dim to see clearly, but the glow of the exit signs outlined the shape in front of me. Maybe it was its height, or its tangled hair. Or maybe it was just its voice, which still immediately made me think *Romeo*—and then made me want to shut myself in my locker and hide for the rest of junior year. Whatever it was, I knew that the person standing there was the new kid from anatomy class.

"What?" I croaked. And I actually *croaked.* Like a phlegmy frog.

He held out a package. "M?" he repeated. "Would you like one?"

I cleared my throat. "You mean *M&M?*"

"Well, I was only offering one. An M. Singular. But if you want more, go ahead."

He was still extending the package. Keeping one eye on his outline, I reached inside. The crinkled paper edges felt real. The little round chocolates in my hand felt real. I squinted down at my palm. In the ruddy light, all of them looked black.

"They're just M&M'S," said the voice. "I haven't laced the bag with anything insidious, I swear."

"No. I didn't think you were going to roofie me with a bag of chocolates." *I just thought you were a hallucinated Shakespearean character.* And now I'd brought date-rape drugs into the conversation. Hopefully the darkness and the red light would hide my burning face. "I'm just trying to see what colors they are."

His silhouette nodded. "I have a specific M&M-eating order myself. That's why I can never get them at movie theaters."

"Too dark," I agreed. *Just talk. You can do this. Just talk, like a normal person.* "What's your order?"

"Red first, green last."

"Ah. I'm *brown* first, green last."

He nodded again. "Everybody saves green for last."

"This one tastes brown. But I suppose all chocolate tastes brown in the dark."

He gave a little laugh—more of a breath, really, but I assumed it was a laugh.

The sound made my skin flush again. What was wrong with me?

We were quiet for a second. I realized my hands were shaking. I clenched them together. The chocolate shell of the candy splintered and melted on my tongue.

"Are you okay?" he asked.

That voice. I could hardly believe I hadn't created it with my mind, making it exactly what I wanted to hear. But he was standing there, waiting. Listening.

"No," I said. "Actually, it feels like my skull's going to explode. Which might be an improvement, because then at least the aching would be over." I stopped. Way too late. "But please don't tell anyone I said that."

"I won't."

"The headache's not even the real problem." Why was I telling him this? Because he couldn't see my face anyway? Because even the fake memory of him beside me in the snow made me want to keep him here?

His silhouette leaned against the stair rail. One long leg bent to brace itself on the edge of a step. "What *is* the real problem?"

"What just happened onstage is the problem. I've been

resting and recovering and waiting, and *still*..." I flung out my hands, and one uneaten M&M clicked away into the shadows. "If I screw this up—this play, this rehearsal—Mr. Hall will give my part away. Everything I've been working for will be over."

"That's not going to happen."

"What?" I said skeptically. "Why not?"

"Because you're really good."

I snorted. "How do you know?"

"Because I watched your scene." His silhouette turned slightly, folding its arms, and now I could see the long, angular lines of his profile. His features were hard and delicate at the same time, like a portrait done in black ink with a fine-point pen. "I was over on stage right, by the ropes."

"Why were you backstage?"

"The counselors here *strenuously* recommended that I join an extracurricular activity. They knew I'd done other plays, so"—he gave a long, lazy shrug—"stage crew it is." His head tilted, and I could tell he was looking down at me. "I've been part of enough school productions to know what lousy performances look like. And yours was not lousy."

"Well." I twisted sideways, remembering—too late—to brush my hair over the scar. "Thanks."

Rob pushed himself away from the railing. He sat down on the step beside me, just far enough away that his sleeve didn't touch mine.

"Check it out." He bowed his head.

Even in the semidarkness, I could see a bumpy, two-inch scar buried in the roots of his hair.

"Impressive," I said. "What happened?"

"I was a twelve-year-old idiot. I borrowed a neighbor's skateboard without asking—"

"So you stole it."

"I stole it *temporarily*. Which is really just unsupervised borrowing."

"Right. Unsupervised borrowing. Which is really just stealing."

"Exactly." He straightened so the reddish light fell onto his face, and I could see that he was grinning. "This was when we were living in Denver. I'd never skateboarded before, but I decided that my very first attempt should be down this long, steep, highly trafficked city street."

"All kinds of good decision-making happening here."

Now he let out a laugh. "Good decision-making is my trademark. Anyway, I managed to stay upright for a while, which is kind of miraculous. I was probably going about forty miles an hour by the time a car shot out in front of me."

"Forty miles an hour? On a skateboard?"

"Yeah. The record for a skateboarder going downhill is over eighty miles an hour."

I started to smile back. "You just happen to know this?"

"I just happen to know all kinds of useless stuff." He leaned back on one elbow. "The hippo's closest relative is the dolphin."

"*What?*" I laughed. "Wait. Stop. We're getting side-tracked. You were going downhill on a skateboard . . ."

"Yeah. So, this car streaked out, I threw myself backward, hit my head, split my scalp open, and sustained a moderate concussion."

"Sounds painful."

"That's the weird thing. I don't remember it hurting. I don't remember going to the hospital, getting stitches, any of that. I don't remember anything after that red car. That's really all I remember—the feeling of not being able to remember."

"I know," I said. "I can't even remember going on that skiing trip. I can't remember hitting a tree, or hurting my head, or getting to the hospital . . . It's like somebody else stole my body and screwed it up and then gave it back to me. I'm sorry—they 'borrowed' my body without supervision."

He laughed again and looked at me closely, smiling. Then he sat up straight again. "I was back to normal in a few days, but I still remember how that sucked. Not being able to trust my own brain."

"Exactly," I said softly. "That's the worst."

It was like he knew what I was thinking. But he wasn't inside my head. This was real. This was actually, physically happening. I had the sudden urge to reach out and touch his arm, just for proof.

I touched my own scar instead. The ache in my skull

had boiled down to a simmer, but it was still there, ready to flare up with any fresh fuel.

"Just so you know," I said, after a beat, "I'm not usually such a freak. I mean, I don't always stumble around accusing strangers of being characters from Shakespeare."

There was enough light on his face to see his widening smile. "It made for a more memorable first day than usual."

"'Than usual'? How many first days have you had?"

"I think this is my tenth school. Well—thirteenth, if you count expulsions."

"Expulsions? With an *s* at the end?"

"Like I said: good decision-making. And we've moved around a lot."

I leaned back on the step behind us. The simmer had nearly stilled. "I've lived in the same city, in the same *house*, for my entire life."

His eyebrows went up. "Wow."

"Not *wow*. Yawn. Where else have you lived?"

He took a breath, and I could see him running the list in his head. "Portland, Seattle, San Francisco, Denver, Chicago, Nashville, but that was really brief . . . Tacoma . . ." He paused. "And Boston and Atlanta. I think that's it."

"God. I'm jealous. Which was your favorite?"

"Probably Seattle." He met my eyes. "But Minneapolis seems interesting so far."

I straightened up, pulling my gaze away. "It's Rob, right?"

"Right."

"See? I knew it wasn't Romeo." I patted the hair over my scar. "Not one hundred percent insane."

"And you're Jaye Stuart."

"You're correct."

He put out one hand with exaggerated formality. To take it, I had to turn toward him again. I watched my own fingers move toward his, my cold palm pressing against his larger, warmer one. His fingers closed around mine. Slightly rough. Familiar. "Pleased to meet you, Jaye Stuart."

"Pleased to meet you, Rob . . . Martin?"

"Mason."

"I was close."

He didn't let go of my hand. His voice seemed to murmur straight into my ear. "'And palm to palm is holy palmers' kiss . . .'"

I jerked. "What?"

"What?"

I put my hands behind my back, against the gritty chill of the stairs. "Did you say something else?"

"Something besides my last name?"

"Like . . . a quote. Something about hands . . ."

Rob frowned slightly. "Maybe you heard somebody on-stage."

Onstage.

Oh my god. *Onstage.*

I straightened up. "Oh, no. I probably missed my—"

The stage door above us slammed open. Multiple sets of feet pounded down the staircase.

"Jaye?"

"Jaye!"

"Here she is!" Hannah grabbed me by one arm and yanked me to my feet.

Ayesha grabbed the other arm. "Geez, Jaye, you can't just disappear like that." She hauled me up the steps, toward the stage door. "Everyone thought you'd wandered out into the snow or something."

"What, like a dying wolf?"

Ayesha ignored me.

As the door swung shut behind us, I glanced over my shoulder. Rob had gotten to his feet too. He was watching us, one hand on the railing, but the red dimness washed away whatever I might have seen on his face.

"Found her!" Hannah blared, leading me onto the stage.

"Well, *good.*" Mr. Hall's voice echoed through the house. "And only ten minutes wasted. Jaye, everything all right?"

"Yes. Mr. Hall, I'm sorry. I just lost—"

"Never mind." His tone was brisk. "Are you able to continue?"

"Yes. I'm fine. I'm able."

"Then let's just move on. We'll start from the top of scene two: Titania enters with her train."

I stepped back into the wings. A knot of fairies was waiting impatiently. A few of them shot me angry looks as I sidled into my place.

"Okay," Ayesha signaled us. *"Go."*

I tried to brush away the embarrassment. Titania wouldn't be embarrassed. She would be graceful and regal and strong. I sailed out into the light, the fairies skipping and tittering around me.

"Come, now a roundel and a fairy song. Then, for the third part of a minute, hence . . ." The words were there without me having to search for them, pulling one another like electric lights on a string. "Sing me now asleep; then to your offices and let me rest."

I sank down on the platform that was supposed to look like a mossy riverbank. Little wire-stemmed flowers sproinged around me as I lay back and shut my eyes.

Other things tried to barge their way in, but I kept my mind locked on the stage. Just because I was asleep didn't mean I could stop being Titania. The fairies sang their lullaby and pittered off into the distance. I kept still, conscious of my breathing, conscious of every little twitch of my face.

The stage lights were warm, glowing red-gold through my eyelids. The velveteen grass tickled the back of my neck. *What would a fairy queen dream about? Fairy dances. Flowers. Charms. Her Oberon.* I turned my head slowly, drowsily, like someone stirring in her sleep—and even though I hadn't opened my eyes, I could see the night-dark hospital room around me, the narrow bed with its plastic railings, the tubes threading out of my arm. I could see him, sitting in the chair beside me. His black hair. His blue eyes. Listening. Waiting.

CHAPTER 10

Everyone onstage for notes!" Mr. Hall's voice called.

The platform rolled backward as Nikki plopped down beside me.

"Nice work," she whispered, leaning back against the crinkly daisies.

"Really?" I sat up. The house lights blinked on, turning the fairy forest back into the auditorium. "Was I okay?"

"You were great. As always."

"Not at first. At first, I was crazy, quoting-the-wrong-play girl."

"Yeah, quoting another Shakespearean play. How unimpressive." Nikki smacked my arm. "You know what? After two weeks in the hospital with a concussion, you're allowed to mess up once. Just once, though. Any more and you're fired."

"Fairies—quiet please," Mr. Hall's voice cut us off. "During the lullaby, we need two full circles around the platform, *then* reverse, then exit. Titania, you can take your time falling asleep. Listen and watch for a while, if you'd like. And Hermia, remember, when you wake up, you don't realize Lysander is already gone, so make sure not to turn in his direction . . ."

I scanned the stage while Mr. Hall went on. There was no sign of the new kid. He'd probably snuck out early. He wasn't here because he wanted to be, anyway. Why would he wait around?

But he *had* actually been here.

He had been.

I was pretty sure.

"That's it for tonight, everyone!" Mr. Hall shouted, throwing both hands in the air. "Get some rest, and we'll see you all tomorrow!"

Nikki pulled me to my feet. "Can you come out for coffee with me and Tom?"

"Yes. You *have* to." Tom skidded across the stage toward us. "We have three weeks to catch up on."

"I'm not allowed. No coffee. No fun. No *out*."

"Just say rehearsal ran late," Tom suggested. "That's what I always do."

"I can't. If I get caught, my mom will pull me out of the show. And then she'll strangle me with her super-strong yoga arms."

"Boo." Nikki tucked a strand of hair behind my ear. "Well, we can at least drive you home. Grab your stuff."

"I'm going to drive her," said another voice.

I whirled around.

Pierce Caplan stood over my right shoulder.

"You are?" I said stupidly.

Pierce smiled in a way that made my rib cage buzz. "Yeah. It's all arranged."

"Really?" Nikki's eyes snapped from Pierce's face to mine. "Because your sister thinks *I'm* bringing you home."

"I talked to Sadie in chemistry," said Pierce, still looking at me instead of Nikki. "I'm taking her." His hand brushed my back. A chain of sparks trailed up my spine. "So. Are you ready to go?"

It would have been more comfortable to tumble into Nikki's rusty old car between her and Tom, breathing the coconut air freshener and spilled coffee and the residue of Nikki's hidden cigarettes. The prospect of riding with Pierce—being alone with him, away from everyone else— was like standing at the top of a snowy hill. Excitement and fear swept through me in freefall. *Pierce Caplan.*

"Um . . . yeah. I'm ready." I gave Tom and Nikki a quick wave. "Thanks anyway, guys. Talk to you later."

"Okay." Nikki took a step backward. Her face was hard to read. "See you later."

Pierce guided me past her, down the stage steps, up the aisle. I didn't look back. I didn't want to know if Nikki and Tom were still watching us with those strange looks on their faces.

Pierce led the way through the school doors and across

the parking lot. Daylight had already drained from the sky. Just a few streaks of indigo seeped up from the horizon.

I tried to remember the last time I'd been alone with Pierce—not counting the two awkward minutes in the greenroom before auditions, or the way he'd surprised me, puffy and unwashed, in my bedroom. It had been years, I knew that much. We'd started to veer apart in middle school, me turning toward plays and him toward sports. Still, every now and then on summer weekends, he'd call and we'd swim together in his family's pool, splashing each other with diving toys, having breath-holding contests under the crystal green water. Or we'd take our bikes and explore new parts of the neighborhood, chasing each other through the alleyways. Dad was always so pleased when he heard I'd spent the day with Pierce. He didn't like my new theater friends. He called Tom and Nikki the Spice Girls. Sad Spice and Scary Spice. I had to beg him not to do it to their faces.

Now Pierce was guiding me toward a glossy black BMW. I didn't recognize the car, which made me realize again how big the gap had grown. Once, I could have cataloged every T-shirt in Pierce's drawers. Now something as huge as his car was totally unfamiliar to me.

"Nice car," I said lamely.

"It's my dad's old one." Pierce stopped. A stricken look crossed his face. "I mean, it's not—"

"No. I know."

The words hung between us in a puff of frozen breath. We both knew what had happened to his dad's *old* car.

Then the breath dissipated, and the words were gone, and we headed to the BMW's opposite sides.

Pierce unlocked the doors. I slid into the passenger seat. The instant I'd buckled the seat belt, a nervous, vibrating sensation nestled into the top of my chest. It beat harder as Pierce started the engine.

We shot out of the parking lot.

I pressed back against the leather seat. My fingers locked around the armrest on the door. That unfinished sentence had tainted everything. I didn't want to be in this black BMW, this slightly newer version of the car that I'd seen, crumpled and bloodstained and surrounded by broken glass in our dark garage. My panicked face stared back at me from the side mirror.

Calm. Cool. Elizabeth Taylor. Marlene Dietrich.

Pierce paused at a stop sign, then streaked forward again. The icy road tugged at the tires. I felt the car skid slightly as we rounded a corner.

He finally broke the silence. "So . . . overall, how was your first day back?"

I swallowed. *Cool. Steady.* "It was okay. I wish I hadn't screwed up in rehearsal, which was totally humiliating. But other than that . . . it was all right." I swallowed again. My tongue was like paper. "How was your day?"

"Not bad."

The BMW squealed around another corner. I gripped the armrest tighter. Days of slumping around like a slug might have messed up my internal speedometer, but I was pretty sure we were going too fast for these streets. Uncomfortably fast.

Another realization hit me. Maybe Pierce was only driving me home as a favor. Maybe he couldn't wait to get this over with. To get me out of his front seat and zoom off to whatever it was he actually wanted to do these days, with whoever he actually wanted to see. Maybe Sadie had even *asked* him to drive me home, thinking his car would be safer than Nikki's rusty old Beetle. God, how embarrassing. How utterly pathetic.

We hit a divot in the pavement. My skull thumped back against the headrest. I heard myself suck a breath through my teeth.

Pierce's jaw tightened.

Of course. He was probably annoyed at having to chauffeur some ex-friend around. Some weird, awkward, injured ex-friend who couldn't even make ten minutes of conversation. The scene I'd screwed up had been *his* scene too. He had plenty of reasons to be irritated.

Before I could decide for sure, Pierce wrenched the wheel to the right, throwing me backward. The BMW skidded to the edge of the road and crunched to a stop.

The pounding in my chest turned from a mallet into a sledgehammer.

My father had done this once. In the exact same way, in almost the exact same place. Just over two years ago.

We'd been halfway between the school and our house. Dad had been silent ever since we left the counselor's office, his fingers clenching and unclenching the wheel, and I'd sunk so low in my seat that my chin rested on my sternum.

Dad had let out a loud breath through his nose. Then, so abruptly it almost made me sit up straight, he veered to one side, nearly planting the front tires in a snowdrift. He jammed the car into park.

He'd whipped toward me, one hand grabbing my headrest. "Just what do you think you're doing?" His voice was a barely smothered yell. "Late for class *eleven times* this semester? Participation grades slipping in every subject? And now, in-school suspension for skipping class?"

I'd stared at the hole in the knee of my purple jeans.

Dad's jaw rippled under his skin. This always made me shiver. "How do you think this makes me look? When it's my job to motivate students? To make them into winners? And here's my own daughter throwing every opportunity away, moping around, turning herself into a loser like she's doing it on purpose?" The veins in his forehead had risen. I could practically hear them pulsing. "So, would you just explain to me, please, *what the hell you think you're doing?*"

"I told your sister I'd drive you straight home." Pierce's voice seemed to be coming from behind a black velvet curtain. "But I figure I'm not breaking my word if we just sit here for a minute. I mean, it's not like I'm driving you anywhere *other* than home."

"Oh," I managed. "Yeah."

"The drive isn't long enough to really talk. You know?" Pierce angled toward me. He didn't have to unbuckle his seat belt, because he hadn't buckled it in the first place.

"Oh," I said again. The black curtain was disintegrating, taking the residue of my father's voice with it.

Pierce cleared his throat. "I have to tell you: When I said I was doing the play because of you . . . it's not just because you made it look like a good time."

I scrambled for an answer. "Really?" *Good one.*

"With what happened . . . you know . . . to your dad . . ."

My spine went rigid. *No. No. No.*

"I knew you probably hated me," Pierce went on. "I knew you maybe even blamed me. At least a little."

Why? I wanted to say. *Because your dad's still alive and mine's not? Because my dad spent his last minutes with you instead of with us?* But I just swallowed one more time and said, "You weren't driving."

"But I was there." Pierce stared through the windshield. I scraped my gaze along his profile like I was honing it. Perfect nose. Strong chin. Dimples that were visible even when he wasn't smiling. The ache pounded harder. "What happened—" Pierce went on "—you know—losing him . . ."

I gritted my teeth. *Shut up. Shut up. Shut up.*

"It was the worst thing that had ever happened to me. And then, as the months went by, it was like . . . I started to realize I'd lost *you*, too. I mean, I understood it—why you wouldn't want to see me or talk to me anymore. But for me, really, that turned out to be even worse."

The thing in my chest thrashed. *I wasn't the one who pulled away*, I wanted to scream.

Suddenly Pierce turned to face me straight on. "I've missed you, Stuart," he said softly.

I slid my papery tongue over my lips. "I missed you too."

He grabbed my hand. His skin was warm and dry in spite of the cold. I found myself cataloging all the ways it was different from the hand that had held mine in the red-lit stairwell. This hand felt smoother. Warmer. Golden.

"When I heard what had happened to you—that you'd been in an accident, and you were in the hospital, and it was serious—that's when I told myself that I wasn't going to waste any more time." Pierce gave me a little smile. "I know it sounds crazy, but it's like the universe was telling me, 'Hey! Here's this thing you lost once, and now you almost lost it again for good, so you'd better wake up and see how much you care about it. Maybe try to get it back, if you still can.'"

The words falling out of Pierce's lips couldn't quite make their way into my brain. I almost said, *That's nice*, because he had stopped talking, and I couldn't figure out what else to say. I just held perfectly still as he wrapped my hand in both of his.

He ran his thumbs over my knuckles. "Maybe that was the point of all of this. Like, these things had to happen to push us apart and bring us back together. And now it means more. Because we both know what we've missed."

He looked so earnest—so almost-joyful—saying this. Like he'd just won some fantastic prize and was waiting for me to congratulate him.

"So," he went on, giving me the half smile that made one of his dimples flicker, "what do you think?"

"What do I think?"

"I mean, I know we can't go anywhere right now, but how about when you're better?"

"When I'm better . . . What?"

"Do you want to hang out? Go to a movie, or out for dinner, or something?"

"Oh," I said, for the eight hundredth time that day. "Sure."

Pierce was still smiling, but now his eyebrows pulled together. "'Sure,'" he repeated, in my dreamy tone.

"Yes," I said, more loudly. *"Sure."*

Pierce gave me one more bemused look. Then he turned back toward the windshield, clicked the turn signal, and edged back out into traffic.

The moment we bumped into my driveway, I threw open

the passenger door. The car hadn't even stopped moving. If I could get away from Pierce fast enough, I might be able to make it indoors without falling apart. I lunged out of the BMW, dragging my bag clumsily after me, and bolted toward the front door.

"Thanks for the ride," I called over my shoulder.

"Good night, Stuart." Pierce grinned at me through his open window. "See you tomorrow." Keeping his eyes on me, he backed down the driveway and peeled away into the thickening dark.

I paused on the porch for a minute, taking a few cold, deep breaths. Once my heart rate felt halfway back to normal, I reached out and opened the door.

Sadie was curled up in the living room armchair. She looked up from her computer as I crashed into the room.

A coy smile spread across her face. "Have a nice ride home?"

I plunked down on the couch. It gave a saggy squeak. "No."

"No? What happened?"

"I acted like an idiot." I tipped sideways until my face was buried in a heap of pillows. "I sounded like someone who's just pretending they can speak English. *Huh? Oh. Yes. Sure.*"

The cushions bounced as Sadie sat down beside me. "What were you two talking about that overwhelmed your powers of speech?"

"Pierce . . ." I turned my face sideways on the slippery pillow. ". . . I think he just asked me out. Sort of."

"Sort of?"

"He said, 'Do you want to hang out or go to a movie or something?'"

"You lucky *brat!*" Sadie shrieked, bouncing onto her knees. "Do you know how many senior girls are going to want to skin you and wear your face?"

"Well, they'll have a handy place to start peeling." I rubbed my forehead. "I don't really know if he meant it as a *date* thing, or as a *just friends* thing, or as an *I pity you, you grotesque weirdo* thing, or—" I sat up, dropping my voice to a whisper. "Oh god. Mom isn't here, is she? Is she overhearing this?"

"I made her go to yoga class. She was getting that long-haul-trucker glaze." Sadie leaned closer, sweeping the hair back from my face with her cool, apple-scented fingers. "You know, you aren't acting like a girl who's just been asked out by the most gorgeous *senior* in our entire school."

My throat tightened. I could feel my face crumpling. For years, I'd tried to learn to cry like Katharine Hepburn: big, barely restrained tears shimmering like diamonds on my lower eyelids, mouth tilting down in a vulnerable but elegant line. I'd practiced in the mirror until I could make my eyes well up and give my mouth that little downward curl—and still, when it came to *actual* crying, I knew I looked less like Hepburn and more like a wet paper bag.

"Sadie," I sobbed. "Today was awful. I made an ass of myself over and over. In front of Mr. Hall, in front of this new kid. In front of everyone at rehearsal. Ever since I got home, I've been waiting to feel like *me* again. I keep telling myself it has to get better. The next day, or the next hour, or the next few minutes have to get better. But it doesn't."

"What are you talking about?" Sadie frowned. "What happened that was so bad?"

"You can't tell Mom this, okay?" I wiped my cuff across my cheek. "Ever since the hospital, I've been having these dreams. Sometimes it's like I'm stuck inside them, and they're so real that I don't even try to wake up, and sometimes I *know* I'm already awake, but pieces of the dreams—people from the dreams—are still there." I snuffled into the pillow. "I *know* they aren't really there. But I can't make them go away. And they're going to ruin everything."

Sadie's hand rested on my shoulder. "Blue Jaye, lots of people see and hear things after a head injury. Medications can make you hallucinate too. That, on top of a concussion . . . It would be weird if you *weren't* a little messed up."

I wound an unraveling thread from my cuff around my fingertip. "Maybe."

There was a beat.

"So . . . who did you see?" Sadie's voice was very soft. "Did you see Dad?"

I froze. I could feel the locked door between us inching open, icy air from the other side blowing in.

I shook my head, looking down.

Sadie's voice turned crisp again. "Well, if this is a symptom of the injury or a side effect of the drugs, either way, it has to get better with time. Right?" She gave my shoulder a brisk pat, and I knew the door was safely shut. "I mean, you just got out of the hospital a few days ago. You probably still have Jell-O in your veins."

I pulled the unraveling thread tighter. "Probably."

"Did you tell the doctors or nurses about this stuff?"

"No. At least, I don't think so."

"Jaye! You should have *told* them."

"But I needed to get back to normal. I had to get back to the play, and school, and I couldn't keep watching Mom walk into that hospital room trying to look like she wasn't going to fall apart if somebody breathed on her too hard . . ."

Sadie wrapped her arm around me. For a minute, I sagged against her shoulder, snuffling, while she patted my messy hair.

"Don't tell Mom," I said at last, into her collar.

Sadie sighed. "I won't. But *you* have to tell her if it gets worse."

"I will."

"You swear?"

"I swear, damn it."

This was an old Dad joke. It was as close to opening the door as we could comfortably get.

Sadie and I smiled at each other for a second. Then she reached for her computer, and I got up and climbed the stairs to my room.

I sank down on the bed and checked my phone.

So glad UR back! Hannah had texted at 2:06 p.m.

Pierce Caplan? said one from Tom. *Yr full of surprises.*

The first text from Nikki read: *Call me.*

The second one, sent five minutes later, read: *CALL ME NOW.*

Nikki picked up her phone on the first ring. "Are you alone?"

"Yes. I'm alone."

"Pierce isn't there?"

"No. That's what *alone* means. He dropped me off twenty minutes ago."

I heard Nikki let out a breath. "What *was* that? Him insisting on driving you home?"

"I don't know. I think he was trying to be nice."

"*Nice?* Pierce *Caplan?*"

I got up and shuffled across the room toward one of my collages. A photo of Tom and Nikki and me in our costumes from *Snow White* was hanging askew. All three of us were dwarves. I pushed it back into place. "I know he's not, like, a friend or anything, but we used to be close. Best-friend close."

"You know what he and Josh Hedlund and Bryson Rayder and those guys did to Anders, don't you? Leaving the specimens from dissection in his locker? Sending him those creepy messages?"

I closed my bedroom door and leaned back against it. "I don't think Pierce was part of that."

"Well, Josh definitely was. He got suspended for it. And he's, like, Pierce's right-hand man."

"Are you saying Pierce *commanded* him to do it or something?"

"No, I'm just saying that Pierce's current 'best friend' is someone like *that*."

The ache twisted behind my forehead, making one eyelid twitch. "You don't know him like I do. Or *did*, anyway."

"I guess not. Because he doesn't talk to people like me."

"I wish you'd give him the benefit of the doubt. I think he's trying to change, trying to do new things. Like the play. To be a little more open-minded and friendly to everybody. I think the stuff with—you know—everything that happened . . . I think it really screwed him up."

Nikki was quiet for a beat. "That's generous of you," she said. There was another exhaled breath. In the background, I heard a blast of her mother's Christian folk music, followed by the loud slam of a door. Nikki was shutting herself in her own bedroom. The music got quieter. "I can try. It's just . . . I've seen what he's like when he loses his temper."

"What are you talking about?"

"Didn't I tell you about this? I suppose not. It's not like seeing Pierce Caplan throw a fit had any bearing on our lives *last* year."

"Nikki, *what?*"

"Okay. Last spring, after some track meet or something, where I guess the team had come in fourth and he was totally furious with everyone, he had this *meltdown* in the parking lot. I was at school late, doing layout for the magazine, and I came out into the lot and saw him smashing his car with a trophy."

I ran my hand across my pulsing forehead. "The BMW?"

"It was scary. He just kept hitting it over and over. He smashed the rear window. He smashed the lights. He just kept hitting it and hitting it until the trophy was in pieces, and then he got in and drove away, with me and a couple of his track friends staring after him."

"You're sure it was Pierce?"

Nikki gave a little snort. "It was him. Plus, I heard from Josh that he'd already punched a couple of the guys on the team who he thought were slacking off or something. But none of them reported him, so the school never did anything."

"I never heard that."

"Well, I *did*."

Silence lengthened between us. There was no point in arguing with Nikki. I hadn't been there; I hadn't seen whatever she'd seen. But she didn't know all the things I'd seen, either. All the good things. Even if they'd happened a long time ago.

"My . . . um . . . my family really loved him." I forced the words out. "They thought he was just the greatest guy."

I heard Nikki let out another long breath. "Sorry, Jaye. I'll try to be nicer. Like I said."

"Thank you. And you know *you're* my very favorite person, right? Way above Pierce Caplan?"

She laughed. "Good night, fairy queen. 'May flights of angels sing thee to thy rest.'"

"That's the wrong show."

"I know. You're not the only person who can quote *Hamlet*. See you tomorrow."

After she hung up, I stood in the darkness for a while, keeping still, letting the ache rumble inside my head until it had worn every other thought away.

CHAPTER 11

The bile-sweet smell of cider vinegar saturated the anatomy room. The class had clustered in the lab, where Mr. Ellison shuffled between the high black tables, arranging a set of dissection pans. I huddled in a corner, staring down at the cuffs of some torn black jeans that I couldn't remember putting on. I couldn't remember brushing my hair or my teeth that morning, either. I couldn't remember smearing deodorant under my arms, or packing my book bag, or how I'd gotten to school. I rubbed one eyelid, and my finger came back blackened. At least I'd remembered eyeliner.

The second bell rang, its buzz exploding through my skull. I jerked away from the wall before the sound and the smell and the headache could combine and make me throw up my breakfast all over the anatomy room floor. If I'd even eaten any.

"Today we embark on our dissection unit," Mr. Ellison announced. "I know you're all raring to go. But remember, scalpels are not toys. Pins are not toys. Your frogs and their parts are not toys. This is science class, not a slasher film."

While Mr. Ellison droned on, I glanced around the room. The new kid wasn't there. I checked each table again, just to be sure. No tall, blue-eyed guys with black hair.

Something inside me sagged.

Was I actually disappointed?

Why was I looking for him in the first place? We'd shared a few M&M'S, he'd touched my hand, and my brain had started spinning a web that connected him to some dreams and a sad old play. If any of that had actually happened.

My stomach tightened. It couldn't all have been a hallucination. Other people had talked to him. Looked at him. Mr. Ellison had called on him.

But in the backstage stairwell, it was only me.

"If anyone needs to step out of the lab for a moment, they may," Mr. Ellison was saying. "But I've been teaching this unit for twenty-one years, and I haven't had a student faint over a frog yet. Fetal pigs, on the other hand . . ." This was supposed to be a joke, but no one smiled, Mr. Ellison included. "All right," he finished. "Go to your stations."

Head down, I edged toward my spot at table twelve.

My partner, Emma Kraus, snapped on a pair of latex gloves. I caught myself starting to imitate her shoulders-back, chest-out posture, then went back to my usual slouch.

In front of us, our frog lay on its back in the tarry pan, its little froggy arms and humanoid legs splayed out. Its belly looked like a cold fried egg.

"I've never seen a frog this size in the wild," said Emma.

"Me neither." I looked at its long, pale toes. "They're probably only found on the frog farms that raise them to ship them off to high school anatomy classes."

"Focus," warned Mr. Ellison, strolling through the aisle between us. "Put your gloves on. Take out your scalpels."

"Want me to start?" Emma offered briskly.

I stared at the frog's delicate yellow underside. "It seems kind of mean, doesn't it? That it died just for us to do this, and then we won't even touch it with our bare hands." I brushed one fingertip over its belly. The skin slid with my touch like a silk water balloon.

Emma gave a skeptical sigh. "Yeah. Okay. I'll cut."

She pulled the scalpel through the skin, and I pinned it gently to the tar at the bottom of the pan. The vinegary smell grew stronger.

"Start identifying the organs," said Mr. Ellison. "You should be able to see the lungs, the heart, the liver . . ."

Something gray and grizzled brushed my cheek.

I turned. Three old women craned over my shoulder. Dirt clung to their matted hair. Smoke seemed to rise from their ragged black clothes. "Stomach, pancreas, small intestine," they incanted, but it was Mr. Ellison's voice coming from their mouths. "Eye of newt and toe of frog . . ."

I jerked. My hand hit the edge of the pan, and Emma's scalpel slashed out of line, straight through the frog's stomach. Emma gasped.

"Sorry." I could barely hear myself over the watery thunder in my head. "I'm sorry. I'm sorry."

The three witches were gone. Mr. Ellison moved closer.

"Careful there, Miss Kraus. You're not giving the frog a gastric bypass." He sauntered on to the next table. "Interesting. This one's liver is substantially enlarged . . ."

"I'm so sorry," I told Emma again. "My hand just slipped."

"It's fine," she said tightly. "Just hold it still so I can make the next cut."

I clenched the sides of the cool metal pan with both hands. *Six and a half more hours until rehearsal. Try to act like a sane person until then. Just pretend.*

Across the room, the intercom buzzed.

"Mr. Ellison?" said an amplified voice. "Would you please send Jaye Stuart to Mrs. Silverberg's office?"

I froze. Had anyone else heard *this* voice?

Several pairs of eyes flicked toward me. Mr. Ellison gave me a drowsy blink. "All right, Miss Stuart. You'll just have to catch up on what you've missed tomorrow."

I reached for my book bag. "Sorry, Emma," I said one more time, although she actually looked relieved to see me go.

Once I was out of the anatomy room, I let my face slip. Nausea and panic bubbled inside me. For a second, I was tempted to go to the nurse's office instead of the counselor's, to put on my best quietly tragic sick face—my toned-down

Camille face—and let her make the decision to send me home.

No. Rehearsal. Six hours and twenty-five minutes to go.

I stacked the bones of my spine into a column, like we did in warm-ups. Each vertebra sliding into place. Skull balanced on top, lightly, like it was hanging from a string. Then I headed toward the second floor.

The counselors' offices were lined up in a row. Name plates glinted on the battered wooden doors. Before I could stretch out the final few steps, the third door in Counselor's Row flew open.

"Jaye!" Mrs. Silverberg beamed out at me. "Good to see you! Come on inside!"

I flattened my face into a pleasant blank and squeezed past her into the room.

Mrs. Silverberg's office was a small blue box. The walls were coated with inspirational posters of stock nature photos and Zen sayings. A dark wood desk and three up-holstered armchairs took up most of the floor space. I settled myself on one puffy seat.

"So!" said Mrs. Silverberg, plunking down on the other side of her desk and clasping her ring-glittery hands. "You've finished one full day and come back for more!"

I widened my smile slightly. "Yep. I'm back."

"That's fantastic!" From her tone, you would have thought we were discussing plans for a surprise party. "And how has it been going?"

"Fine." I made my smile even wider. "I mean, I've got a lot to catch up on, but everyone's been really understanding."

"And you're feeling good about coming back so quickly?"

I flexed the corners of my mouth, trying to keep the smile from going tight. "Yes. I'm really, really glad to be back."

Mrs. Silverberg nodded. "That's nice to hear. Well, if you *do* feel that you need some additional time or help, just let us know. Some of your teachers are concerned that your regular schedule might be pushing you too hard."

Who's concerned? Mr. Hall? I corked the questions. *No fear on your face. Keep your voice calm.* "No, I'm fine. I wanted to get back to my regular schedule."

"Of course." Mrs. Silverberg braced her chin on one glittery fist. "We just want you to know that if you need a little leeway—extra assistance, or extended deadlines, or a break from certain activities—the staff here would understand. And we're all one hundred percent committed to helping you graduate on time."

I scanned Mrs. Silverberg's features. Everything was sparkly and steady. "That's nice. Thanks."

"Well—that covers the academic front." She leaned forward. "And how are you doing emotionally? The accident must have been a lot to deal with."

She paused. I kept my face attentive, my smile pleasant. I didn't answer.

"And then coming back here, to all the stresses and

responsibilities of high school . . ." Mrs. Silverberg trailed off, waiting for me to pick up the cue.

If she was watching closely, she might have seen my nostrils flare. I needed to work on my breathing. "It's been a little overwhelming. Like you said." I looked down at a framed photo on her desk to keep her from looking straight into my eyes. In the picture, three dripping children stood in front of a sun-splotched swimming pool. "But I think wanting to come back here, to rehearsals and classes and my friends, is what keeps me motivated. It's what helped me recover so quickly."

"Are rehearsals going well?"

I caught a flinch just in time. Had Mr. Hall talked to the counselors? Had he told Mrs. Silverberg that he was worried about me? Was that why I was sitting on this squishy chair in this little blue room right now?

Mrs. Silverberg's smile gave no clues.

"Pretty well." *Hopeful. Light.* "I mean, I *think* they are. I'm a little behind, but I love the play. I love my role. I want to do my best. I don't want to let this stupid thing hold me back." I patted my forehead. The scent of vinegar shot up my nose, and I suddenly remembered that I hadn't washed my hands since touching the pickled frog.

"And I'm sure it won't. Not with an attitude like that." Mrs. Silverberg's smile softened like melting butter. "Your father would be so proud of you."

The words were a kick in the lungs. *Wrong,* I wanted to

shout. He wouldn't have been *so proud* of my commitment to some wordy old play. He would have been nonplussed, at the very best. Nonplussed and disappointed. Nonplussed/ disappointed/bored. I sat, paralyzed, for a second, fighting the fury back before it could explode through me.

Then I put on my graciously humble face. My Vivien-Leigh-accepting-an-Oscar face. "Thank you," I murmured. Below the edge of the desk, out of Mrs. Silverberg's sight, I wiped my froggy fingers on the upholstered chair. "That's nice to hear."

Mrs. Silverberg sent me back into the hallway with a sloppily scrawled pass. I stood there on the scuffed tiles for a few seconds, trying to imagine going back to anatomy class, the sliced-open frog on the tabletop, the witches whispering in my ear, and felt the hallway begin to smear around me. The walls wavered. The floor dribbled like pancake batter. I reached out for something solid, and felt my hand lock around the corner of a plastic desktop.

"Everybody with me?" said a voice.

Mr. Costa turned away from the board and let his gaze sweep the algebra classroom. His nearsighted brown eyes traveled from face to face, landing at last on mine. He waited for a nod.

I managed a tiny head twitch.

Mr. Costa turned back to the board, and I looked down at my desk, trying not to hyperventilate. There was my notebook. There was my pencil from American Players

Theater. How had they gotten here? How had *I* gotten here? How had I gotten through the last six hours?

I squeezed my eyes shut. Still, sealed inside my eyelids, I could feel the room rocking from side to side. *Less than an hour until rehearsal. Almost there.*

"So, if we add 2b squared, c to the fourth, and 5b squared c to the third . . ." Mr. Costa's voice marched on.

You're all right. No one noticed anything. Empty stage. Empty stage.

Cautiously, I lifted my eyelids.

Mr. Costa's jowly face had narrowed. His forehead was higher. His hair was longer. A gold hoop dangled from one ear.

"2b, anyone?" His now-blue eyes met mine. "'To be, or . . .'"

The kid in the desk in front of mine turned around. He wasn't a red-haired junior anymore. He was Hamlet in a Pink Floyd T-shirt.

"Are you following any of this?" he whispered, holding up a skull covered with pencil-scrawled integers.

I shot out of my desk. Everyone around me looked up.

"Um—Mr. Costa?" I croaked. "Can I be excused?"

Mr. Costa's brown eyes settled on me. He gave an understanding little nod before tapping the board and pulling everyone's attention back. "So, how can we simplify this?"

I grabbed my books and tore out of the classroom.

In the nearest bathroom, I took out my phone and stared

at the date and time until the digits began to swim. At least I'd only lost a few hours this time, not days. Still, the thought that my body had been wandering around without my mind was frightening. Violating. Like something had been stolen right out of my pocket.

I soaked a brown paper towel in cold water and pressed it against my forehead. Its fibers were rough on the raw skin. The stalls were empty, so I stood there for a few minutes, leaning against the sink and blinking into the water-specked mirror. My eyes were bloodshot. My skin looked like wax.

When the rocking feeling had settled slightly, I rinsed my mouth with a handful of rusty water and staggered back into the hall.

There was no way I could go back to algebra class. I'd already come dangerously close to blurting something bonkers and giving myself away. Better to have them all think I was hurting than know that I was crazy.

Without being sure where I was headed, I hurried off in the opposite direction.

After the fluorescent light of the hallways, the dimness of the auditorium was a shock. I had to stop just inside the doors. I leaned back against the solid wood for a while, letting my eyes readjust while the headache swelled and slowly shrank again.

A row of work lights burned above the stage, probably left on by crew members working on the set over lunch.

When I was sure I wasn't going to trip over my own shoes, I shuffled down the aisle toward them.

Titania's platform was positioned upstage left. I dropped my stuff in the seats, climbed the steps, and sank down onto the grass-colored velvet. The buzz of the lights was lulling. The padding under the velvet was soft. Very slowly, the panic began to drain away. I could feel it trickling down through the platform, into the boards, filtering through the hollow darkness under the stage. I pictured myself floating on a swell of muddy water, like Ophelia, my skirts buoyed up by pockets of air. My body weightless.

"There is a willow grows aslant a brook, that shows his hoar leaves in the glassy stream . . ." I heard myself say the words aloud. I was pretty sure they came from *Hamlet,* but I didn't know how or when I'd learned them. They drifted through me like that muddy stream. I kept my eyes shut and let the words pull me. "There with fantastic garlands did she come of crow-flowers, nettles, daisies, and long purples, that liberal shepherds give a grosser name, but our cold maids do dead men's fingers call them—"

"Hey," said a deep voice.

I screamed something that might have been a word. Probably a rude one.

Something lanky and black flickered in front of me.

"God—I'm sorry." The thing held out both hands. "I didn't mean to scare you."

I rolled to a sitting position, tilting my face away. My heart was pounding. Each pulse sent reverberations through my skull. Through the messy strands of my hair, I peered out at the flickering thing in front of me.

Blue eyes. Black hair. Dark clothes.

Romeo.

No, *Rob.*

Rob.

"You," I said blearily.

His face was worried. "Are you all right?"

I skipped the question. "I didn't think anyone would be here. It's still sixth period."

"I know."

"You know? Then what are you doing here?"

"Skipping chemistry. You?"

"Skipping algebra. Sort of." I tried to rearrange my floppy hair. "Mr. Costa won't care if I don't go back. The teachers are all pretty tolerant, considering . . ." I indicated my monster scar. "So, you're skipping another class?" *God. Are you the hall monitor?* "I mean —I didn't see you in anatomy this morning."

"Yeah. They're pretty tolerant of us new kids too. If I say I got lost, or I didn't understand the schedule, or I didn't realize that the day ended at three o'clock instead of two fifteen, they usually buy it. For the first week, anyway."

"You've done this before."

"Skipped class? Yes. Terrified a girl with a head injury—I think this is a first." He took a step away from the platform. "I'm really sorry. I'll leave you alone if you want."

"No," I said. Too quickly. Then, partly to cover it, partly because the question was pounding harder and harder in my head, I said, "How can I be sure you're even really here?"

Rob's left eyebrow went up. "The fact that I just scared the crap out of you isn't proof enough?"

"Nope." I shook my head carefully. "I've seen other people who I know weren't really there. And I've heard them too, so hearing you doesn't count."

"Hmm." Rob reached into his back pocket. Then he crouched down on the floor in front of the platform. "There. Proof of my identity." He held out a leather wallet.

I took it. Its leather was ancient, buttery and smooth at the corners. It fell open at the folds like a broken-spined book.

"So this is what an Oregon driver's license looks like." I raised the card toward my nose and read the small print aloud. "Robert Coltrane Mason. Coltrane?"

"Family name. My mother's side."

"I don't know. It seems pretty improbable."

He pointed to the wallet. "You can cross-check it with my other IDs."

I opened the pocket behind the license and pulled out a

wad of paper and plastic. "Geez. How many library cards do you have?"

Rob settled on the stage floor, folding up one long leg beneath him. "I never throw any of them away. They help me remember where we've lived."

I flipped past the library cards. "It might be a challenge to earn this free latte at Seattle's Finest Coffee," I said, holding up a blue punch card. "You decided this was worth saving too?"

He shrugged, smiling slightly. "You never know."

"Here's a card reminding you that you had a dentist appointment eight months ago . . ." I pulled out a ticket stub. "And you saw something called The Ravages at someplace called The Morgue."

"Oh, yeah." He laughed. "A punk show in Portland."

"How was it?"

"Pretty bad. But really loud."

"At least you got your money's worth." I leafed to the bottom of the pile. "And . . . oh." The last thing in the stack was a photograph. It was in black-and-white, its corners almost as battered and soft as the wallet itself. In the picture, a beautiful girl with long, wavy dark hair and an old-fashioned swimming suit leaned against a boulder, with a rocky seashore spreading out behind her. The photo could have been an antique, or it could just have been a filtered shot of a cool vintage girl. The kind of girl who knew how to make pin curls and where to find Bettie Page–style swimsuits and who probably went to punk shows in Portland.

I felt a jolt of ice in my stomach.

Was it actually jealousy? *Don't be an idiot, Jaye. Or at least don't act like one.*

"Who's this?" I asked, keeping my voice light.

Rob craned to look at the picture in my hand. "Oh. That's Vera."

Even lighter. "Is she a friend of yours or something?"

"I don't actually know her name." Rob sat back again, bracing one arm on his raised knee. "She just looks like a Vera. When I bought the wallet at a secondhand shop in Belltown, she was inside."

"Oh." I ran one fingertip over the photo's most battered corner. "And you just left it in here?"

"Well—yeah. It seemed right. I mean, she'd been there for decades already." He nodded toward the photo. "Look at the back."

I flipped it over. A message was written in faded, feminine cursive: *To Teddy with all my love. June 1942.*

"I wonder what happened to Vera and Teddy," I said, after a beat. "If they ended up together, or . . ."

"Me too," said Rob, when I didn't finish. "He kept the picture for a long time, anyway. Or somebody did. And then whoever it was eventually gave his wallet to the Salvation Army."

I put the picture at the bottom of the stack of cards and slid them all gently back into the leather pocket. "It's sweet," I said. "That you kept it."

"So." Rob held out a hand. "Now you know all the weird contents of my wallet. Does that qualify as proof?"

I tilted my head to one side, considering. "I don't think so. I could have come up with all of this in my own subconscious." I handed the wallet back. "Well—maybe not Vera. But everything else."

Rob's eyes caught mine. Looking into them felt like edging my toes into a cool stream. A shiver raced up through my legs, into my spine, and for a second, I wanted to plunge the rest of the way in, to know everything, to tell everything, to be completely *there*—but then I remembered the hideous gash on my forehead, and all the mess that went with it, and a second later, I remembered Pierce. Gorgeous Pierce. Perfect Pierce.

I pulled my eyes away.

"How's your head feeling?" he asked.

"Not great." I scraped my hair over the scar. "Like an ugly mess inside and out."

"Most people can't lie around and quote *Hamlet* perfectly if their heads are a mess."

"So that *was Hamlet*. See?" I crossed my legs on the platform, angling slightly away from him. "I didn't know I knew that speech. I didn't even know what it *was*."

"Maybe that head injury gave you some kind of crazy

gift. Like those people who have a seizure and can suddenly play every piano piece Mozart ever wrote."

"But it's not like I can recite all of *Hamlet*. Or any other play. It just—it comes out in these weird little pieces, at the worst possible times."

"Okay. Maybe it's Shakespearean Tourette's."

I laughed. The tightness in my skull was loosening. "How did you know that was from *Hamlet*, anyway? Have you done that play?"

"We were studying it in lit class at my last school."

"But you said you've been in other plays, right?" I felt the sudden need to move the conversation away from myself, away from real thoughts and feelings. "Which ones?"

Rob leaned back on his elbows. "In reverse order: *Much Ado About Nothing, Our Town, Tom Sawyer, The Three Little Pigs,* and *Alice in Wonderland.* I was the Dodo."

I felt a faint, deep sting at the words *Alice in Wonderland.* I rubbed it away. Put on a smile instead. "The Dodo? I love it. And please tell me you were one of the Three Little Pigs."

He grinned. When he smiled, the shape of his chin sharpened, and asymmetrical laugh lines appeared on either side of his mouth. I found myself studying that smile, feeling my own face trying to imitate it, even though I knew I'd probably never get it right. "I just built sets for that one," he said. "I like being offstage more than having to be on."

"Really? I *love* being onstage." I shuffled my feet against the fake grass. "My favorite thing is that feeling when you're waiting in the wings, in the dark, totally hidden, but you can *feel* the audience out there, and then you step out and the lights hit you, and you're blinded for a second, and you could be anywhere, but you know you're inside this thing that you're helping to create, and it's like—it's like electricity. I'm completely addicted to it." I gestured to my forehead. "That's why I was in such a hurry to get back here. Even with this giant thing on my head."

"I get it." Rob watched me for a second. His smile had softened a little, but it changed again before I could figure out what was behind it. "What's been your favorite role so far?"

"Probably this one." I pulled a petal off one of the silk daisies. "I've played a lot of crappy parts."

"Such as?"

"Oh, god. Let's see. The stupidest of the seven dwarves. An ear of corn. A talking tumor —"

"A tumor?"

"It was an anti-smoking skit."

His left eyebrow went up. They were great eyebrows. Stage makeup eyebrows.

"I don't know," he said. "I think a talking tumor is cooler than a fairy queen. For sheer messed-up-ness, anyway."

"Maybe. But the tumor had fewer lines."

Rob laughed out loud. I felt myself smiling too, the constriction in my body starting to release. There was something about having him near—something exciting and comfortable at the same time. Something familiar yet totally new.

But it *wasn't* familiar. My brain was stretching feelings that didn't belong over moments that hadn't happened at all. I yanked another petal off of the daisy, making it tremble on its wire stem.

I'd been quiet for longer than I'd realized. When I looked up again, Rob was watching me closely. His eyes made my neck tingle.

"Are you remembering your roles as other inanimate objects?" he asked.

"No," I said, looking away. "Actually, I was thinking that maybe it would be better if I *was* imagining all of this. Because then at least I wouldn't be acting like such a freak in front of everyone. And then I was thinking that maybe it would be worse, because this is the most realistic hallucination I've had yet."

"So you need, like, *metaphysical* proof of identity. Yeah. I don't carry that in my wallet." He paused, looking thoughtful. "You're supposed to pinch someone who thinks they're dreaming, right?"

I pulled my legs out of his reach. I actually heard myself giggle, like a girly idiot. "Don't pinch me."

"I wasn't going to. I swear." He extended one hand toward me, palm out. "What if we just shook hands?"

"We've done that before."

"And it was real."

I shook my head. "Not every time."

Now he frowned, but he looked more intrigued than confused. "What do you mean?"

The red-spattered hole in the snow. The hospital room. Rob lifting my hand, kissing the back of my wrist . . .

"Nothing. I'm—don't listen to me."

"But I like listening to you." Slowly, Rob reached out and ran one fingertip down my forearm, over the place on my wrist where I could almost feel that kiss. Then he leaned back, meeting my eyes. "Feels real to me."

My stomach fluttered with paper-thin wings.

"Hey," he went on. "After rehearsal—"

Before he could finish, the final bell blared through the auditorium.

The sound tore through my brain. I hunched over, squinting. Red spots flared in my half-open eyes. The sound hadn't even died away when the auditorium doors slammed open and cast members started to pour in.

Anders and Hannah and Tamika were some of the first down the aisle. Nikki and Tom showed up together, laughing about something as they threw their bags into the seats. Pierce strolled in several steps behind them. His light gray sweater seemed to glow with its own magical spotlight. His hands were tucked casually into his pockets. He saw me, and his face curved with that crooked half smile that made my heart jump halfway to my larynx. Then he noticed Rob.

His eyes flicked from my face to Rob's, the two of us caught alone in the onstage dimness. His expression shifted. Then he turned back to me, and his smile was even deeper than before.

"There," Rob whispered to me, under the noise. "I think that might have been proof."

I didn't give any sign that I'd heard him. I inched backward up the sloping platform, keeping my eyes on Pierce instead.

"Hey, Stuart." Pierce leaped onto the stage. "Look what I found in my parents' storage room." He crossed to the platform and stopped in front of me, his foot almost crushing Rob's outspread fingers. Rob leaned out of the way. Pierce didn't glance down.

I stared at the framed photograph in Pierce's hand. Five-year-old Pierce and four-year-old me stood side-by-side in the Caplans' dining room. Pierce wore a tie and a plastic top hat. I was dressed in someone's antique lace nightgown. Several paint-splotched tissues were pinned to my stringy brown hair.

"Ohhhh!" Hannah cooed over my shoulder. "That's adorable!"

More people clustered around us, craning for a look. Rob didn't move.

"That was the day we decided to get married," said

Pierce. "I think my dog was the ring bearer. Didn't we tie a sofa cushion to his head?"

"Oh my god." I cupped my hands over my cheeks. My palms were as hot as my face. "Snooks. That's right. Then he ran around smashing everything off the end tables."

"Look at those chubby cheeks!" someone squealed in my ear.

"Is that toilet paper on your head?" asked someone else.

"Kleenex."

"And I realized," Pierce went on, "we're still technically fake-married. So we should probably get fake-divorced."

Around me, people were laughing. Someone nudged me. Someone else said something I didn't hear. I glanced down at Rob out of the corner of my eye. He was watching all of this, his eyes cool, amused. Catching everything.

"I'll start." Pierce raised one hand. "I, Pierce Charles Caplan, do hereby untake you as my unlawfully wedded wife."

The ache in my head twisted. I didn't feel like being watched by a crowd. Not now, when I was only my bruised, messed-up self, with makeup I couldn't remember applying and the hairstyle of someone who'd just had a frontal lobotomy. But Pierce was grinning. Pierce was as golden and glowing as a trophy.

I put on a matching smile. "I, Jaye Eden Stuart, do hereby untake you as my unlawfully wedded husband."

"You may kick the bride!" someone shouted.

Before Pierce could move, I gave him a kick in the shin. I turned to run. Pierce dove after me, laughing. His arm locked around me from behind, pinning my arms to my sides.

"Let go!" I shouted, pretending to laugh too. "I'm not your wife anymore!"

Pierce lifted me off the ground. His chest was warm and solid against my back, and his arms were like metal bands. They were crushing me. Blood rushed to my head, making it pound, but I didn't really care. Because Pierce Caplan had his arms around me. *Pierce Caplan.* Then I felt like an idiot for not caring. And then I remembered Rob, with his cool blue eyes and his wallet full of interesting memories, watching all of this. My stomach went sour.

"All right, everyone!" Mr. Hall's voice rang through the house. He clapped his long pale hands. "Let's finish the wrestling match, shall we? Ensemble assemble! Center stage, please!"

Pierce gave me one last squeeze before setting me on my feet. I staggered toward the group, still laughing, feeling feverish and dizzy. Rob had disappeared.

"Wrestling with the girl," said Nikki's voice from behind me. "Jock Flirting 101."

"Quiet please!" Mr. Hall ordered. "I'd like to run Act Three, then go back and work a few scenes as needed. Bottom and the players, we'll start with you. And Tita-nia?" His eyes traveled around the circle until they caught me. I tried to brush my hair into place. "Remember, you're already asleep upstage at the start of the scene. Ayesha, call for places."

I turned toward Nikki, but she had already darted off into the wings.

Tom skipped across the stage toward his mark and stopped next to me. He put a hand on my shoulder. His too-large sweater had holes in both cuffs. "Are you okay?"

"Yeah. I'm fine."

"You look a little shaky."

"I'm *fine*."

"Are you sure? You *did* just get divorced."

"Shut up." I smiled and gave Tom a shove. He moved into place, grinning back at me.

The platform squeaked slightly as I settled down on the fake grass again. Downstage, the other actors were milling, murmuring. I spread my hair over the fabric and rested my uninjured cheek on my palm. The lights clicked and dimmed above me.

Tom, as Bottom, and the other players began their scene. Their voices rose and fell in the distance. But it was another voice that whispered in my ear.

"Here lies Juliet, and her beauty makes this vault a feasting presence full of light."

My eyes snapped open.

Shakespeare sat beside me on the green velvet. Stage light frosted his soft brown hair.

"I'm *onstage*," I breathed through my teeth. "Why do you keep showing up at the worst possible times?"

Shakespeare shook his head. "Confusion's cure lives not in these confusions."

"So stop confusing me." I lowered my eyelids to a squint, hoping that from offstage they would look shut.

"In the meantime, hither shall Romeo come, and he and I will watch thy waking—"

"Wrong play," I muttered, struggling to keep my voice and my eyelids down. "And you're not here. You're not here, *you're not here*, you're NOT here."

Shakespeare's voice breathed close to my cheek. "What thou seest when thou dost wake, do it for thy true love take."

At least that was from the right show. I widened my eyes just a sliver. Stage lights made feathery rainbows on the tips of my eyelashes. Downstage, Tom and Adam and the others were reciting their lines; I could hear them, but I couldn't see them from where I lay. Instead, I gazed out past the lip of the stage, into the blurry blackness. If Pierce was out there, or Rob, or anyone else, I couldn't see them, either.

Besides, you're already *awake*, I reminded myself. *You're awake. You're awake. You're awake.*

CHAPTER 12

Oh my god." Nikki reached across my lap and grabbed Tom's hand.

The three of us were sitting on the rolling platform, waiting for Mr. Hall to finish with notes. My mind kept wandering away from his voice, away from the stage, into the darkest corners. I hadn't seen Rob since rehearsal began. Had he watched my scenes from the wings again? Was he still even here? I rearranged my hair and straightened my shoulders, just in case.

Nikki held Tom's shiny purple thumbnail in front of my face. "You forgot to take off your nail polish from last weekend."

"I didn't forget," Tom whispered back. "I'm out of remover, and it wouldn't scratch off. Besides, Jonah already saw it."

"What did he do?" I asked.

"I told him I hammered my thumb in shop class. He was happy."

Nikki blinked. "You're not in shop class."

"He doesn't know that."

"I bet he doesn't know that you've got a bigger nail polish collection than me, either."

Somewhere farther off, I could hear Mr. Hall dismissing the cast, other voices breaking out. Rehearsal was over. I let myself imagine what Rob had been about to ask. *After rehearsal, would you like to . . .* Don't flatter yourself. *After rehearsal, could I look at your anatomy notes?* That was probably it. *After rehearsal, can I hitch a ride home with you?* Or maybe: *After rehearsal, could you get me that girl Michaela's phone number?* My eyes scanned the house, checking each shadow, each silhouette. They were still focused on the blurry darkness when a pair of blue jeans walked straight in front of me.

Nikki and Tom went silent.

I glanced up.

"Ready to go?" asked Pierce.

"Oh," I said, feeling like he'd caught me in front of my bedroom mirror all over again. I raised my chin. Smoothed my face. "Are you driving me home? Because Nikki and Tom and some other people were going to go—"

"Your sister made me swear that I'd drive you straight home again today." Pierce held up my coat and bag. "I got your stuff. So. Are you ready?"

"Oh," I said again. ". . . Sure."

"'Sure.'" Pierce imitated my dreamy tone. "You use that word a lot, don't you?"

"Sure."

Pierce didn't seem to notice the sarcasm. Slinging my book bag over his shoulder, he stepped down from the stage and headed up the aisle.

"Bye, guys," I murmured before hurrying after him. I checked each row of seats as I went, but there was no sign of the new kid. Pierce was walking so fast, I may have missed him anyway.

Outside, a thick, fast snow was falling. The pavement of the parking lot was slick. Without speaking, Pierce grabbed my arm. I couldn't tell if it was to keep me safe or to keep me close.

He opened the passenger door of the BMW, waiting until I'd climbed in and grasped the seat belt before closing it again. This was charming. I should have been charmed. I should have seen the waves of his lion-colored hair and the jut of his chin and the shape of his shoulders and felt fluttery and flattered and happy.

"What a piece of work he is . . ." Shakespeare's voice sighed from the backseat. "In form and moving how express and admirable, in action how like an angel . . ."

My concentration shattered. *"Shut up,"* I growled over my shoulder.

"What?" asked Pierce. He slid into his own seat.

"Nothing. I just—I caught my hair in the seat belt."

Pierce shook his head. "You need to stop hurting yourself, Stuart. You've got little enough hair left as it is."

I felt my face ignite. I turned aside, shaking the hair back across the scar.

Pierce streaked out of the lot. My spine pressed back against my seat, my brain knocking inside my skull. In the rearview mirror, I could see a pair of heavy-lidded blue eyes watching me.

"It's crazy how fast this semester's going," said Pierce, after a silent minute.

"Yeah," I said, still facing away from him. "It goes even faster when you miss a bunch of it."

"You know, after the play, there are only eleven weeks until graduation. It's crazy."

I braced my elbow on the door as he zoomed around a corner. "You must be excited to get out of here."

"Well, I'm just going to U of M, so it's not like I'll be going far." He glanced at me. "It's a sixteen-minute drive from my future dorm to your house. In case you know anyone who's interested."

Now my stomach started to flutter.

"Hey." Pierce's tone changed like he'd just remembered something. "Who was that guy you were with?"

"What guy?"

"On the stage. Tall. Skinny. Wearing black. Looking like some death metal reject."

"Oh." *Proof,* said Rob's voice in my head. Pierce *had* seen him. The wallet, our conversation. It had all been real. Relief and joy streamed through me. "He's new. The counselors made him join the stage crew."

Pierce's profile went rigid. Of course, I realized a second too late, all he'd seen was me beaming at the memory of another boy.

"What's his name?" he asked.

"Rob, I think. Rob Mason, or something."

The BMW was moving faster. We skidded toward a stop sign, barely decelerating before racing on to the next block.

Pierce stared straight ahead. A muscle in his jaw clenched and unclenched. "How did you two get to rehearsal so early?"

"Um . . . Well, I left algebra class because my head was killing me. And I guess he got lost on the way to chemistry or screwed up his schedule or something." *Casual. Careless. Like you can barely remember.* "So we both ended up in the auditorium, like, fifteen minutes before everybody else. Maybe ten minutes."

"So it was just a coincidence? You two being there alone?"

"Yes. Total coincidence."

Pierce gave something so small it might not even have been a nod. "Was he bothering you or something?"

"Bothering me?"

The tires skidded around another corner. My head slammed sideways, and I let out a little gasp. Pierce didn't look at me.

"He looks like—I don't know," he said. "Like a creep. Like one of those guys who think they're a rock star even if they're just a loser who wears jewelry and black leather. That kind of guy."

"He's not," I said, too quickly. "I mean—he seems fine. We were talking about other plays we'd done. That's it." *Change the subject. Quick.* My mind threw itself at a question I hadn't planned to ask. "Hey . . . did you ever smash this car? Maybe a year or two ago?"

Pierce frowned. There was a beat that stretched so long, I almost repeated the question. But then he said, "Smash it? Like in an accident?"

"No, like—with a trophy or something? Somebody told me they thought they saw you."

The frown flickered and broke. "Oh, god. Yeah. Not too long after—uh—after your dad was gone, we placed fourth at a meet for the first time. The first time *ever.* Like, we had *never* not placed first—or maybe we placed second once, like ten years ago—but we had never gotten *fourth.* I was pissed. So, yeah, I smashed the car with that fourth-place trophy." A smile raised the corner of his lips. "Then I had to pay to fix it, of course. But that's what happened."

"Oh," I said.

It was believable. It made his anger seem fair. Almost noble.

Still, imagining Pierce's fist swinging a heavy trophy, denting metal, shattering glass . . . My stomach twisted.

I wasn't going to ask any more questions. Shakespeare's eyes shifted back and forth between us in the rearview mirror.

Pierce didn't speak again. A not-totally-uncomfortable quiet filled the car, and gradually, I let my head sag against the window. The cold glass was soothing. At that angle, the dark blue gaze from the backseat couldn't quite reach me.

After another minute, I let my eyes slide shut. I could still sense Pierce beside me. The warmth of him. The silence that had started to feel less angry than protective.

There was a gentle bump as we turned into my driveway. The car stopped. I heard Pierce shift the gear into park. A second later, something brushed my cheekbone.

I opened my eyes.

Pierce's face loomed over me, gigantic and golden. A strand of his wavy hair touched my skin. His eyelids were lowered. His lips were moving toward mine. It was like the sun had slid out of the sky and crashed into the car beside me.

I was so startled I almost smacked him.

Instead, I jerked backward. My head slammed against the windowpane. There was an audible *thunk*.

"Jesus." Pierce sat back. "Are you okay?"

Behind me, Shakespeare was laughing so hard, he wheezed.

"I'm fine," I said, even though fissuring black clots were shooting back and forth in front of my eyes. "I'm fine."

"Are you sure? That sounded like it hurt."

"No. I'm fine." I groped for the door handle. "I just—I just need to get out."

Before Pierce could unlatch his own door, I flung mine open. I toppled out backward, not even trying to catch myself. Shakespeare let out another hoot of laughter. My bare hands landed in icy slush. I could feel the wetness soaking through my jeans.

Pierce jogged around the front of the car. "Hang on," he said, pulling me to my feet. "Just hold on to me." He hauled me up the walkway to the front door, one arm wrapped tight around my waist.

The door flew open in front of us.

"Oh my god." Sadie appeared on the threshold. "What happened? Are you okay?"

"I just bumped my head," I muttered, pulling up my collar to hide my flaming face. Pierce released me, and I shuffled forward into the warmth of the living room. "I'm fine."

"You don't look fine. Should I call the hospital?"

"God, Sadie, no. I'm just a klutz." I turned back to Pierce, waiting in the doorway, but I couldn't force my eyes any higher than the collar of his coat. "Sorry, Pierce. I'll be better tomorrow."

"Okay." He hesitated, glancing at both of us. "Well— I'll see you then."

His feet thumped away down the porch steps.

Sadie closed the door after him. Neither of us spoke for a second. Then Sadie asked, "Which part of your head did you hit?"

"The back. Not the bad part."

"Do you want an ice pack? Or some water, or anything?"

"No. I am really, truly *okay.* I just want to go lie down for a while."

I trudged toward the staircase, dragging the weight of Sadie's stare behind me.

Without taking off my coat, I sank down on my unmade bed. If I turned my head sideways, there was less pressure on the bruised spot. Unfortunately, it also forced me to look straight at the dressing table, where Shakespeare had settled himself on the ledge.

"My care hath been to have her matched," he began, as if he were talking to an invisible crowd. He picked up a nail file and began grooming his left hand, his face and voice exasperated. "Having now provided a gentleman of noble parentage, stuffed, as they say, with honorable parts . . ." He filed faster. "Proportioned as one's thought would wish a man . . ." He pointed the file at me. "And then to have a *wretched puling fool*—"

I whipped a pillow at him. It hit the closet door instead.

Flopping over, I buried my face in the blankets, not caring that the fabric rubbed my raw skin, or that the weight of my own skull pressed the ache forward until the world turned gray.

My father's eyes were brown. *Had been* brown. So it definitely wasn't the color that made Shakespeare's eyes remind me of him. It was the way they looked at me.

God, I'd seen that look so many times. Disappointed. Scornful. Faintly disbelieving, like I might be some imposter who'd snuck into Jaye Stuart's skin. I'd seen it when I broke curfew and lied about why. I'd seen it when I claimed I couldn't miss rehearsal, so I couldn't come along on the family trip to watch Dad run in Chicago. I'd seen it on the awful night of the eighth-grade spring dance. I'd tried to let this memory fade, but it clung to my brain like a tooth hanging by a stringy root.

Empty stage, I thought. *Empty stage.* But the words were just noises. I couldn't turn the memory off.

We weren't going to go to the dance at all, Nikki and Tom and Anders and I. We weren't the kind of people who went to school dances. We weren't the kind of people anyone asked. But that Saturday night, as we lounged on the swaybacked couches in Nikki's basement, *not* going had started to seem even stupider than going.

It was Nikki who came up with the plan: We'd go to the middle school, but instead of just joining the crowd in the gym, we'd sneak into the costume shop, put on the craziest things we could find, and then make a grand entrance on the dance floor. Two of Nikki's older cousins from North Minneapolis were with us that night—I'm still not sure why; the two of them spent most of the time talking to each other and laughing in a way that made it impossible to tell what they were laughing at. But it was one of them who managed to pick the lock on the costume shop door.

The shop was full of clothes from last fall's *The Wizard of Oz* and our upcoming *Alice in Wonderland,* mixed with leftovers from a bunch of thrift shops and fairy tales. Nikki dressed up as a flying monkey. Anders was a tree—one of the apple-throwing ones. Tom found a dinosaur suit somewhere. I was playing the White Rabbit in *Alice in Wonderland,* so I zipped myself into the fuzzy bodysuit, complete with hood and floppy ears. The cousins, who were really too cool for any of this, just put on long black robes. They looked like scrawny executioners.

There was a little stir when we all strutted out onto the dance floor. Some people pointed and stared. A few came up to us, laughing, complimenting. Most of them ignored us completely.

Standing around on a crowded gym floor in heavy costumes got dull pretty fast. I can't remember if it was one of the cousins who suggested the next part, or if it was Nikki, or if it was just something that happened because we were bored and restless and tired of being noticed and not noticed at the same time. I just remember that it was already dark when we crept out of the gym and through the side doors onto the athletic field. Anders led the way across the grass, his papier-mâché branches rattling softly. A stack of crates was propped against the back of the field house, and suddenly we were all climbing up onto the broad tar-papered roof.

We lay down on our backs and stared up at the night sky. Above us, the stars were small and white as spilled sugar. The fuzz of the rabbit suit tickled my neck. One of the cousins took out a little tin box and some rolling papers, and we all passed the first joint around. The smoke seemed to swell inside of me until my lungs ripped like cotton batting. Tom had some cigarettes and a bunch of tiny plastic bottles of brandy, all stolen from his stepdad, and soon I was floating, and the stars were cycling gently, and we were all laughing, and I don't know if it was the smoke or the brandy or just being together at night on top of the school field house in a bunch of ridiculous costumes, and then the police came.

The next hour is a blur. The entire crowd from the dance—all the students and teachers and chaperones—lining up to stare while the officers questioned us. Police lights strobing with the music that still poured out the doors. Red and blue flashes on Tom's fabric scales, Nikki's wings, my own fuzzy white feet. Tom's mom and stepdad. Nikki's mother. My father coming to pick me up. The terrifyingly silent drive back to the house.

All at once, the whole night seemed impossible. I couldn't really be sitting next to my dad in the front seat of the car, with a brain full of mist and stars, wearing a white rabbit suit. I could hear Dad breathing beside me. Like a dragon. If he'd turned toward me and started yelling then, I'd have been crackled up in a rush of fire.

But he didn't. He didn't say anything.

Somehow that was worse.

When we pulled into the driveway, Dad still hadn't spoken. He got out of the car without looking at me. I followed him inside, keeping my eyes fixed on the tight, straight line of his back, feeling like my own feet weren't quite touching the ground.

Mom was waiting in the living room. Her eyes flicked between the two of us. "Go up to your room," she said.

I shuffle-floated up the steps. Shut inside, I took off the rabbit suit and hung it awkwardly over the back of my chair. Its fur smelled like smoke. Then I sat down on the very edge of my bed, like it didn't belong to me.

My parents' voices simmered softly through the door. I couldn't decipher any words—just the low, angry thrum of Dad's, and the higher, almost inaudible tone of Mom's. Eventually things got quiet. A few minutes passed before I heard the thud of the front door.

I got up, swaying slightly, and went to the window. In the patches of light beneath the streetlamps, I could see Dad in his running clothes, flying up the sidewalk, dwindling quickly out of sight.

My heart rocketed up into my head.

He was leaving. I'd pushed him away. It was too late to catch him; he was already gone.

I scrambled back down the steps.

Mom looked up, startled, as I raced into the kitchen.

"Where is Dad going?"

"He needed a run." Mom turned back to the dishes in the sink. "It'll help calm him down."

"Oh." I hung on to the doorframe. My heart was still torn loose, knocking around somewhere in my skull. "So . . . what's going to happen?"

Mom's lips were tight. "We'll talk about that later."

"Am I grounded?"

"Jaye—"

"Am I? Please, just tell me."

"Yes. You're grounded. No visitors. No phone. No after-school activities."

"For how long?"

"A while, Jaye."

"What about the play?"

Mom sighed, bracing her hands on either side of the sink. "Your dad thinks you should be done with that too."

"What?" *Don't scream. Calm. Mature. Head spinning. Heart floating.* "But everybody—Mom—the show's only three weeks away."

"After what you kids did tonight, you'll be lucky if the school lets any of you participate. Did you even think about that before you made these great choices?"

Of course not. My stomach writhed. "Mom, please . . ."

Mom lifted one hand, not looking at me. "Stop. I'm not doing this with you. And your dad feels even more strongly than I do."

"When will he be back?"

Mom stared down into the dirty water. She let out a long, slow breath. "A while."

I hurried through the living room, out the front door, and sat down on the top of the porch steps. The night had gone pitch-black. I had no idea how late it was, but the air felt cold and wet, and the streetlights shut out all but the very brightest stars.

After a few minutes, I started to shiver. I wasn't sure if it was cold or anticipation. But I wasn't going to go inside to get a sweater and risk missing the moment when Dad jogged up the driveway, risk having him *not* find me here, looking humble and cold and sad and small. I wanted him to see me shiver.

It seemed to take forever. I started to wonder if maybe he wasn't going to come back at all. If running until he wasn't angry at me anymore would take him all the way out of the state, find him still racing along at daylight, somewhere far away. But at last I heard the soft slap of shoes on the sidewalk, turning up into our driveway. His gray WILSON HS TRACK T-shirt flickered through the shadows. His breathing, still fiery, but steady now, came closer.

He jogged up to the steps, stopping a few paces away

from me. In the yellow glow of the streetlights, I could see tiny wisps of heat rising from him, floating out with each breath.

He didn't say anything.

I waited for a second. "Dad . . . I'm really sorry."

A stiff nod.

"I won't ever do anything like that again."

He didn't even nod this time. He picked up his left foot, stretching his quads. I thought I heard him give a snort, but it might just have been an exhalation.

I put on my most mature voice. *Meryl Streep*. Plus a little Julia Roberts, for charm. "I totally agree that you should ground me."

Now I heard the snort. "I'm glad to hear that."

"But I'm . . . please . . ." I swallowed the panic. "*Please* let me stay in the play. Please. Not for me. I'd be letting everybody else down."

Between breaths, Dad's voice was low. Sharp. Hard. "What do you think you did tonight?"

"I . . ."

"And since when do you worry about 'everybody else'? When do you worry about *anybody* else?"

I felt my mouth fall open, but my brain was still too fuzzy to put the right words in it.

Dad dropped his left foot and picked up the other. He wasn't looking directly at me, I realized, like he didn't even want to touch me with his eyes. "Do you know how many strings I'll have to pull to keep you from getting suspended? Or expelled?" His jaw rippled. His voice got even lower. "Don't you get enough attention? Now you have to get caught by the police, on drugs, on a rooftop, in a rabbit costume, in front of the entire school? What kind of statement are you trying to make?"

"I'm not—it's—it was just a mistake."

"Yeah, it was. And you've been making plenty of those lately. Did you think, for even a second, about how all of this reflects on us?"

"No. It's not about you."

For a beat, I thought Dad was going to explode. His mouth tightened. His eyes got wide. I shrank back against the steps.

Dad glanced around, quickly scanning the street. He dropped his right foot and leaned against the front of the house with one hand, moving on to the next stretch. If any neighbors were watching, all they would see was him going through his usual routine, me sitting nearby, watching him.

"You think this doesn't reflect on us? You think what you do doesn't damage and embarrass all of us?" Dad's voice rang softly off the wall as he leaned forward. "You know what? Things are not going to go on like this."

"What do you mean?"

"I mean I don't want you spending time with Tom Leung or Nikki Vega or Anders Larson anymore. They are messed-up kids from messed-up families. You need better people in your life."

"But they're my friends." *Don't panic. Calm. Pitiful.* "They're my *only* friends."

Dad frowned. "What about Pierce?"

He might as well have said *What about your unicorn?*

"Pierce?" I repeated. "He's in *high school.* We're not even in the same building anymore. And even if we were, he doesn't—we aren't—he hasn't even talked to me in months."

"Have you talked to him?"

"Dad, we don't—we're just different people now. I have more in common with people like Nikki and Tom and—"

"God, I hope not," Dad cut me off. "And if those are the kind of kids doing theater, maybe you shouldn't be doing *any* plays for a while."

These words tunneled straight through the mist. I felt each one of them hit me.

"What?" My voice came out in a weird, choked squeak.

Dad switched legs, going on with his routine as if everything in the world wasn't falling apart. "You need to take a break. Focus on your grades. Try something new. Or go back to something else—tennis, volleyball, anything. But this"—he nodded toward me, his eyes still not meeting mine—"this isn't you. This isn't going to go on."

I felt my chin start to wobble. "Dad. Please. You can't make me stop forever."

Dad sighed, exasperated. "Did I say forever? I said *for a while.*"

"No." I was crying now. Not Katharine Hepburn crying. Not Meryl Streep crying. Ugly, out-of-control crying. "You can't do this."

"Keep your voice down," Dad growled, jaw tight. "I am not discussing this in front of the entire neighborhood."

"You can't take this away from me! You can't take *every-thing* away from me!"

"I'm done." Dad lunged forward so suddenly that I cowered against the steps. But he just charged past me, up the steps, through the porch door. "No one can even talk to you when you're like this. I'm finished."

I sat on the porch steps for a long time, sobbing into my arms. Maybe neighbors were watching me. Maybe no one even noticed. I kept my face hidden and my posture as tragic as possible, just in case. Finally, when I couldn't cry anymore and my toes had fallen asleep, I got up and trudged inside.

The house was quiet. All the lights except the one in the upstairs hall were turned off. Mom and Dad's bedroom door was shut. I went to bed in my clothes.

Sometime just before dawn, I heard the front door thump again. I hurried to the window.

Dad ran up the sidewalk below me, looking fuzzy and faint in the lavender light. In seconds, he was gone.

We didn't speak to each other for days.

In the end, I got to stay in the play. Mom must have softened. Dad didn't come to any of the performances, and he didn't come to the show I did that summer, either. Eventually Nikki and Tom were allowed to come over again, and things went on almost as usual, even though I could feel something emptier in the space between me and Dad, as if both of us had just taken two big steps back.

Sometimes, when I look out the window in that just-before-sunrise part of the morning, I can almost see him running away up our street, his body frozen in that hazy blue light, disappearing. Sometimes I wish I'd called out to him. Sometimes I wish I had run after him, even though I know I could never have caught up.

CHAPTER 13

You *have* to hear this." Tom grabbed me by the arm and yanked me down over the side of the stage.

Mr. Hall had just dismissed the cast, and everyone was forming little clumps of conversation. I could see Pierce in the seats far to the right, surrounded by a cluster of fairies. Tom, Nikki, Anders, and some others stood in a huddle just below the stage, laughing. When Tom pulled me down, I found myself wedged between Anders's skinny arm and someone else's shoulder.

I glanced up.

Rob Mason.

We'd had a test in anatomy that morning. Rob, as the new kid, was excused. He hadn't even glanced at me when Mr. Ellison stopped him at the door and sent him to the library. But he looked at me now.

He gave me a quick, friendly smile. Then his eyes went back to Nikki.

"Wait, Nikki, start over," Tom commanded. "Jaye missed the first part."

I moved my arm just enough that Rob's sleeve wouldn't touch it. "What's going on?"

"Okay." Nikki rolled her eyes. "You know that guy I've been seeing?"

"That *college* guy," said Anders.

"In a year, half our grade will be *college guys*," Nikki shot back.

"Not third-year college guys," said Tom.

Nikki smacked his arm. "He's in his *second* year. Anyway, last night, my mother found out."

"*What?*" I asked. "How?"

"Because she was going through my drawers, like she does periodically. Which is why I keep everything *actually* incriminating in my car, or hidden at the bottom of the old toy chest in my closet."

"Smart," said Rob from beside me. "No one ever suspects a teddy bear."

"Exactly. But Declan left one of his sketchbooks under my bed when he was over the other night." She turned to Rob, explaining, "He's an art student."

"Of *course* he is," Tom and I said at the same time.

Nikki smacked both of our arms.

"And his name is Declan?" asked Anders.

"Like Elvis Costello," said Rob.

"Exactly!" Nikki's face lit up. "Like Elvis Costello."

"And he's almost the same age as Elvis Costello too," said Tom.

"Shut *up!*" Nikki smacked his arm for the third time, and Tom grabbed her in a restrictive bear hug.

"Anyway," said Nikki, over the crook of Tom's arm, "Declan's name and address and phone number were written right there on the cover. And the sketchbook is from his life-drawing class . . ."

I started to laugh. "Oh, no."

". . . So the book is full of drawings of naked people. Mostly girls. And my mother decides that the guy who draws these must be some kind of perverted slut-monster, and that one of the girls in the drawings looks like me, even though *that* girl has long hair and is obviously about two feet taller than I am."

Rob and Anders and I were all rocking with laughter now.

"Wait; it gets better," said Tom.

"So," Nikki continued, "I got to have dinner last night at Denny's with my mother and her pastor. The *youth* pastor."

"Oh, god!" I laughed. "Oily Eric?"

"Oily Eric. And he ordered some giant breakfast-for-dinner, five-thousand-calorie Denny's thing, and then— I'm serious—he used the fried eggs and the sausage links to teach me about how—"

A hand landed on my shoulder.

We all looked up.

Pierce.

Anders stiffened, pinning his eyes to the floor. I remembered what Nikki had said about Pierce and Josh Hedlund and his other friends, rumors about the bloody things they'd left to rot in Anders's locker. Everyone went quiet.

"Where's your bag?" Pierce asked, ignoring them. "I'll drive you home."

"*Actually*," said Nikki, "since rehearsal ended early, you could come out for coffee with us for a whole half hour and your mother would never even know. New Kid's coming too. Right, New Kid?"

"Right," said Rob.

"Come on." Tom released Nikki from the bear hug and grabbed my hand. "We haven't done this in *forever*."

"You could come too, Pierce," said Nikki, a little haltingly. "If you want." She turned back to me. "So? Yes?"

"She can't," said Pierce.

Nikki frowned. "Why not?"

"Because. She can't."

"Wait. That was crazy." Rob smiled, looking back and forth between me and Pierce. "Nikki asked *her* a question, but the answer came out of *your* mouth. Are you a ventriloquist?"

Pierce's face tightened. "Is this any of your business?"

"Not really," said Rob. His eyes came back to me. "I'm just trying to figure out how things work here."

Pierce pulled me backward—fairly gently—and waited

until I met his eyes. "Are you going to risk doing this play for a cup of coffee?" he asked.

It was a good question.

I would have to be some sort of idiot to do that. The kind of idiot who was just about to run happily off with her friends. Breaking her promises. Forgetting her reasons for all of this.

"No. You're right." I turned back to the circle. "Sorry, everybody. I wish I could go."

"Grab your stuff," said Pierce, before anyone could answer me. "I'll meet you at the doors."

I lurched toward the corner where I'd left my coat and bag, disappointment curdling in my stomach. But Pierce was right. He was being mature and wise and responsible, just like I was supposed to be. Or at least pretend to be.

I reached the top of the aisle and looked back. The group had dissolved. Only Pierce and Rob stood in the space between the rows. Pierce reached out with one hand, not quite touching Rob's chest, and said something that made Rob lean back. Then he turned away and stalked up the aisle toward me.

"What was that about?" I asked as we shoved through the doors into the chilly twilight. "What did you say to him?"

"To that Rob kid? Nothing."

"Nothing?"

"Yeah. Nothing." Pierce met my eyes. His own were steady. "But just so you know, I've heard things about him. Like the reasons they've moved around so much. Why he's gotten kicked out of so many schools." Pierce's voice got harder and louder as we reached the BMW. "You don't need someone like that around you."

"Oh my god. You sound just like——" I stopped.

Pierce didn't prompt me.

We climbed into the car. There was a flash of motion in the rearview mirror, and I looked around to see Hamlet and Ophelia making out in the backseat. Delightful. I sank down in my own seat, feeling prickly and trapped and uncomfortably warm in spite of the freezing air.

Pierce steered the car out of the lot and accelerated up the street. He didn't speak. I didn't say anything either. And Hamlet's and Ophelia's mouths were too busy for talking, which was good, I guess. And awkward. And kind of gross. The ache in my head, which had maintained a low boil all day long, began to bubble faster. I closed my eyes. The car swayed and surged. I swayed along with it, feeling more and more irritated with the ice on the roads, with the kissing sounds from the backseat, with the gorgeous boy sitting next to me. Even if he was right. Maybe *because* he was right. Maybe because, with my eyes closed, I could practically see my father's arm slung around his shoulders, his proud, pleased smile coating Pierce with its warmth.

Pierce turned a sharp corner, and the car slowed to a crawl, then stopped. Bright gold light slipped under my eyelids. I looked up.

"Wait." I stared out at the big stone-and-glass house ahead of us, its facade hung with enough lights to help land an airplane. "This is *your* house."

"I told Sadie I'd bring you straight home." Pierce grinned at me. "So it wasn't really a lie. It's just *my* home." He opened his door. "Plus, we've got that extra half hour."

"But—"

"Come on." He was already climbing out of the car. "I've got some stuff to show you."

I hadn't been inside the Caplans' house in almost three years. And they'd moved to this place not long before that. After the expansion, when C&S Outdoor Outfitters went from one store to a chain, the Caplans had started turning up to get-togethers in their BMWs and sleek haircuts, bringing food and wine that definitely didn't come from the supermarket. I guess their investment had paid off in ways that Dad's hadn't.

I blinked around the foyer. The Caplans' new house was huge and minimalist, with shiny dark wood floors and chalk-white walls. The furniture looked like it had fallen out of a Scandinavian design magazine. Abstract paintings hung in carefully lit nooks. It was perfect. Like everything else about them.

Pierce's mother, Michelle, was in the kitchen. She was a

clothing buyer for a big department store, and she'd always looked like I'd imagined Audrey Hepburn's older sister would look—spare and elegant and effortlessly lovely. She looked up from a magazine as we walked in.

"Hi, honey. How was—" she began. Then her eyes locked on me.

The bare spot on my scalp suddenly felt even barer.

"Jaye?" She stepped closer. "Oh my goodness. It's been such a long time."

"Yeah." I tipped my head, trying to conceal the scar, and put on my Vivien Leigh smile. "How are you?"

"How are *you*?" She took one of my hands. Hers was smooth and cool, with nails like petals. "We were so sorry to hear about your accident. God, your mother must have been . . ." She broke off, erasing her expression and putting on a brighter one. "Do you want a soda? Or can you stay for dinner? I was just going to order from Royal Thai."

"I can't. But thank you."

"Are you sure?" Michelle still hadn't let go of my hand.

I felt my cheeks getting hotter. I wanted to run away, hide my face inside my collar, transform into the kind of beautiful person who belonged in the Caplans' gleaming glass-and-metal kitchen.

"We're just going up to my room for a few minutes," Pierce stepped in. "Then I'm driving her home."

"All right. But help yourselves to anything in the kitchen if you change your mind." Michelle leaned in and gave me

a quick kiss on the cheek. I could smell her delicate perfume. "So good to see you," she whispered before picking
up her coffee cup and wafting out of the room.

"Come on." Pierce nodded toward the staircase. "I'll try
not to get you home too late."

I followed him up the steps.

Like the rest of the house, Pierce's room was white-
walled, wood-floored, and expensively accessorized. A few
books stood on the bookshelves between dozens of glinting
trophies. World Cup posters and track photographs hung
over the bed in subtle silver frames.

I touched the navy bedspread. "No more Star Wars?"

"I'm saving those for college." Pierce grinned. "Have a
seat."

I sat down on the end of the bed as Pierce pulled a stack
of boxes from the floor of the closet. Watching him open
them felt too much like eavesdropping, so I stared across
the room at the only object I recognized: a little plush wolf
with a green collar. Wolfgang. Pierce used to bring him
everywhere. Now he sat on the dresser between a skinny
metal lamp and a silver MVP plaque.

"I can't believe how clean you keep your room," I said.
"You've always been such a freak that way."

"A freak who can actually find a pair of matching socks."
Pierce looked up from the boxes, grinning again. "How
many times did I catch you wearing two different ones?"

"I don't know. Infinity?"

"I bet you're wearing them right now." His hand flashed out and grabbed my ankle. "Let's find out."

"Don't!" I giggled, writhing backward as Pierce started to pull off my shoe. "Give my socks their privacy!"

Pierce pulled my shoe the rest of the way off. "Say uncle."

"Are you serious? Are we nine years old again?"

Pierce smiled wickedly. "Say it, or I'm going to tickle you under your toes."

"No! Please!" I thrashed, laughing, but Pierce's grip was tight. "Uncle. *Uncle!*"

Pierce released me, giving me another smile that made my entire rib cage vibrate. He pulled something out of the open box.

"Here it is." He crossed in front of the bed, holding a bundle in both hands. He set it in my lap.

I looked down. The outside was a gray T-shirt, soft and weathered with washing and wearing. WILSON HS TRACK was printed on the front in dark red letters. On the back, in capitals, was the word COACH.

The room went watery. My hands shook so hard, I could barely unwrap the rest of the bundle.

Tucked inside the shirt was a pair of red-and-white shoes. Dad's running shoes.

"I kept a couple of his things," said Pierce, when I hadn't spoken for several seconds. "You know. From when he was staying here. I guess my mom called your mom, but she just said to donate all the rest of his stuff to charity. I thought—I don't know. I just wanted to keep a couple of the important things."

I dropped the edges of the shirt. The shoes lay inside it like scraps in a napkin. "What?"

Pierce blinked down at me. "What?"

"When he was staying here?"

"Yeah." Pierce nodded. "You know. When he stayed with us for a while."

"For *a while?*" Repeating the words only made them seem stranger. "When?"

"You know . . ." A little frown appeared between Pierce's eyebrows. "The last couple of months. When he was living with us."

The watery room froze. It tilted sideways, everything sliding out of place. "What are you talking about?"

"Like—from November to February, I think. Yeah. When the accident happened."

"You're saying . . . my dad *lived* here with you? For months?" I almost laughed out loud. "No, he didn't. That's— No. He didn't."

"Yeah, he did." Pierce went on frowning at me. This clearly wasn't unfolding the way he'd expected it to. "Maybe you don't remember, because of your . . ." He pointed to his own forehead. "You know."

Anger lanced through me. "No. I didn't *forget* it. It didn't happen."

"Yeah, it did. For, like, three months, he was—"

"That's crazy."

Pierce leaned back, his jaw hardening. "Oh. *That's* crazy. Okay."

My mouth fell open. I couldn't put the right words together before Pierce went on.

"Where did you think he was all that time?"

"When he was gone? Well, first, it wasn't for *months*. It was just a few weeks. Off and on. He and your dad were traveling, for the business. Checking the new stores."

Now it was Pierce's turn to look confused. "You thought he was just on some business trip?"

"He *was*." I clenched my fists on his fancy bedspread. "Stop trying to gaslight me."

Pierce looked even more confused. "Gaslight you?"

I sighed. "Never mind. It's—Ingrid Bergman. This old movie. Her husband tries to make her think she's crazy by messing with the lights in their house."

Pierce stared at me like I'd started speaking in Pig Latin. "That's not what I'm doing. Your dad came to stay here because your mom threw him out."

Now I actually laughed aloud. "My mom? My mother threw my dad out?" I got to my feet, shoving the shoes and T-shirt off onto the bed. "I can't even . . ." The ache was pulsing. I rubbed my forehead with both hands. "I don't know who told you that, or if you just made it up, but that did *not* happen. That could never have happened."

"Okay. Fine." Pierce's voice was cool. He took a step backward. "I'll drive you home. And you should take that stuff, either way. I kept it for you."

I wadded the shoes and shirt under my arm. I didn't want them. I didn't want their nearness, their memories, the ghost of Dad's scent still on them. But I wasn't going to leave them here either, where they could be some kind of proof for Pierce's messed-up story. I stalked past him, back down the steps and out the front door into the cold.

He drove me home without saying a word. When I opened the car door to climb out, he finally turned to face me. "I didn't—"

I hesitated, halfway out of the car.

"I didn't mean to *upset* you," he finished.

"I'm not upset." Total lie. But I kept my face blank.

"Okay." There was a beat. "I'll see you tomorrow." He flashed me that perfect half smile, the one that makes the dimple in his left cheek deepen. "Good night, Stuart. Go check your socks."

I gave him a half smile back. "Shut up."

On the front porch, I stopped to stuff Dad's shirt and shoes into my book bag. Then I let myself inside.

According to the clock, I was only twelve minutes later than I should have been. No one would have noticed the difference. If anyone had been around to notice. Mom still wasn't back from work, and Sadie was out of sight. As I climbed the stairs, I heard the sound of the shower running, and I caught a hint of green apple shampoo.

I lay down on my bed and closed my eyes. The ache swung back and forth in my skull like a wrecking ball. If I didn't move, it seemed to swing a little less, but furious thoughts still crashed and tumbled around it.

Pierce had remembered wrong. Or heard wrong. Or gotten something wrong. There was no way. *No way.*

God, I wished we'd just gone out for coffee with the rest of the group. Maybe they were still at the coffee shop. All of my friends, without me. And Rob with them. He could be sitting between Hannah and Nikki right now. Tomorrow he'd probably be dating Hannah. Or in love with Nikki.

Empty stage. Empty stage. Empty stage.

The spotlight, the shining boards, the rippling curtain drifted into place.

Titania's lines. Act Four. "Come sit thee down upon this flowery bed..."

As fast as I could, I filled the stage with words. Soon there wasn't room for anything else.

CHAPTER 14

I was still lying on my bed, eyes closed, when damp fingers touched my ankle.

I jolted up.

Ophelia stood beside me. Rivulets of muddy water dribbled from her hair onto the carpet. Her eyes were blue-white. Dead eyes. Corpse eyes. She touched the book bag where Dad's stuff was hidden. "I have remembrances of yours that I have longed long to redeliver . . ."

"You what?" I whispered.

"I said, what did Pierce do to you that it brought on a fainting spell?" Sadie folded her arms over her pale green bathrobe. "Are you okay?"

"Yeah." I wormed up onto my elbows. "I'm okay."

"Was it a better day at school?"

"I think so. I mean, yes. I don't know."

"Very confidence-inspiring." Sadie flicked a strand of shower-wet hair over her shoulder. "Are you sure you're all right?"

"I'm fine. I just have a headache. I *always* have a head-ache. I have arms. I have knees. I have a headache."

"Okay." Sadie stepped back, raising her hands. "And you've got a great attitude too." She moved toward the doorway. "Would you like a grilled cheese sandwich? I told Mom I'd feed you."

I rubbed my forehead. "That makes me sound like a guinea pig. Thank you very much."

"Guinea pigs don't eat grilled cheese." Sadie gave me a sharp look. "Did you and Pierce have a fight or some-thing?"

"What?" I sat up, crossing my legs and looking away. "Why would you think that?"

"Because you look like you do after every fight. Kind of sulky and sad and Victorian."

I snorted.

"So, what did you two fight about?"

"Oh my *god*, you're nosy."

"I'm well-informed." Sadie mussed her hair with one hand, sending little droplets over the quilt, over the bag where Dad's stuff was hidden. "If you don't want to talk about it, fine. I'll just assume Pierce was the one who was wrong."

I gave a tiny laugh.

Sadie stepped through the door. Before she could disap-pear down the hallway, I called out, "Sadie?"

She turned back. "What?"

The door with the cold wind on the other side inched open.

"You don't—I mean—this is going to sound weird, but Dad didn't ever *stay* with the Caplans, did he?"

Sadie's face did that thing it always does when we talk about Dad. Or I should say, the thing it's done the few times we *have* talked about Dad. The color washed out of it until she was like a sketch of herself. Flat. Gray. Incomplete.

"Stay with them? Like, for a weekend?"

"No." I shifted, crossing my legs tighter. The ache in my head reared again. "Like—for a few months. At the end."

Sadie's nose crinkled. She looked almost disgusted. "What? No."

"That's what I said."

"Pierce told you he was *staying* with them?"

"Yeah."

"Well, he's wrong. Or confused."

"That's what I said. I remember Dad being gone a lot—"

"They were opening the new stores. They had to spend, like, a week at each one. And then they had that conference in Chicago or somewhere, and all those trade shows . . ."

"Yeah. I know. I *knew* Pierce was wrong, but he wouldn't believe me."

"Well . . ." Sadie shrugged. "Who knows what he heard? He just obviously got things mixed up."

"Yeah. Obviously."

"Okay, guinea pig." She stepped back through the door. "I'm going to go make dinner now."

"Sadie . . ." My mouth was there before my mind. "Why don't you ever talk about him?"

Sadie stopped. She turned to face me. "Why don't *you*?"

"I asked you first," I said, like we were eight and nine again.

Sadie glanced through the doorway, listening for a second to make sure the downstairs was still empty. "Because of Mom," she said, turning back to me. "Because even hearing his name makes her just—shut down. I guess she . . ." Sadie paused, tightening the belt of her bathrobe. "She can't deal with some of it at all. Yet."

"Yeah." The memory of Mom's face during the months afterward clawed its way to the surface. Gaunt and white and haunted. Literally haunted, as if something the rest of us couldn't see was clinging to her with all of its weight. "But . . . even when she's not around . . . why don't *we* ever talk about it?"

"Because it hurts," Sadie answered. "There. Your turn."

"Because I think . . . maybe it's because I don't want to remember. But I'm remembering anyway. All the time."

Sadie leaned against the doorframe. Her long, slim body looked graceful, even in a bathrobe. "Sometimes that helps, though," she said quietly. "Remembering the good things."

"That's not what I mean." Behind my right eye, the ache

moved like a piston. "I can almost hear his voice some-times. Telling me what to do. What *he* would want me to do. Telling me everything I choose is wrong." I pressed my fingers into my temples. *Keep going. It's still your line. Say it.* "Sometimes all I can remember is how bad things were at the end. All the stupid things I did. How disappointed in me he always was. How angry he was."

"Jaye—you were in *middle school.* Of course you did stupid things."

"Oh? What did *you* do in middle school? Mouth off to Mom a couple of times? Everything I did was wrong. *Everything.* Dad hated everything about me. My clothes. My friends. Things I liked. Things I didn't like anymore. He thought I was just—I was a loser. He *said* it."

Sadie folded her arms again. Her face was stern. Teacher-like. "Jaye. You did some dumb things. You got scolded. Like every thirteen-year-old."

I shook my head. "That's not all it was. Did he ever say that to you? That you were pathetic? That he didn't want to raise someone like you?"

"No. And I'm sure he didn't say that to you, either."

I sat up straighter. "Yes he did."

"Oh my *god,*" Sadie burst out. "You're so overdramatic. You turn getting grounded in eighth grade into some Cin-derella story. Poor little Jaye, huddled in the corner, while the family goes off to the ball— "

"That's how it was!" I shouted back. "You all went

off together on trips, to games, out for meals, all kinds of things, and you didn't even—you just left. Without me."

"You *stopped coming*. You whined and complained about *everything*. Or you wormed your way out of it. Like those trips? Oh my god. Mom and Dad would try to plan something special, and—"

"I was terrified! I was afraid of heights, and I wasn't good at the things all of you could do, and I *knew* I was going to hurt myself, and I was just supposed to suck it up because we were going skiing or hiking or waterskiing or—"

"I am so sick of hearing about the skiing trips!" Sadie shouted. "This is what you do: You play this sad outcast role, but nobody put you in it. You *chose* it. You chose it for yourself."

"Did he ever lock you in your room? Did he stop coming to your events? Did he say you were ruining your life? Did he tell you that you couldn't see your friends anymore?"

"No." Sadie spoke loudly and clearly, as if she were confronting an idiot on the opposite side of a stage. "And he *didn't do that to you.*"

I threw up my hands. "Why is everybody talking to me like I'm crazy?"

"If *everybody* is, maybe that should tell you something."

The words struck like a slap. I sucked in a breath.

Sadie stopped, her hand clenched around the doorframe. "I'm sorry," she said. "But he was just trying to make you better. He was trying to push you to the right choices. That's what parents *do*. It's what they're *supposed* to do."

I shut up. If I opened my mouth, I wasn't sure what would come out. I didn't want it to be a sob. I stared down at my socks instead. Pierce was right: They were two different shades of black.

"Let's stop," said Sadie. "You're not supposed to be getting upset. I shouldn't have gotten into this with you." She shook back her damp hair, straightening her shoulders. "Okay." She took a breath. "Back to cheese-related subjects. Do you want tomato soup with your sandwich?"

"I'm not very hungry," I whispered.

Sadie gave an exasperated sigh. "Jaye——"

"Fine. Soup. Sandwich. Whatever."

I heard Sadie's footsteps thump down the staircase.

When I was sure I was alone, I opened my bag. Then I bundled Dad's T-shirt and running shoes into an old blanket, dropped down on my knees, and stuffed the whole thing under my bed, as far into the dusty darkness as it would go.

CHAPTER 15

Water splashed my face.

Too much of water hast thou, poor Ophelia . . .

I threw my head back, gasping, and banged into some-one in a letterman jacket. The guy—some senior whose name I didn't know—gave me an annoyed look as he strode away.

Shaking, I wiped the droplets off of my cheek. My hand was dry. I wasn't drowning. I was in the science hall, stand-ing next to a drinking fountain, with my book bag slung over my arm.

I pressed myself against the wall, getting out of the flow of traffic. The hall was jammed with people talking, slam-ming lockers, hurrying in all directions. I pulled my phone out of my bag. 9:04. I'd already gotten through anatomy. *Had* I already gotten through anatomy? I looked down at my body. Boots. A skirt and snagged gray tights. A different sweater from yesterday. I'd managed to dress myself. If I'd avoided talking to anyone so far, maybe no one would have noticed that I was a body wandering around without its brain.

I shoved the phone back into my bag. My anatomy text-book and notebook were inside. Nothing else. American literature came next. I needed . . . What were we reading? Something about *red.* Scarlet. Crimson. *Beauty's ensign yet is crimson in thy lips and in thy cheeks, and death's pale flag is not advanced there.* Who said that? . . . Romeo. In the tomb. God, *stop it.*

I stumbled down the hall in the direction of my locker. *The Red Badge of Courage. The Scarlet Letter. The Crimson and the Black.* There were too many books about *red.* Red petals melting into the snow. Red spatters in my hair. Romeo lifting my hand.

No. No. No.

The ache swung.

I put out a hand to catch myself and almost groped a passing freshman. For a second, I leaned against the bricks, trying to steady myself. Then I shuffled to the end of the hall, staring at my feet the whole time.

But as soon as I turned the corner, there he was. Pierce. Leaning against my locker door, his hands hooked in his pockets, his perfect profile turned away as he scanned the crowd. Waiting for me.

I lunged into the nearest classroom.

Inside, a bunch of freshmen were setting up a DNA helix made of marshmallows. They stared up at me.

"Um . . ." I groped for the first freshman theater kid name I could find. "Is Lia Gomez in this class? I have to tell her something about rehearsal."

They shook their heads.

"Oh. Thanks anyway."

I tiptoed back through the door.

Pierce was still leaning against my locker, looking like a magazine ad.

I couldn't do it.

I couldn't walk up to him and smile and act sane. Not after the things he'd said last night. Not after the argument with Sadie. Not with this giant blank spot dragging right behind me like a weight chained to my ankle. What if I lost myself again and said something, did something that gave everything away?

I took a step backward. Then I turned and ran.

I ran all the way up to the third floor, winding past the art rooms, keeping my head down, walking like I had somewhere important to go. I was already going to be late for my next class. There was no way I could go back to my locker, get my things, and make it up to English on the second floor.

I picked the third-floor bathroom tucked away at the end of the choir hall instead. Most people forgot it even existed, maintenance workers included. It was still full of hand-cranked towel and soap dispensers, and probably hadn't been painted in forty years.

It was empty when I entered and locked myself in a stall. Curdled things sloshed in my stomach. My head seared. I leaned my forehead against the cool metal wall. Fragments of magnified graffiti blurred in front of my eyes: *Lisa H. is a . . . 412-83 . . . B&S 4 EVER.*

A bunch of choir girls burst in.

They gathered at the mirrors outside, checking their hair, their voices ricocheting off the tiles.

"Can't believe she gave *her* that solo . . ." one of them said, slamming into the stall next to mine.

"Apparently she loves nasal, slightly flat sopranos." The lock on my stall rattled. A fist knocked at the door.

"Knock, knock, knock," Shakespeare's voice muttered. He'd appeared next to me, wedged between my side and the toilet paper dispenser. "Who's there, i' th' name of Beelzebub?"

The fist knocked again.

I realized I'd been holding my breath. "I'm—someone's in here."

"Oh. Sorry."

Another stall door creaked. Flushing. Talking. Someone sang an arpeggio. Then the bell rang, and the choir girls scurried out.

The bathroom went echoingly silent. I closed my eyes, still leaning against the divider. The ache was like a presence beside me.

When I finally opened my eyes again, Shakespeare was gone.

Now what? I couldn't avoid Pierce forever; rehearsal was creeping closer. If I could make it until then.

I slipped back out of the bathroom. 9:16. Already late for American literature. Still bookless. As I climbed down the staircase, my vision began to swim. By the time I reached the first-floor hallway, I was squinting like a driver with a dirty windshield. The ache thrummed. Walls were melting. Doors and lockers and posters and windows all smeared into each other until there was nothing to hold on to—except for one dark, solid shape headed straight toward me.

I blinked. The windshield cleared.

Rob Mason was walking swiftly in my direction. I felt a strange surge in my stomach, like something that had been crawling had suddenly grown wings. He was wearing a long black wool coat, and a bag on a leather strap hung over his shoulder. He'd clearly just arrived.

He saw me and slowed. His face stayed blank.

"Hi," I said.

"Hey," he answered. There were melting snowflakes in his hair.

I couldn't think of what to say next. The new thing in my stomach was too distracting. Rob didn't say anything either.

For a second, I thought he might not have recognized me. But how many girls with patchy hair and giant head wounds could he know? Unless . . . Unless I'd imagined every conversation we'd ever had. I rewound through our interactions as Rob stood still, watching me with his cool blue eyes.

"You're running late too?" he asked.

I wasn't ready for him to speak. I think I actually jumped.

"What? Oh. Yeah. I mean, no." I laughed idiotically. "I was here already. I just—I didn't get to class on time. You?"

"Overslept. And I earned my first tardy slip." He flashed a yellow note. "At *this* school, anyway."

"Congratulations."

Rob still didn't smile. Suddenly what I wanted more than anything was to make him smile at me again.

"Hey," I began. "Did I . . . do something?"

He frowned slightly. Getting worse. "What do you mean?"

"I mean, you just—you seem—I don't know. Different. I just wondered if I did something."

Rob shook his head, still frowning. "No. Not at all." He turned toward the stairs. "I'd better get to trig. The teacher seems like the angry type."

Keep him here. Keep him talking. "Oh? Who do you have?"

"I can't remember her name. The one who looks like Hillary Clinton with Bill Clinton's hair."

I laughed. Rob's face stayed blank.

"Mrs. Duvall? I never thought about it, but that's exactly what she looks like."

"Well," said Rob. "See you later."

"Yeah. See you."

He turned around. Watching him go jerked something awake in me. Something that wanted to see his face again, even after it had just turned away.

"Wait," I called after him. "How would you feel about being a little bit tardier?"

He stopped. "Why? What do you mean?" His tone was polite.

I moved toward him, glancing at the closed classroom doors to either side. "We're running out of days when we can use our New-Kid, Head-Injury-Girl excuses. So . . . let's go somewhere."

"You're asking me to cut class with you?"

"Yes. Unless—you can't. Or you don't want to."

A tiny smile started to reshape his mouth. "Where do you want to go?" he asked. "We could hang out in the auditorium for a while . . ."

"No. I want to get out of here."

Rob nodded. The smile grew deeper. "I've got a car."

We drove through a neighborhood of huge Victorian houses that had been turned into boutiques and cafés. The streets were snowy and narrow. Thickly bundled people hurried up the sidewalks. Rob pulled up in front of a brick building surrounded by empty patios and crooked wrought iron gates. Dead vines clung to the bars, rustling softly. An old-fashioned neon sign reading CAFÉ burned above its deep-set windows, and warm reddish light glowed from inside.

"How did you know about this place?" I asked, looking out through the passenger door.

"I saw it while I was driving around the other night. It looked like a good spot." He unlatched his seat belt. "Have you been here?"

"No. I never even noticed it." I unlatched my belt too. "Do you do that a lot? Just—drive around?"

"Yeah. Me and Merle." He patted the dashboard. A huge silver belt buckle was glued above the stereo. "He came with me across the country from Oregon. All that time stuck alone together. Now we're like cell mates: I know he's a piece of crap, but I like him anyway."

I smiled. "Does that make Minnesota the prison?"

Rob shrugged. "I thought it would be. I'm still figuring it out." He opened his door. "Come on."

Inside, the coffee shop was dim and warm. Mismatched paisley couches and lamps with silk shades filled the corners. Steam coated the windows, beading into pearls that froze and melted again as they dribbled downward. No one gave us a second glance. Still, the excitement of doing something wrong zinged in my chest like miniature fireworks.

We took our red enamel mugs to a table at the back.

I rearranged my scarf, making a partial shield for my

face. "Is it way too obvious that we're not supposed to be here?" I whispered, tugging one side higher. "Like—could someone just look at us and *know?*"

Rob gave the rest of the shop a quick glance. He shook his head. "No. They probably think we're just two more college kids talking about our godawful folk-punk band."

"I think I look more like a terrible poet, personally." I twirled the spoon in my cup of coffee. Regular coffee. Rebellion coffee. "I haven't done this in a long time."

"Stirred your drink?"

I grinned. "Skipped school. *And* had actual coffee." I took a sip. Bitter and dark and delicious. I could practically taste the caffeine. "I've had to be obnoxiously good ever since the head stuff. My sister drives me to school. Pierce drives me home. I haven't been anywhere but there and the hospital in weeks. Oh—and Pierce's house, last night. But that was kind of a kidnapping situation, so I don't think it counts."

Rob leaned back in his chair. His face was distant again. "Kidnapping?"

"Friendly kidnapping. Friend-napping."

"Wow. Even the felonies are nice in Minnesota."

I laughed. Still, I wished I hadn't brought up Pierce's name. I didn't want the thought of him, perfect and golden, hanging over my shoulder.

"So," I picked up. "Where did you and Tom and Nikki and everybody go yesterday?"

"Someplace with eight thousand kinds of pie."

"Norske's?"

"That was it. I think Tom ate four slices. For such a skinny guy, it was truly impressive."

"Yeah . . . there aren't a lot of family dinners at his house."

Rob nodded. "I picked up on that. He's a nice guy. And Nikki. She's very cool."

"Yes, she is." I looked down into my mug again. "I wish I could have gone with all of you."

Rob shrugged. "You were with your friendly kidnapper."

I wasn't sure if this was just a joke. There was something hard and chilly inside it, like a chunk of ice sliding down into a warm shoe.

"Hey. Yesterday, did he—did Pierce say something to you? After rehearsal?"

"Not really." Rob was still leaning back in his chair, almost as far from me as he could get. "I just hadn't realized you two were together."

"Me and Pierce?" It still sounded so impossible. "We're . . . It's not like we're dating. We've never even gone out for coffee. I mean—" I heard the words and wished I could reel them back in. My cheeks burned. "Not that that would mean—I don't know. Where did you hear that?"

"From him. Well—he sort of implied it."

I made myself meet his eyes again. "What do you mean?"

"He told me to stay away from you, or I'd be very sorry."

"*That's* what he said to you after rehearsal?" I put my face in my hands. "God. I'm so sorry. It was—he doesn't understand."

"I get it." Both his voice and his face were harder than usual. "I've known a lot of guys like him."

"He's just being protective. Misguidedly protective, but . . ." I felt a sudden need to explain him. To explain what he was to me. At least, as long as Rob went on watching me with those unnervingly beautiful eyes. When had I started thinking of them as beautiful? I stared down into my coffee again. "We practically grew up together. Pierce and my sister and me. His dad and our dad were best friends. Business partners. Unofficial brothers. They used to laugh that Sadie and Pierce should get married someday and then we'd all finally be related for real, and the business could become this family empire. Sadie and Pierce were the same age, they were into all the same things. But they were never actually that close. I think they were both too competitive. It was me and Pierce who were best friends." I turned the mug between my palms. "We grew apart eventually. For the last two years, we didn't even talk. But now—I don't know. He's trying to fix things." I turned the mug again. "There. That was way too much stuff that you probably didn't even want to know. Let's talk about you instead."

"If you want to." Rob picked up his own mug. "But you're a lot more interesting."

"Me? Are you serious?"

"Yeah." He nodded at me, frowning and smiling at the same time. "I have this theory that there are about ten basic people templates. And everywhere you go, you just meet slight variations on these templates. I mean, every place I've lived, every school I've been to . . . it's the same models, over and over. You can tell right away. But you're not—I don't know. I'm not sure you fit any of the templates."

"Maybe I'm damaged goods. Like factory seconds or something."

"Or maybe you're a limited edition." Now only his smile was left. "Or maybe my whole theory's BS."

I spun the spoon in my coffee again. "I think most of us try to fit in categories. You know, so we'll feel like we belong somewhere. But we really *don't* fit. We're really meant to be these totally weird, complicated, different-from-anybody-else things. That's part of why I love acting. I don't have to just be me, in my little category. I get to dye my hair every color and wear insane clothes and say things I'd never normally say. I get to be a whole bunch of weird, complicated things."

"See?" Rob was smiling wider. "Interesting."

My cheeks prickled. *Change the subject.* "I know. Tell me your favorite movie. No, wait. Tell me what movie you've seen the most times. And you have to be honest."

"Hmm . . ." He gazed into the distance. "Probably

Labyrinth. I watched that movie pretty much every day between the ages of six and ten."

"Really?"

"Yeah." He grinned. "I still have confusing feelings for David Bowie."

I laughed.

"What about you?" he asked.

"Me? I'm not sure."

"Fast and Furious Two: 2 Fast 2 Furious," Rob suggested.

I laughed again. "Nope. I've seen *Breakfast at Tiffany's* a lot. And there was the summer I got obsessed with Emma Thompson and watched *Much Ado About Nothing* and *Sense and Sensibility* about a hundred times. Wait . . . I know what it has to be. *Ferris Bueller's Day Off.* All of elementary and middle school, that was my go-to movie. It's probably the reason I skipped school for the very first time."

Rob shook his head in mock reprobation. "Hollywood and its propaganda. Corrupting the youth."

"I thought it would be this wild adventure. We'd be dancing through museums, eating in fancy restaurants. But actually we just hid in Nikki's basement and ate stale Doritos."

"Did you get caught?"

"Of course. We got a week of detention, all of our parents got called, it was this whole big mess. Well—Nikki's mom didn't care. I don't think Tom's parents even noticed. But *my* parents . . ." I snorted. "I thought my dad was actually going to crack a tooth, he was clenching his jaw so hard."

"He's really strict?"

"He's dead."

The words flew out before I could stop them. Like a sneeze.

I expected Rob to look startled. But he didn't flinch. His eyes widened very slightly, and his eyebrows went up, but he kept looking straight at me.

"What happened?" he asked.

"A car accident. It was winter, two years ago." I stopped. "You know what's weird? I don't think I've ever told anybody the whole story before. Everybody I know already knows. Or they think they can't ask. So it's like—like I don't have anything rehearsed." I let out what was supposed to be a laugh, but it didn't quite sound like one. "I almost don't know what to say."

Rob waited for a second. "If you don't want to talk about it—"

"No," I broke in. "No. I can. I . . ." *Just talk. You're Jaye Stuart, and you're sitting in the back of a coffee shop, across from a guy who's waiting for you to speak again. You don't have to be anything else.* I took a long breath. "Like I said, it was winter. We'd been having blizzards, ice storms. The roads were really bad. Afterward, they told us—I mean, the police said—they skidded out of their lane, clipped another car, and slid off the highway into a tree."

"They?" Rob repeated. "Was he with your mother?"

I shook my head. "The Caplans. Pierce and his father."

"Oh," said Rob quietly. "Wow."

"They were both all right. I guess Patrick had a broken rib and some cuts on his face. He was driving. Pierce was in the backseat, and he was fine. My dad had a fractured skull, kind of like . . ." I pointed briskly to my head. "But he had a serious hemorrhage, and there wasn't much they could do. He just never woke up."

I stared down at the edge of the tabletop.

I wondered what my face was doing. I wondered what Rob saw when he looked at me. I didn't have a mask ready for this. I felt cold, and uncovered, like I'd just stepped outside without a jacket on.

Rob didn't speak for a moment. Then, under the table, I felt his foot bump against mine. I didn't move away. Neither did he.

"I'm sorry," he said.

"Yeah." I looked up again. "Me too."

"So . . . is that why you haven't been talking to Pierce for the last two years?"

"Sort of. Maybe." I shrugged one shoulder. "It was starting to happen before the accident, and afterward—I don't know. It was like the door had already shut, and now it was locked."

Rob nodded. For a while, we both kept quiet. But it wasn't the kind of uncomfortable quiet that feels like somebody has forgotten a line, and the pressure starts to build, and everything's messed up and awkward. It was more like a deep breath.

"What was your father like?" Rob asked, after the minute had passed.

"Um . . . god." I leaned my head on my hand. "I don't know what . . ."

"Sorry—I shouldn't have asked. I'm being an ass."

"No," I said quickly. "You're not at all ass-like. I just—I don't ever do this, either."

"Describe him to asses?"

"Talk about him. With anybody."

"Not even with your family?"

"No," I said. "Especially not them." I picked up a sugar packet from the center of the table. "My dad was . . . he was always moving." I flipped the packet between my fingers, turning it around and around. "He was a runner. He ran marathons. He coached the high school track and cross-country teams. He was out on the streets before dawn every single morning, running for miles. Even when he sat on the couch, he'd be moving. Writing lists, jiggling his feet, flipping through paperwork. He could never sit still long enough to read a book or watch a whole movie." I gestured to myself with the sugar packet, giving a little laugh. "I guess I'm like that. In a fidgety way. In every other way, we were pretty much exact opposites."

"How do you mean?"

"Oh god. Everything. He hated my clothes. He hated my dyed hair. He *hated* my friends. He hated that I quit sports to have time for drama. He thought theater was weird and boring and pointless, because according to him, it didn't make money, it didn't teach you any real world skills, and it didn't get you in better shape. He stopped coming to my shows. He stopped including me in everything. Toward the end, he practically stopped talking to me. Even when the rest of the family went away on trips, they didn't bring me along."

"That's kind of messed up," said Rob softly.

I shook my head, looking down at a constellation of spilled sugar crystals on the tabletop. "It was my fault. I'm the one who started to pull away. They just . . . They just let me."

Someone behind the counter switched on the coffee grinder. Rob and I went still for another minute. I could feel his eyes on me the whole time.

"You know . . ." I began as the whirr of the machine faded. "You know how when someone dies, everybody just wants to remember the good things about them? Well, *everybody* knew my dad. And they all thought he was this great, likeable, wonderful guy. He and my mother were like the ideal couple. My sister adored him. Pierce *worshipped* him. When he died, it was like—like suddenly, as far as everybody could remember, he had been completely *perfect*. So, if he didn't like *me*"—I shrugged again—"he must have been right. And I was wrong." I picked up my mug. The coffee had grown lukewarm, almost cold. "Oh my god. I really don't know why I'm telling you all this. Please ask me to shut up now."

Rob leaned on one elbow. I could practically feel the pull of his eyes. "I think it's easier to be who you really are with someone who doesn't think they already know everything about you."

I looked straight back at him. For a breath, it felt like there was nothing between us. Not the table, not the air. I wanted to reach out and touch him.

I sat farther back in my chair instead.

"You know there are all kinds of rumors going around about you, right?" I made my voice a little cooler. "Like that you've moved so much because you've been expelled so many times. That you have some crazy criminal record."

He laughed, waving a hand dismissively. "I've only been expelled four times."

"Oh. *Only*" I laughed too. "Why must teenagers exaggerate everything?"

Rob nodded at my cup. "Want another coffee?"

"Yes. But first I want to know about the expulsions."

"Fine." He leaned back again. "My dad gets transferred around a lot for work. Something in IT training or networking—I don't really know what he does, so don't ask." He grinned. "Anyway, because we were always moving, I was always the new kid. The *weird* new kid. I was this skinny little bookworm with long hair, and I always liked the wrong teams or talked the wrong way or whatever. At first I got picked on. Then I became a smartass, so I got picked on and beaten up. And then I got mean." He spun the dregs of coffee in his cup. "I got expelled from my first middle school in Chicago because I broke a kid's nose. But that was basically an accident."

"Basically?"

"He knocked me down, and I was lying there, flat on my back, with him above me, so I swung at him with my American history textbook. I got expelled for the second time because I brought a knife to school—"

"Like, a butcher knife?"

"A little Swiss Army knife. This bigger kid said he was going to kill me, and I was a twelve-year-old moron, and I believed him. Expulsion number three . . ." Rob looked up. His face began to curve into a smile. "This was in Denver. I was fourteen. I stole a teacher's phone—she was really mean, so I still don't feel bad about this—and I sent a text to everyone on her contacts list."

"What did it say?"

"It was something like, 'I don't know how to tell you this, but I've had intense physical feelings for you for a long time now. Please come over tonight so we can talk . . . or not talk. Your choice.'"

"Oh my god!"

Rob's smile grew broader. "I heard about six of them showed up. Including a relative."

I hooted with laughter.

"Expulsion number four wasn't even really an expulsion," Rob went on. "My parents took me out of the school before anything could officially happen."

"What did you do that time?"

Rob hesitated. "This was in San Francisco, a couple of years ago," he said, instead of answering the question. "I'd started hanging out with this group of guys who thought they were punks. They were into skateboarding. And tattoos. And vandalism. And drugs. And petty theft."

"I know how well things went with you and skateboards . . ."

"Yeah, well, the other stuff went even better." Looking almost sheepish, Rob set his forearm on the table. His hand stretched toward me, palm up.

For a second, I wondered if he was reaching for me. If I was meant to put my own hand in his. I remembered the texture of his skin, the rough-smooth of his palm, the long fingers raising my wrist to his lips—

Stop it.

Before I could make a total fool of myself, Rob shoved his sleeve up to his elbow. A skull cut in blurry blue ink grinned from the middle of his forearm.

"Alas, poor Yorick," Hamlet's voice whispered from somewhere close by. "I knew him, Horatio . . ."

I put both hands over my ears. Then I remembered where I was and who I was with, and pretended to be rear-ranging my hair. "Ouch."

"Yeah, well, at least it's not a nipple ring." Rob pushed his sleeve back down. "Some of the other guys decided to tattoo *and* pierce themselves."

I glanced over both shoulders. No Hamlet. I turned back to Rob, sitting up straighter. "Is that what you told your parents?"

He gave a dry smile. "Actually, they barely cared about the tattoo. They were a lot angrier about the whole break-ing into the principal's office, spray-painting his walls, and stealing a bunch of stuff part."

"What did they do to you?"

"They pulled me out of school, had me do a ton of community service and take online classes . . ." His words slowed. "And then Dad found out he was transferring to Seattle. And Mom decided not to come with us."

"So—what? She just stayed in San Francisco?"

Rob nodded. "She said she didn't know how to deal with me anymore, and she thought my dad should take a more active role in my life, so . . . That was two years and three moves ago." He met my eyes again. "I basically ended my parents' marriage." He gave another very small, very dry smile. "That's worse than getting expelled for a fourth time, right?"

"I'm sure it wasn't just about you," I said quietly. "I mean . . . there must have been stuff going on that you didn't even know about."

He tipped his head to one side. "I don't know. They always try not to blame the kids, but . . . sometimes it's the kids."

A little cyclone started to spin in my stomach. I could see Dad running up the sidewalk, away from home, away from us, his gray T-shirt fading out in the half-light. "Maybe," I said.

Rob pushed back his chair. "So. Now you know my whole history. Including some things I don't usually talk about with anyone either." He stood up and took my empty mug. "Another French roast?"

"Sure." I started to smile back at him. "Wait. Am I keeping you here too long? What about the other classes you'll miss?"

He shrugged, picking up his own mug. "I'd rather keep talking with you."

For a second, I thought he was going to say something else. But then he straightened up again, putting a friendly distance between us, and headed toward the counter.

I turned to watch him place our order. From a distance, he was striking. The lines of his profile were so interestingly carved. An arc here. A point there. Different from every angle. The tangled black hair that swept across one eyebrow made my heart beat faster.

The girl at the register twitched her shoulders in a flirtatious way. But Rob looked past her, straight at me. One side of his mouth began to curve upward. I looked down at the table, feeling something in my heart swell and fracture into a thousand tiny sparkling things.

When he set my refilled mug down in front of me, I asked, "Would you rather be really, really good at one thing, or pretty good at everything you try?"

"One thing," said Rob, falling back into his seat. "Wait. Would I be terrible at everything else?"

I laughed. "Not *terrible*. Bad at some stuff, okay at other stuff."

"Yeah." Rob nodded. "One thing. Definitely. You?"

"One thing. Also definitely." I took a sip of the fresh coffee. "What's the one thing you'd want to be great at?"

Rob squinted into the distance for a second. "When I figure that out, I guess I'll know what to do with my life. What about you?"

"Oh." I shrugged, looking down. "You already know." I pressed my hands around the mug's warm sides. "I think I'm not doing a very good job at it right now, though. Rehearsals, everything . . . I just feel like I'm disappointing everyone. I'm disappointing *myself.* Because I know I can do better, but I just can't—I can't hold on to anything long enough to change it. You know? And then there are those people . . ." *Pierce.* ". . . those people who can do something for the first time and be perfectly good at it. Then they do something else, and they're good at that too. They never even have to try."

"What's the value in that?"

I met Rob's eyes. "What do you mean?"

"I don't know. I just think anything that comes really easily doesn't have much power."

"Yeah." I nodded slowly. "*Yeah.* I like the work. I like trying. I like getting better. I even kind of like screwing up, because that means I have to figure out how to fix it. It makes it something *alive,* you know? Not just—something that can't change. That's stuck forever in its perfectly-good-ness."

Rob was smiling at me, his head tilted to one side.

"What?"

"Nothing." He straightened up. "I was just thinking that you're really good at more than one thing."

"Well, I *am* pretty good at drinking coffee." I picked up the mug and took another sip. "See? Not spilling. Not burning myself." Rob clapped, and I took a little bow. "Thank you. Thank you very much."

He narrowed his eyes at me, smiling again. "How are you with chopsticks?"

We took our time finishing our second cups of coffee. Then Rob drove us to a tiny white storefront where we ate spicy noodles from paper boxes. We spent the hour after that wandering through a giant secondhand shop, looking at creepy old toys and racks of battered, dust-scented books.

By the time either of us thought about rehearsal, we were already ten minutes late.

CHAPTER 16

The auditorium was in chaos.

The crew had been trying to work the scene change from Act Four to Act Five, and a set piece that should have drifted down from the flies and settled lightly into place at the back of the stage had instead plunked down on something else and crushed it. Everyone in the cast and crew was either standing around complaining or running around complaining about the ones who were standing around, and some miscommunication with the music department meant that a grand piano was still positioned center stage and eight people were trying to move it.

Because of all of this, there wasn't a single person left over to notice Rob and me creeping in through the backstage door.

"I think we're safe," I whispered as we slunk through the wings. "The truancy gods have smiled on us."

Rob grinned. "Thanks for coming out with me."

"Thank *you*. It was my suggestion. And you drove. You even paid for the coffee."

He shrugged, grin widening. "You can pay next time."

Then he turned away, heading into the crowd surrounding the broken set.

I almost followed him. Just to get one more look. Just to make sure he was still real. But someone grabbed my arm.

"Hey, you're here!" Ayesha squinted down into my face. "Somebody told me you were out sick today."

"Me?" I put on my innocent/mildly surprised expression. "No. One hundred percent healthy."

"We're starting Act Five in three minutes. If we can get that freaking piano out of here, anyway. *What?*" she snapped into her headset. "No, there will be a music cue there." She whirled away, still speaking into the microphone. "No. Not until *after.*"

I edged around the cyclorama. On the far side of the stage, Pierce was surrounded by a knot of fairies flitting their new tulle-and-wire wings. I was pretty sure he hadn't seen me, or I would have thought he was ignoring me deliberately. His smile seemed too wide. His laugh was too loud. I dove back out of sight into the wings.

Focus, I told myself, pressing my temples with my fingertips. *You got lucky that no one noticed you. Now you need to make them think there was nothing to notice in the first place.*

Act Five. *Oberon says, "And this ditty, after me, sing and dance it trippingly." And you say, "Speak the speech, I pray you, trippingly on the tongue—"*

No. That's Hamlet.

I pressed harder. A double pulse beat between my temples and my fingertips.

There was a cheer as someone finally got the piano's wheel locks unlatched. With several crew members barnacled around it, the grand piano creaked off into the wings. I backed out of the way, half listening, while Mr. Hall shouted directions and Ayesha marshalled everyone into place.

Theseus and Hippolyta began Act Five's opening scene. The lights formed pools of red and gold around their feet.

"Lovers and madmen have such seething brains, such shaping fantasies that apprehend more than cool reason ever comprehends . . ."

Speak the speech, I pray you, trippingly on the tongue.

Speak the speech, I pray you, trippingly on the tongue.

The words looped in my brain. I tried to push them back, to catch the words that belonged there. I'd been feeling fine. *Better* than fine. Better than happy. Now something I'd been ignoring for the last several hours crept up on me in a tide of panic.

Speak the speech, I pray you, trippingly on the tongue.

Speak the speech, I pray you—

Speak—

"Hold, please!" shouted Mr. Hall.

Devon, as Theseus, stopped mid-line.

Mr. Hall's voice echoed through the auditorium. "Are Rob Mason and Jaye Stuart here?"

I froze.

The cast went silent, waiting.

Across the stage, I could see Rob's tall, dark shape separating from the shadows. I inched out of the wings.

Mr. Hall and Vice Principal Carter stood side by side at the lip of the stage. Mr. Hall's face was rigid.

"Would you two come with me?" said Mr. Carter in his quiet voice.

There were rumors that Mr. Carter had once been a Green Beret, or some other kind of military assassin. He never raised his voice. He didn't have to.

My head began to swim. I teetered across the boards and down the steps. Rob stepped down from the stage's other side.

Behind us, the whispering began.

We followed Mr. Carter's broad back up the central aisle. I could feel Rob's presence behind me, but I knew I shouldn't turn around. Not as long as anyone—or everyone—was watching. The more distance between us, the better. I moved closer to Mr. Carter instead.

In the fluorescent brightness of the hall, the vice principal turned to face us. His perfectly bald head gleamed like marble. He seemed to loom over both of us, even though I noticed he and Rob were almost the same height. I could practically feel myself shrinking.

"The two of you left school grounds without permission after first hour," Mr. Carter began in his low, calm voice.

"You skipped your remaining classes, and returned to the building just after the final bell this afternoon. Is that correct?"

I looked down at the toes of his polished brown shoes. "Yes."

"Yes," said Rob, beside me.

"Mr. Mason, you've come to us with a long record of infractions, suspensions, and expulsions. I assume that's a pattern you don't want to continue here, especially when doing so could jeopardize your chances of graduating. Is that also correct?"

"Yes," said Rob. "It is."

"Were the two of you aware that an unexcused absence during the school day precludes you from participating in any extracurricular activities for the remainder of that day?"

I sucked in a breath.

"I wasn't," said Rob. "I guess I should have read the student handbook more thoroughly."

There was a short, scary pause. Then Mr. Carter said, "That would be a good place to start. For now, you will leave school grounds immediately. Before the first bell tomorrow morning, report to the main office to receive your detention assignment. A notification regarding your unexcused absence will also be sent to your home. Understood?"

"Understood."

"Good night, Mr. Mason."

I felt Rob hesitate next to me. Mr. Carter's eyes were fixed on him, waiting. Finally Rob turned away. His footsteps dwindled around the corner and faded out.

"Miss Stuart." Mr. Carter's voice snapped my eyes upward. "We're all aware of your situation. But as you're not a new student here, I assume that you're familiar with school rules and policies."

"I am," I said to the pin on Mr. Carter's navy silk tie. "I just . . . forgot."

"I hope you haven't 'forgotten' our expectations for our students. Do you need a reminder of those? Maybe a conference with your mother and the school psychologist?"

"No," I said quickly. "I know what I did wrong."

"Did your injury have anything to do with your decision to leave school without permission?"

"No," I said again. "Not like . . . No. I knew what I was doing. I just made the wrong choice."

"Yes, you did. And I hate to see that happen." Mr. Carter's voice got even softer. "Your father had high expectations for you."

My skin began to burn.

"All of us here at Wilson do," Mr. Carter went on. "And because I believe what you say, that this was a bad choice made due to your situation, or to the influence of another student, I am going to waive the usual consequences." He lowered his chin and stared into my eyes. "In this *single in-*

stance. You may participate in today's rehearsal. But I don't want to see this kind of poor judgment from you again. Understood?"

"Understood."

Mr. Carter nodded toward the auditorium doors. My face searing, I turned and staggered back inside, into the dimness.

Rehearsal had resumed. Everyone was in the middle of Act Five, the play-within-a-play for Theseus's court. Nobody broke the fourth wall to look back at me.

I crept down the aisle and through the stage door, up the steps where Rob had offered me the package of M&M'S, winding my way into the wings. The ache in my skull was a frozen explosion. The scene onstage was ending, but I couldn't hear it. I could only hear Hamlet's voice reciting, *Speak the speech, I pray you, trippingly on the tongue,* louder and louder, over the rhythm of my own hammering pulse.

Pierce waited for me at our entrance. He didn't glance up as I crept closer. When our cue came, he raised his arm. I placed my palm on the back of his hand, and we strode together into the stage lights.

Somehow, I managed to spit out my only line in the scene—"First rehearse your song by rote, to each word a warbling note . . ."—without scrambling any *Hamlet* into it. But my voice sounded thin and distant, as if it were coming from the other end of a long, chilly hallway.

And then it was over. We exited, my hand still hovering on top of Pierce's warm skin. The instant we were offstage, Pierce dropped his arm. He walked away without a word.

I stood where he left me, my legs shaking.

What an idiot. What a wretched, puling fool.

I'd screwed it all up. I'd done the opposite of what I should have done, the opposite of what everyone had asked me to do, the opposite of what I'd promised my mother. The opposite of what my father would have wanted.

And now something even worse was coming. I could feel it thrumming closer, vibrating with each thump of my heart. I stood there, trembling, while Nikki recited the play's final words.

> *If we shadows have offended,*
> *Think but this, and all is mended:*
> *That you have but slumbered here*
> *While these visions did appear.*
> *And this weak and idle theme,*
> *No more yielding but a dream . . .*

The spotlight that encased her tightened to a pinpoint. As she reached the very last line—*So, good night unto you all*—the fragile light winked out.

"All right!" Mr. Hall shouted. "Lights up, please! We won't do notes tonight, but I'd like Bottom and the players to stick around; we're going to go through the Pyramus and Thisbe bit one more time."

Someone nudged my side. I swayed, losing balance.

Pierce was beside me. The line of his jaw made me flinch.

"Where's your stuff?" he asked, in a clipped, quiet voice.

"Oh. I . . . um . . ." I stammered. "If you're tired of going out of your way every night, I'm sure Nikki could drive me. I don't—"

"I'm driving you," he cut me off. "Get your bag. Let's go."

Pierce followed me out of school and across the parking lot. I got the sense that he was monitoring me, like a warden with an unpredictable prisoner.

The inside of the BMW was frigid.

I huddled in the passenger seat. My head felt like a blender. The ache was a clump of ice cubes whirling and clattering between the blades.

Pierce waited until we'd put two blocks between the car and the school. Then he said, very softly, "I was looking for you all day. I even waited at your locker between classes. And you were cutting with that freak the whole time."

I swallowed. "He's not a freak."

"Really? He hasn't been expelled from like fifteen schools for drugs and fighting and whatever else loser wannabe rebels do?"

The hardness in Pierce's voice sharpened mine. "No.

His father has to move a lot for work. That's why he's been to so many schools. And he's not doing any of that other stuff anymore."

"You know him so well already? That was fast."

The tires shrieked around a corner.

"Pierce—don't be angry." I hated the pleading that edged into my voice. "I was feeling really out of it today, and I ran into him in the hall, and I just—I needed to be somewhere quiet. We went to a coffee shop and talked. That's it."

"That's it," Pierce repeated flatly.

"Yes. I just needed to get out of there. To talk to somebody."

"Why couldn't you talk to me?"

I looked at the white knuckles clamped on the steering wheel.

It wasn't just that Pierce would never have suggested skipping school, or taken me to an out-of-the-way coffee shop, or browsed used books for more than an hour. I couldn't tell him the things I'd told Rob. I couldn't ever show him the weak, flawed, disappointing, terrible-daughter truth.

Of course, I couldn't tell him *this*, either.

"I'm sorry," I said.

We bounced into my driveway. Pierce threw the car into park. He grabbed my hand in a way that made his fingernails dig lightly into my skin.

"Next time, talk to *me*," he said. "Please."

"I will," I lied. "I will. I'll try."

His grip loosened slightly. "Is this because of last night? Because I wasn't trying to make you mad."

"No. I know," I said quickly. "That's not it. That's— nothing."

"I'm not trying to force you to do anything you don't want. I just hate watching you do stupid, dangerous things." He shook his head once. "But I guess that's your choice. Right? If you don't have any feelings for me, then what you do is none of my business. I just—I thought you did. I thought we were finally in the same place."

"Me too," I said. "And I do. Have feelings."

Pierce's face mellowed. He leaned closer until I could feel the heat of him radiating straight through me, and I could barely breathe, and then his lips were on mine, and the blender in my head went from *mix* to *liquefy*, and my body seemed to have evaporated, because I couldn't move a single thing.

This was real. This was really happening. Pierce Caplan— perfect, beautiful, out-of-reach Pierce, the boy I'd loved for most of my life—was kissing me. That he was now some- where between a friend and a stranger made it seem both meant-to-be and frightening. But maybe that was how it was supposed to feel. Maybe that was how fate felt.

Pierce's lips were warm and firm. I felt his breath against my cheek, and realized that I was holding mine.

After a few seconds, he pulled away.

He gave me that dizzying half smile. "Good night, Stuart."

I hurried through the double beams of his headlights, up the porch steps, to the front door. I shoved my way into the living room without looking back.

Then I froze.

Because Mom was home. Early. And it was clear from the way she stood in the dining room door, still dressed in her work clothes, her fingers clenched around her upper arms, that she'd come home early for a reason.

Sadie was curled up in her usual chair, her eyes flashing between me and Mom with a mixture of dread and glee.

"Jaye," said Mom. "I need to speak to you."

Not talk. *Speak.* Always a bad sign.

"Okay," I said slowly.

"Come into the kitchen." Mom spun around.

Sadie raised an eyebrow at me before turning showily back to her textbook.

I followed Mom through the dining room and around the corner.

Mom leaned against the yellow enamel counter next to the fridge. Her arms were still clamped across her chest, and the line of her mouth was tight. I couldn't meet her eyes. I shuffled to the opposite corner, putting as much distance between the two of us as the kitchen would allow.

For several seconds, she just waited. I could hear her

soft, methodic breathing. Her yoga breathing. It's probably as close as Mom gets to a prayer.

Finally she said, in a quiet voice, "Jaye . . . would you please tell me what is going on?"

Suddenly I almost resented her. For worrying about me. For needing me to be all right. "What do you mean?"

"Don't pretend not to know what I mean. Your vice principal called me at work an hour ago."

Our kitchen linoleum was supposed to look like brick, but it was too worn and shiny to fool anyone. Sadie and I used to pretend that if we stepped on the cracks between the bricks, we'd be burned by bubbling lava. I followed the zigzag of fake mortar with my eyes.

"Oh. I didn't—I didn't know he'd have called you already . . . Yeah. That."

"What were you thinking?" Mom's voice got a tiny bit louder. "Skipping school, leaving the building, driving around with some stranger *one week* after getting out of the hospital?"

"He's not a stranger."

Mom let out a breath through her nose. Her eyes got a little more desperate. "Do you really want to argue about this?" she asked, without waiting for an answer. "Mr. Carter said he was a new student. I've never heard you mention him before. How long could you possibly have known him? What *do* you know about him?"

"He's new," I said. "And he's nice."

"Nice," Mom repeated. "Nice enough to convince you to cut class?"

"He didn't convince me." The ache tightened. I touched the rubbery line of the scar. "My head was really hurting. I just needed a little break."

"Jaye, if your head is hurting so badly that you can't be at school, then you shouldn't be *at school*."

Panic flashed through me. "No, Mom. I didn't mean— That's not what I meant."

Mom gazed at me for a beat. Her eyes were bloodshot, cupped by purplish shadows. I wondered if she'd gotten a full night's sleep in the last two weeks. "Is it hurting that badly?" she asked.

Before I could answer, Shakespeare stepped out from behind her left shoulder. He stared at me too, with eyes that were deep and dark.

"No," I said. "Not all the time. I shouldn't have put it that way."

"Maybe we should move up the date of your next appointment. I'll call the hospital and see if they can fit us in tomorrow."

Shakespeare glided past the end of the counter and slid behind the refrigerator, like someone onstage stepping behind a curtain. I dragged my eyes back to my mother.

"Mom, it's okay. I—"

"Because if things aren't getting any better, you just can't take this kind of risk."

Something was beginning to seep out from beneath the refrigerator. Something red and wet and spreading.

"Mom, I swear, I'm not going to skip class again."

"I mean the risk of going to school."

The pool of blood widened across the fake brick floor. It trickled into the mortar lines. It was already only inches from the side of Mom's foot. Polonius in *Hamlet*, stabbed behind a tapestry. The puddle around the crushed BMW.

It's not real. It's not real.

"Mom . . ." I inhaled slowly, smoothing my voice down. *Katharine Hepburn. Cate Blanchett. Meryl Streep.* "The headache isn't that bad all the time. Really." The pool was trickling closer. I forced myself to keep still as it lapped toward my toes. "I just slept badly last night, and then I made one stupid decision. That's it. I won't do it again. I promise."

Mom held her own arms tighter. It looked almost like she was hugging herself. I imagined stepping forward, hugging her with mine instead, but I couldn't make my body do it. Besides, the pool of blood now completely filled the floor, widening the space between us.

"I thought we were clear on this," Mom said. "I'll say it again, just in case. You are not allowed to go *anywhere* but school until the doctors and I agree that it's safe. All right?"

"Yes. All right." I pulled my eyes away from the puddle again. My head spun. "I won't."

"That means nothing with Nikki, or Tom, or Pierce. And it means nothing with this new kid, Ron Whatever-his-name-is."

I could almost feel the warmth of the blood now. "Rob."

"Fine. Rob," Mom repeated. *"Nothing."* She released the grip on her arms. She rubbed her forehead with her fingertips, and I noticed for the first time that her hand was shaking. "Please don't scare me like that again."

"I'm sorry," I whispered.

I looked down at the floor, because I couldn't look at her anymore.

Blood. Pooling. Sticky. Warm. Melting holes in the white snow.

"Jaye . . ." Mom's voice came from far away. "If all of this is just too much for you right now—classes, home-work, the play—please tell me. Because you getting better matters more than any of that."

I closed my eyes. "I know. I will."

The kitchen was quiet for a moment.

"I'm afraid I haven't done a good enough job of pro-tecting you lately." Mom's voice was fragile. I wished I could wrap it in a cast, like a broken bone. "Of making sure you're all right."

"Mom, I'm fine."

"I think I've felt so guilty about the things you don't have—things I can't give you—that I've just let you make your own path. But I need to do better. I need to take care of *you.* Not the other way around." Mom's voice grew a little stronger. "I can't let you make all of these choices. You're not ready. So much of the time, you still choose wrong."

I kept my eyes shut. "I know."

"If you do something like this again, something that could put you in danger, that is it for the play. You'll be done."

My eyes flicked open. The pool of blood was gone. I inhaled, focusing on a piece of lint that clung to the front of Mom's cardigan until I was sure that my voice wouldn't come out in a wail.

"All right," I said. "I won't. I promise."

"Good," said Mom gently. "Now get thee to bed and rest, for thou hast need."

The linoleum sagged under me.

Lady Capulet's line. *Romeo and Juliet.*

"What?" I breathed.

Mom gazed back at me, her forehead crinkling with worry. "I said, go get a little rest. Are you all right?"

"Yeah. Fine." My throat tightened. I took a breath, trying to force it open again. "I just . . . must have misunderstood you."

I lurched away, keeping my face down until I was safely around the corner and out of her sight.

As I crossed the living room, the set began to change. Our furniture drifted silently up into the fly space. The carpets rolled back. Painted stone walls settled down onto the black wooden floor. I climbed the steps, which were now just wooden slats leading up to a stage-craft balcony.

By the time I reached the top, I could hear new sounds coming from below. Clanking. Rasping metal. Hard footsteps. I leaned out over the railing.

Two actors were dueling on the stage below. Their long, thin swords hissed when they touched, like water on a hot burner. At first, from their clothes—one in a white tunic, the other all in black—I thought they must be Laertes and Hamlet, acting out their final scene. But when they changed direction, I could see their faces for the first time.

It was Pierce and Rob.

I held the railing tighter. What play was this?

They moved in a tight pattern across the floor. Spotlight glittered on their swords.

Pierce slashed at Rob's rib cage. Rob leaped out of the way, but the blade caught his side, tearing a slash through his shirt. Red drops spilled from the fabric.

Too real. Too real to be stage blood.

Rob didn't pause. He swung around, lashing out as Pierce charged forward. A streak of red appeared on Pierce's shoulder.

"They bleed on both sides," a voice whispered in my ear.

Hamlet stood beside me. His cracked-ice eyes seemed to give off their own light. "What is it you would see?" he asked, gazing past me, at the fight below. "If aught of woe or wonder, cease your search."

"Why doesn't anybody stop them?" I whirled away from

Hamlet, ready to run back down the steps, but the wooden staircase had disappeared. We were stuck on our little platform. I held the railing and leaned out as far as I could. "Somebody stop them!"

Rob and Pierce fought on. They were both staggering now. Blood left wet petals on the boards. Their boots crushed them, dragged them into streaks.

"Stop them!" I tried to scream, but no sound would come from my mouth. "It's real! This is real!"

Why hadn't I seen it coming? Everyone knows how the play ends.

But I'd been an idiot. I'd let it happen.

Hamlet took hold of my arm. I tried to shake him off, but he wouldn't let go.

"Stop them!" I shouted at him. At anyone. "Please! *Please!* It's real!"

A hand grabbed my other arm.

"Jaye. *Jaye.*"

Faint light on my face. Someone turning me around. Pulling me down to the carpet. The smell of blood thinning in the air.

I blinked. The upstairs hallway snapped back, solid and familiar. Moonlight blurred the hanging picture frames. Sadie was crouched in front of me, holding me by both arms. A tennis racket lay on the carpet beside her.

"Jesus, Jaye," she whispered. "I thought somebody had broken into the house. What, were you sleepwalking?"

I looked down. I could see the fuzzy plaid of my own pajama pants. Below us, the living room was silent. Mom's door at the far end of the hallway was shut.

"I don't know. I must have been," I whispered back. My heart was slamming so hard against my ribs, I wondered if Sadie could hear it. "I was dreaming . . ."

"About what?"

"About . . . someone fighting. I was trying to stop them. I kept yelling and yelling, but no one could hear me."

"I hate that. Or when you dream that you're trying to run, and you're working as hard as you can, and your legs won't even move." Sadie got to her feet. She offered both hands and pulled me up too. "Let's get you back to bed."

"Were you going to serve a burglar to death?" I asked as we stepped over her tennis racket.

"If I had to," Sadie answered. "I would at least have returned him to the bottom of the stairs."

She tucked me back under my rumpled purple quilt. For a second, I almost asked her to stay and sleep beside me, like we'd done when we were little, and I thought packs of hungry monsters hid under my bed. But I couldn't quite get the words out.

"Sadie . . ." I whispered. "Thanks. For getting there before Mom."

Sadie nodded. "Don't worry about it. I'm sure she didn't even hear us."

"You won't tell her, will you?"

Sadie looked hard at me. "Does she need to know? You've never sleepwalked before. You could have fallen down the steps and hurt yourself."

"I'll tell the doctors at my next checkup. I promise. I just don't want to scare Mom any more."

Sadie paused in my doorway, turning back to the bed for a second. The Beatles' faces on her T-shirt looked blue and ghostly. "Do I need to barricade you in here?" she asked. "Set up any booby traps?"

"I don't think so."

"Okay." She hesitated again. "Good night, Drama Queen."

The door clicked shut.

I lay still, staring up at the ceiling.

I'd lost a few hours. But I was safe at home.

Pierce was safe in his own house, a couple of miles away.

Rob, wherever he was, was safe too.

I promised myself this.

It was only a dream. Or mostly a dream. Or a dream with real things scattered inside. Fake swords, real blood.

Still, even though I'd woken up before the end, something dark and heavy lingered inside of me, telling me that I was already too late.

CHAPTER 17

It wasn't until I reached the backstage door that I realized my shirt was inside out.

I traced the exposed seam around my wrist and up my arm. Yep. Definitely inside out. This meant I'd been wearing it that way, with the seams sticking up and the tag poking out, all day long.

It meant my mother hadn't noticed it that morning, when she'd let me sleep in until after ten, because Sadie *had* told her about the night before, that traitor. She hadn't noticed it at the breakfast table, while she sipped her third cup of coffee and I wasn't allowed to have a single one, or while she drove me to school with an excuse note for the office. I'd watched her hands clenching and unclenching on the tabletop, in her lap, around the steering wheel, like she was trying not to let go of some invisible thing.

There was something else I had to hold on to. Time had gotten slippery, and my memory was a mess of things that appeared and disappeared on their own, but I had to hang on tight to yesterday. I ran through the events again and again, like I was learning my lines. Everything that had happened—my promise to Mom, getting in trouble with Rob, Pierce's anger, the way he had kissed me—

He'd kissed me.

Pierce Caplan had kissed me.

And that awful thing I'd seen. Blood seeping across the kitchen linoleum. Blood on the stage's black boards. I had to hold on to that too, before it sank back into the mess. The kiss. The blood. It meant something. It had to mean something.

I tiptoed into the back of the wings. The crew was on-stage, attaching the pillars of Theseus's palace to the fly rods, and I could hear the voices of the rest of the cast coming from the house. All afternoon, I'd managed to avoid seeing Pierce or Rob or anyone else who would ask about yesterday's stupidity.

But as I crept into a corner to stow my bag, I heard Tom's voice. "Ooh, it's our favorite outlaw!"

He hurried through the wings, wearing a sweater and a smile that were both too big. "What's this stuff about you cutting with the new kid?"

I looked around, making sure no one else was near enough to overhear. "A mistake."

"You mean it didn't happen?"

"No. It happened. But it was moronic. I shouldn't have done it."

"I don't know." Tom pulled me down onto the edge of

Titania's platform. "He's . . . well, he's not cute. *Cute* isn't the right word."

"No." I agreed, looking down at my feet. "He's . . . something else."

Tom started to smile again. "Jaye and the new kid . . ." He bumped me teasingly with one arm. "You *strumpet*."

"Shut up."

"It's just what Shakespeare would say about you."

I rubbed my head. "You don't know what Shakespeare would say about me."

Tom raised his eyebrows. "Oh, I think I do. Because aren't you already *with* Pierce Caplan?"

I threw up my hands. "I don't even know. I mean— we're something. Sort of. I don't know."

"Well, that clears *that* up." Tom kicked my shoe lightly with the toe of his. "You know, it's a little weird to not even know who your best friend is dating."

I let out a breath. The ache in my head thrashed. "I'm sorry." I leaned against his baggy woolen shoulder. "It's not even clear to *me*."

Tom patted the side of my head. "Next time you feel like cutting class, you should tell me. We haven't gotten to talk in forever."

"I know." I sighed into his sweater. "I miss it. I'm—"

"Hey, Bottom!" Tri, the costumer, poked her head into the wings. "Come try on your new mask."

"Coming!" Tom gave my head a final pat. "See you later, harlot."

When Tom had scrambled past me, I slumped over, putting my face between my knees. I must have been imagining it, because the ache seemed to be worse than ever. And it *couldn't* be worse. I had to be getting better by now. Had to.

The seams outside my sleeves ticked the sides of my face. As long as I was hiding, I might as well take my chance. I scrambled around the back of the platform and crouched down between the fake riverbank and the wall. I yanked the shirt over my head, whipped it right side out, and pulled it back down.

Backward.

I wormed both arms into the body of the shirt. I'd wriggled it halfway around when a deep voice said, "Hey."

Rob stood on the other side of the platform. He smiled down at me. "Nice shirt."

It was like someone had opened a window. Suddenly there was air and light and a potential escape route, and a view of things I hadn't even realized were there. Even squatting in a corner, my clothes on sideways, knowing I must look totally ridiculous, all I felt was happy.

Then I smelled the blood.

Remember.

I looked away. "Thanks."

"You weren't in anatomy," his voice went on. That voice. God. I loved that voice. "Skipping two days in a row? Pretty ballsy."

"I wasn't skipping." I stood up, circling around the far side of the platform. Keeping my distance. "I wasn't feeling well this morning."

"Are you okay?"

I took another step away from him. "I'm fine." *Keep the conversation short. Face blank. Voice calm.*

"I shouldn't have kept you out for so long," said Rob. "I'm really sorry."

No. I'd wanted the afternoon to go on and on. *Keep your face blank. "I shouldn't have suggested it." Say it. That's your line. SAY IT.*

"It was my fault." My chest was tight. "I'm sorry I got *you* in trouble." I put one hand on my head, half hiding from view. "What did they do to you?"

"One week of morning detention and a stern warning. You?"

"Nothing."

"Nothing?" His tone was impressed. "Well played."

"Well. You know." I pointed to my head. "Get Out of Jail Free card."

Rob took a step toward me—just near enough that I could catch the scent of his clothes. Detergent. Soap. Something else, dark and spicy, like cloves. It made my heart beat faster.

"Don't," I said stupidly.

"Don't what?"

I had to be clear. I had to push him away. Even though what I suddenly wanted to do more than anything was reach out and wrap both arms around him, feel the solidity of his body. Tall. Warm. Real.

"Don't talk to me anymore." The tightness filled my skull. "Yesterday was idiotic. My head was hurting, and I was tired, and I made a mistake." The words came faster. "We shouldn't have done it. Now they'll be watching you, like they're already watching me. We can't give them anything to see."

God, I sounded paranoid. I sounded insane.

From the corner of my eye, I could see Rob's smile disappear.

"What would anyone have seen? Two people drinking coffee?"

"That's not all it was."

"Oh. Right." Now his tone was almost sarcastic. "There were some noodles too."

"That's not what I meant. You know that."

"Look: I didn't do anything out of line. You seemed confused and out of it and like you needed somebody to talk to. So I talked with you. You made it clear that there's something going on with you and Pierce—although actually you seemed pretty confused about all of that too—and I listened. And then I brought you back here."

Anger flared in me. "Don't say I was *confused.* Don't just blame all this on my head."

"Isn't that what you're doing?" He shrugged, taking a step back. "You don't want me to talk to you anymore. I hear you. Sorry if I did something wrong."

I darted after him before he could turn away. "No. You didn't do anything wrong." I stopped myself just in time to keep from grabbing his hand. "*I* did. I keep screwing up. I keep choosing the wrong thing."

Rob looked down at me. His beautiful eyes were cool. Slightly hurt. Unsurprised. "It's fine," he said. "I'm not making more out of this than it is. I thought we might be friends. That's it. But I can leave you alone."

"Please—" I had to clench my hands into fists to keep from grabbing him this time. "I'm saying this for you, not for me. This isn't what I want."

"For me? What do you mean?"

"If you don't stay away from me—" Blood pooling on the floorboards. Blood dripping from a gash in his side. My mother's haunted face. My father. My father. "You need to stay away from me," I nearly whispered. The sword in Pierce's hand. "Or bad things . . . really bad things . . ."

And then Pierce was actually there. Standing in the gap in the curtains, his face stiff with rage. His hands clamped around the hanging velvet.

"What the hell?" he demanded.

Rob glanced over his shoulder. "Hey," he said civilly. "Could you give us a minute? Thanks."

"She just told you to stay away from her." Pierce's voice was low and tight as a tripwire. "Now back off."

"I asked you first," said Rob. "I did it more politely, but I meant the same thing. So: Could you give us a minute? Thanks."

Pierce's jaw flexed. "No. I'm not giving you anything. She told you to leave her alone."

"Pierce—that wasn't what I meant," I faltered. "It isn't like—"

Pierce's eyes didn't even flick toward me. "Stay away from her. I don't want to see you talking to her. Sitting near her. Even *looking* at her."

"I'm sorry. I forgot that *you* are in charge of what she does," said Rob, with increasing courtesy. "Hang on. What year is it in Minnesota? Did I move to 1850 when I moved here?"

"I'm not telling her what to do." Pierce stepped closer. "I'm just trying to protect her from some pathetic stalker."

"I don't know—the guy lurking behind the curtains to eavesdrop on her conversations seems more like the stalker to me."

Pierce lunged so close that his chest bumped Rob's. His shoulders were broader, his body thicker, but Rob was a few inches taller. Pierce had to jut out his chin to glare up into Rob's cool blue eyes.

The ache in my head was fracturing. "Pierce. Stop." I shoved my hands between them, trying to grab Pierce's shoulders. *"Listen to me."*

"I'm not going to say it again," Pierce growled, like some actor in an action movie.

"Good," said Rob. "Because I'd really like to see what you're going to *do* instead."

Pierce's face twisted. Suddenly, I couldn't even recognize him. He wasn't the boy who'd been my best friend. He wasn't the gorgeous stranger I'd watched from the other end of the school halls. He bumped me aside, grabbing Rob by the front of his black shirt. I heard threads pop as he whipped Rob around and shoved him out of the wings, onto the stage.

Clusters of actors scattered as Rob and Pierce plowed between them. There were gasps. Somebody shouted Pierce's name.

I heard my own voice yelling *Stop* as I lurched out onto the boards behind them. But the word only ricocheted around inside my skull, never making it out into the fire-colored air.

Pierce's arm went up, aiming a punch at Rob's face. Rob ducked to the side. The propulsion of his fist sent Pierce staggering after it. Smoothly, Rob put out one leg. Pierce tripped over his ankle, sprawling onto the stage.

Mr. Hall's voice came from somewhere in the red-streaked distance, but I couldn't make out what it said. The air was too thick. The fire in my skull burned hotter.

Pierce rolled gracefully back to his feet. He spun around, pounding forward, the force of his whole body aimed at Rob's chest. There was a glitch in my vision as they collided, their bodies frozen mid-fall, the stage simmering away into a wide stone floor. Queen Gertrude and King Claudius, positioned for the final scene of *Hamlet*, watched from their raised thrones. Gertrude raised a cup to the fighters. Over its brim, her glassy eyes met mine.

There was a thud as both bodies hit the floor. Someone's foot connected with a plywood pillar, knocking it aside. More gasps. More shouting.

Pierce reared back, his fist connecting with Rob's cheekbone. It came down again. And again. My stomach heaved. Rob's elbow flashed up to block the next strike. His free arm levered him upward, toppling Pierce sideways. There was a thud as Pierce slid to the boards. Rob pounced, pinning Pierce to the floor. His hands locked around Pierce's wrists.

"Enough!" Mr. Hall's voice seared through the noise.

He dove between Pierce and Rob, arms out. The rest of the cast surged inward, dragging Pierce and Rob apart. Mr. Carter and two school security officers were already jogging down the center aisle. One officer jumped onto the boards, heading for Pierce, while the other pulled Rob off of Pierce's body.

Rob had already gone still. His face went blank as the officer grasped his elbows, yanking him to his feet. A red welt was forming on his cheekbone. A trickle of blood ran from the corner of his lip to the edge of his jaw.

"A touch, a touch, I confess . . ." Hamlet whispered into my ear.

Wake up, I begged myself. *Wake up.*

"All right, Mr. Mason," said Mr. Carter. "It looks like you made your choice." He gave a nod. The officer marched Rob toward the steps, one arm pinned behind his back. Rob didn't struggle.

Mr. Carter spun toward Pierce, who was still thrashing in the grip of the other officer and several cast members. "Mr. Caplan, I expected much better from you. My office. Now."

Pierce threw off the other students' hands. Sullenly, he stalked off between the officer and Mr. Carter, his footsteps hammering the hollow floor and echoing away up the aisle.

There was a moment of stunned silence. No one moved.

Then, without thinking, I flew after them.

I leaped off the edge of the stage, barely feeling the jolt of my brain against my skull—the pain couldn't get any larger anyway—and raced up the narrow strip of carpet, chasing them straight through the auditorium's closing doors.

"Mr. Carter!" I yelled. "Mr. Carter! Wait!"

The vice principal halted. A few steps ahead of him, Pierce and the security officer hesitated too.

"Mr. Carter." I skidded to a stop beside him. "Please. It wasn't Rob. Pierce started it. He grabbed him. He tried to hit him first."

Down the hall, Pierce shot me a look of such fury that my searing skin went cold.

Mr. Carter scanned my face. His eyes traveled upward, to the scar. I'd been truant with this new kid just yesterday. Now he was caught fighting with the school's golden boy, and I'd come running, out of breath, probably looking like a delirious fever patient, to defend him.

"We'll take that into consideration, Miss Stuart," he said slowly. "You take care of yourself." He pivoted on his shiny brown shoes and strode away.

The officer gave Pierce a nudge. They set off after Mr. Carter, Pierce throwing me one last look that lingered on my skin like frost.

Back in the auditorium, rehearsal had dissolved into a total mess.

Cast members stood in knots onstage, their voices overlapping. Tom and Nikki and Anders and a few others formed one tight group. Michaela Dorfmann had planted herself at the center of another knot. I could hear her loudly repeating, "I can't *believe* Pierce would do that. He would *never* do that." Upstage, the crew was trying to repair the damaged set pieces. Just below the stage's lip, Mr. Hall was stalking back and forth between Ayesha and the first row of seats, his face red and furious.

"That's if we're even going to *have* a show at this point," I heard him shouting as I inched down the aisle. "Our Oberon's in a brawl, our crew members are getting expelled, our Titania's falling apart——"

Ayesha's eyes landed on me. They went wide.

The other voices died as people turned to stare.

Mr. Hall spun around. "Jaye," he said quickly, "I didn't mean that you——"

"I'm not falling apart," I said. "I am *fine.*"

"I am but mad north-north-west," Hamlet agreed, looming over my shoulder. "When the wind is southerly, I know a hawk from a handsaw."

"No," I muttered. "*No.*" Even when I cupped both hands around my eyes, I could feel him waiting behind me, a terrifying shadow. "I can't——I'm not——"

Wake up. WAKE UP. But the room wouldn't fade.

I turned and plunged back up the aisle, moving so fast that I hardly felt the wet weight dragging at my legs.

"Jaye?" Tom's voice called after me.

I slammed through the doors into the brightness of the hall. The weight around my legs was getting heavier. I glanced down. My gray jeans were soaked with blood. It rose up from the cuffs, as if I had waded into it. It was

climbing even higher now, creeping over my calves, dyeı.
the fabric with its warm, patient crawl.

A blast of freezing air hit me as I rushed out into the
parking lot. Cold sliced through my clothes. The blood
crystalized, making the damp denim stiffen. Still, I struggled forward, arms wrapped around myself, leaning into
the wind that kept trying to force me back.

CHAPTER 18

Did you just *walk* home?" Sadie demanded as I scurried past her into the living room. "It's almost two miles."

My chattering teeth were enough of an answer. I grabbed a blanket from the couch and sank down beside the radiator.

Sadie towered over me. "And where the hell is your coat?"

"I for-forgot it at s-school."

"You forgot it. In January. In below-zero wind chill."

"I'm—wearing a thick—sweater."

Sadie grabbed the afghan from her chair and draped it over me like a giant doily. She plunked down in front of me. "What happened? Is this because Pierce and that weird new kid got into a fight over you?"

"What?" I shoved a flap of afghan off my face. "How did you hear that?"

"Word travels at the speed of texts. Faster than a stupid girl with no coat can walk home."

I wrapped both hands around my throbbing head. My

brain ground against bone. "It wasn't a fight over me. It was idiotic."

Sadie picked up my right boot. For a second, I tried to jerk my blood-stained leg away, but when I looked down, the blood had disappeared. Sadie pulled off the boot and tucked my foot under the blanket. "You'd better hope you don't have frostbite," she said, yanking off the other boot. "I guess the new kid is going to be expelled."

"What?"

"That's what everybody's saying. Pierce might get suspended too, but Mr. Hall is trying to pull strings, for the sake of the show."

Oh god. The show.

The reality of what I'd just done sank into my thawing brain. I'd just run away from rehearsal, like the damaged little psycho I'd sworn I wasn't. If there had been any way to make this mess worse, I'd probably just done it.

And the whole mess was my fault to begin with. If I'd never spoken to Rob, he wouldn't be getting expelled, or gotten punched in the face. And Pierce would have stayed the near-perfect thing I thought he was.

God, I wished I had never seen that look in his eyes. I wished I hadn't seen the way he'd pounded his fist into Rob's face again and again . . .

My stomach lurched.

"I'm going to lie down," I mumbled, heaving myself toward the stairs.

Sadie called after me. "You know, taking care of you would feel like less of a waste if you'd take any care of yourself."

Still wrapped in the afghan, I fell face-first onto my bed.

Maybe Sadie had heard wrong. Maybe Mr. Carter had believed me. Maybe Pierce had told the truth. Maybe Rob wouldn't be expelled after all.

But there was no way to find out. I'd left my phone with my bag and coat and everything else in that backstage corner. Besides, I realized, I didn't have Rob's number. And I'd never given him mine.

What was I thinking? There was no way he'd ever want to speak to me again. I'd staggered into his life, stayed until it was almost as messed up as mine, and then told him to keep away.

Purple and blue bursts spread across my vision. Burying my head under the pillows, I tried to take deep, slow breaths, but the ache was a spear twisting in a wound, and the flashes of dark color fizzed inside my eyelids.

I'd ruined everything. Rob had no idea how I actually felt. And now he'd never know.

He probably hated me anyway. I'm sure Pierce detested me now. And Mr. Hall had every reason to give up on me at last. I'd thrown it all away.

I'd been warned. I'd been warned, and I'd screwed up in spite of it all. Dad had been right. Pathetic. Stupid. Sad. Wrong.

A hand came to rest on my ankle.

I could have sworn I heard someone say, in a voice I hadn't heard for two years, "What's the matter, Blue Jaye?"

I flipped over. Pillows tumbled to either side.

Shakespeare sat at the end of my bed. His forehead was puckered with concern. "How now? A conduit, girl? What, still in tears?"

I kicked his hand away. "Don't touch me."

Shakespeare tilted his head. "But still thy eyes, which I may call the sea, do ebb and flow with—"

"Please. Stop." I sat up straight. My throat clenched, and I could feel my face crinkling into ugly-cry position. "Please stop doing this to me. Stop talking to me in quotes and riddles, stop appearing out of nowhere, stop judging me and spying on me and trying to make my already ruined life *worse*."

There was no answer this time.

After a moment, I turned my head. Shakespeare was gone.

I pressed my face back into the blankets.

Downstairs, there was the thump of a door. "Hello!" called Mom's voice. Sadie answered.

Other sounds trailed through the house. Water running. Cabinets clicking. The distant, nasal ring of the phone.

My skin went cold.

Mr. Hall: It had to be. He'd have called the landline instead of a cell phone. He would have waited until my mother was likely to be home. And now he would tell her what had happened. He would tell her that he had no choice but to give my role away.

I held my breath, listening. I couldn't hear any voice at all—just the sound of footsteps squeaking up the staircase.

There was a knock at my door. Before I could get up, it swung open, revealing Mom on the other side.

"May I come in?" she asked softly.

"Yeah." I wiped my face, sitting up. "Come in."

Mom sat down so delicately on my bed that the mattress barely moved. She didn't speak.

I sniffed and wiped my face again. "Who called you?"

Mom stroked my quilt absently. "Mr. Hall called me at work. He said that you'd just rushed out of rehearsal, leaving all your things behind. He said there'd been some kind of fight during practice, and you'd been involved somehow, and no one was sure where you'd gone. So I tore out of the office and drove up and down the streets between here and the high school, looking everywhere for you. That's when Sadie called me and told me that you'd walked home and had just gone up to your room."

"I didn't mean to make anybody worry," I said. "I just came straight home. I didn't do anything you said I shouldn't do."

Mom sighed.

I looked down at the ragged ends of her fingernails. "So Mr. Hall didn't—did he say he was going to replace me?"

"Jaye . . ." Mom sighed again. "No. He didn't."

I relaxed for a split second, flush with relief. "So—who called just now?"

Mom's eyes moved away. "That was Patrick Caplan."

Relaxation over.

"Mr. Caplan called you? Why?"

"He wanted to let me know that Pierce had just been disciplined for fighting some new boy with a long record of behavioral problems who has recently been hanging around with *you.*"

I kept still.

"I'm guessing this is the same boy you skipped school with." Mom paused. She still wasn't looking at me. "Am I wrong?"

". . . No."

"Didn't I tell you that I didn't want you spending time with him?"

"You just said I couldn't do anything outside of school and rehearsal with him. And I haven't. You didn't say I couldn't even *talk* to him, or—"

"Fine," Mom stopped me. "Apparently I wasn't specific enough. I don't want you around him at all. Is that clearer?"

"But—he's in one of my classes. And he's on the stage crew. I can't just—"

"Jaye, do you want to be pulled out of school entirely?"

"No. Of course not."

"Then just agree."

I took a breath. Put on my disappointed/resigned face. "Okay. Fine. I'll try."

Mom was silent for a minute, looking at me, and I wondered if she'd somehow seen through the mask. But then she leaned back, looking around at my collage-covered walls. "Patrick is worried, of course," she resumed. "Pierce isn't the type to pick a fight, so I'm guessing he had a very good reason." When I didn't speak, Mom took another breath, her narrow shoulders rising and falling. "Fortunately, because of his record, Patrick thinks the school is going to take it easy on him this time."

The words shot out of me. "But—Pierce started it."

Mom didn't look surprised. "That's what Patrick said. Pierce admitted it. He said he got involved because he was trying to protect you."

"Protect me? From *what?*"

"Jaye." Mom shook her head, gazing at the window. There was a beat. "You know, loving you is pretty hard on the people who try to do it."

These words hit like a punch. Like four punches, really. One for Mom. One for Sadie. One for Pierce. One last knockout for my father.

I couldn't speak for a minute. I stared at Mom's hand again. Besides the ragged fingernails, her knuckles looked red and chapped. She obviously hadn't been wearing gloves on her morning jogs, or using lotion to combat the dry winter air.

I touched one knuckle, gently, with my fingertip. "I'm not the only one who doesn't do a great job of taking care of herself."

"I know." Mom gave me a tiny smile. "Maybe you got that from me. We're both very good at making our own mistakes."

"When did you ever make a mistake?"

Mom met my eyes now. "Oh, I make them. I just usually make them by being too cautious. Too quiet." She smiled again. "That's something you definitely *didn't* get from me. And I'm very glad about that."

My eyes started to sting. "I don't know." I pushed the hair over my scar, trying to hide my face. *You're fine. At least* pretend *you're fine.* "Being me apparently means doing lots of things wrong. Even when I know I should do something else, it's like . . ." *Stop crying, you idiot.* But I couldn't put the mask back on. "I know I disappoint everybody. I know Dad was—"

I stopped. I turned my face aside, so Mom wouldn't see the tears sliding past my nose and over my jaw.

"I don't think you *do* know," said Mom, very softly.

For a few minutes, we were both quiet.

But I knew. I remembered. I remembered perfectly. It was just the blank spots between the memories that made me doubt myself—the things Pierce had told me, the things Sadie had said. They were like gaps between the slats of a high, swinging bridge. I needed more to hold on to.

"Mom," I began, "why was Dad with the Caplans when it happened? Why wasn't he driving his own car?"

Mom sat up a little bit straighter. "You know why."

"I know. Just—tell me again."

"He and Patrick had been on a business trip together. They'd had several trips that winter. Meeting with designers, visiting suppliers, opening the new stores. Remember?"

"Yeah, I remember." I toyed with a fold of my purple quilt. "Just . . . if it was a business trip, why was Pierce with them?"

"Because—" Mom hesitated for a second too long. "They were on their way home from the trip. They must have picked Pierce up after school."

"Then . . . why didn't they pick up me and Sadie? We couldn't drive yet."

Mom's voice hardened. "Why? Are you wishing you were with them?"

"No. That's not—that's not what I mean." Flashes of Dad's face. Smiling at me. Angry at me. His tanned forearms. His half-empty closet. I rubbed my head. "I'm just trying to remember. Because Pierce said—"

Even harder. "What did Pierce say?"

"Nothing. He just said that Dad had been with them a lot. Right before."

"That was nothing new. He and Patrick were together every day."

"No. I know."

"Jaye . . . I think I know what's going on." The edge in Mom's voice dulled again. "You're trying to make sense of things. Why what happened to him happened. Why what happened to *you* happened. Why they ended differently." She touched my ankle. "It isn't fate. It's nothing anyone did wrong. It's just what happened. And I'm so glad—" Her voice choked a little. "I'm just so glad you're here."

I couldn't answer.

We sat next to each other on my bed for a while. I rubbed itchy tears away with the back of my wrist. Mom stroked my leg so lightly I could barely feel it.

Then she leaned over, gave me a kiss on my forehead, and stood up. "Come down and be with us when you're ready."

I waited until the door had shut behind her. Then I slid over the edge of my mattress and pulled the bundle out from under my bed.

I buried my face in Dad's old T shirt. Faint scents of sweat and detergent, laced with Coast soap and his usual cologne. I had to breathe deep to catch it all. Most of it had already faded away.

I remembered when those scents had disappeared from

the house. It had happened gradually. Not finding him already in the kitchen when I woke up, checking the online news, sipping his black coffee, his eyes tired and his mouth tight. Not having to step over his running shoes on the doormat. Dinners without him. Weekends without him. And the times when he was home, when he and Mom were shut behind their bedroom door, just the wisps of their overlapping voices escaping through the cracks.

I breathed in the scent one more time. Then I pushed the bundle back under my bed. This time I didn't push it quite so far.

CHAPTER 19

Saturday is usually the best day of the week. But when you're stuck at home in the middle of winter without even your phone, and you know that people on the outside are doing things without you, or talking about you, or hating you more and more as the hours tick by, Saturday is just a few degrees away from hell.

I spent the morning in my room, trying to concentrate on the script for *A Midsummer Night's Dream*. But my mind kept wandering away, imagining what Nikki and Tom were doing without me, replaying Mom's words from last night. *Loving you is pretty hard on the people who try to do it.*

But most of all, I thought about Rob.

Who was probably expelled.

Who must hate me.

Who I might never see again.

The thoughts lit up like igniting matches, one after another, until my whole head burned.

Ophelia sat at my dressing table for a while, singing softly and combing her long wet hair.

"And will he not come again? And will he not come again?" She stared into the mirror with foggy eyes. "No, no. He is dead. Go to thy deathbed. He never will come again."

When she vanished, the smell of river water lingered after her.

Daylight faded from gray to blue.

I was lying on my bed, staring up at the ceiling, when I heard a knock at the front door.

Three voices spoke, two higher, one lower. I recognized them even through my closed door.

I flew out into the hall.

Over the railing, I could see Mom holding the knob of the front door. Tom and Nikki hovered on the threshold.

"I'm sorry," Mom was saying. "She's not allowed to have visitors right now."

"Can we just say hi?" Nikki wheedled. "We'll stay for just ten seconds. Twenty seconds. Thirty seconds."

Tom bumped her arm. "That's not how bargaining works."

"Hey, guys!" I called over the banister. "Mom, can't they come in for just a second?"

"Or thirty seconds?" said Nikki.

"We brought you your stuff." Tom held up the bag and coat I'd abandoned backstage.

I ran down the stairs. "Mom, please? Just a minute?"

Mom sighed. "Fine. One minute." She turned, giving me a pointed look before slipping away toward the kitchen.

Nikki hugged me violently. "Are you okay? That was *crazy* yesterday."

"Everybody is talking about it," said Tom. Nikki smacked his arm. "What?"

"She doesn't want to know that everyone's talking about it!"

I pulled my bag out of Tom's hands. "What are they saying?"

"Stuff about the new kid, mostly," said Nikki. "But we just ran into Jeremy Stiles—"

"Who?"

"The hot one on the swim team."

"The blue-haired hot one," Tom specified.

"—and he told us something about Pierce."

The pressure in my head twisted. "What did he say?"

"You know how Pierce told everybody he was quitting swim team so he could do the show? He didn't actually quit. He was going to be kicked off."

"What?" I glanced over my shoulder. Mom was out of sight. "Why?"

"For fighting with some swimmer from another school. It was in the locker room at an away meet last year. Jeremy said the other kid needed dental surgery, Pierce beat him up so badly."

"But—then—" The ache got tighter. "Why didn't Pierce get expelled?"

Nikki snorted. "Because the school *loves* him. And his family's rich, and everybody knows them—"

"And nobody knew for sure who started it," Tom interrupted. "Or if they did, they wouldn't say."

"Don't be mad that we told you," said Nikki, when I didn't speak. "We thought, with what happened on Friday, and what I saw in the parking lot a couple years ago . . . It's just obviously not the first time. Are you mad?"

I struggled to keep my face clear. "I'm not mad."

"Okay. Good."

"You guys had better go." I looked over my shoulder again, lowering my voice. "Hey . . . you haven't heard anything from Rob, have you?"

They shook their heads.

"I don't have his number anyway," said Nikki. "Why?"

"Nothing. I just hope he's okay." I grabbed the door. "Thanks for bringing my stuff."

"See you Monday." Nikki and Tom hugged me again before backing out the door.

I scurried up to my room and dumped the bag out onto my bed.

There were six missed calls on my phone. All from Pierce.

None from any unknown numbers. Nothing that could possibly be from Rob.

Of course not, I reminded myself. *You got him detention.*

You got him expelled. You got him beaten up. You told him to leave you alone.

Still, I stared at the screen for a while, as if looking at it and wishing could make something appear.

Sunday dragged by. Pierce called twice. I didn't pick up.

I didn't know what I'd say to him if I answered. And I couldn't get that image out of my mind. His fist. Rob's face. Blood. A dripping sword—

No. That wasn't real.

But the rest of it was.

I was certain. Almost certain.

The more time passed, the more the image seemed to warp, until the truth seemed impossible, and the ache in my head seemed about to break free.

Eventually all I could do was lie on my bed and try to sleep. Lines from *A Midsummer Night's Dream* and *Hamlet* and past conversations tumbled through my mind. I heard fairies singing. A siren wailing. A machine beeping along to someone's heartbeat. And, in the distance, the sound of a ringing phone.

There was a knock at my door.

I didn't get up. It was probably only in my mind anyway. If I answered it, Hamlet and that cracked skull, or Shakespeare and a pool of blood, or something even worse would be waiting on the other side.

The knock came again. The door creaked open.

Mom stood in the doorway. "It's for you," she said, holding out the cordless phone. Her eyes were cool. Distrustful.

I slid off the bed and took the phone. Mom gave me a long look, but she didn't say anything else. I waited until she'd turned away, her steps fading down the staircase, before putting the receiver to my ear. My heart pounded so hard, both my hands shook.

"Hello?"

"Hey," said a deep voice.

That voice. I felt it reverberate through my whole body.

"I didn't think you—" I cut myself off. "How did you get this number?"

"I called every Stuart in the phone book in alphabetical order." His voice was warm. Not angry. I could almost hear the smile in it. "I'm just lucky you're not unlisted. And that your mom's name is Heidi, not Zoe."

I let out a little laugh. Dreaming. Not dreaming. I dug the fingernails of my free hand into my palm as hard as I could. "God. Rob, I'm so sorry. Are you okay?"

"I'm fine. A little bruised. I've had it a lot worse."

"I heard you got expelled."

"Suspended. And they're still going to let me graduate, depending on my future behavior."

"Oh, good. God. I'm so glad." My fingernails had left red half-moons in my palm. Not dreaming. Not dreaming. "What I said—about staying away from me—this is

266

why. Not that I thought Pierce would do this," I went on quickly. "Or I would never have . . . I mean, he didn't used to be like this. At least, I didn't see it. I just knew that *something* was going to go wrong, because I mess up everything I touch. It's not because I don't want—I don't want to . . ."

I couldn't finish.

There was a beat. I listened to the quiet coming through the receiver, and suddenly I might as well have been holding a seashell up to my ear. Just imagining that I heard the ocean.

"Are you there?" I whispered.

"I'm here." His voice. Deep and clear. "I was just waiting to see what you'd say."

"I'm not sure what to say. I mean, I want—I want *God*." I rubbed my fingers through my hair. The scar. The shaved spot. Still there. "I don't like this. Just talking, not being able to see you. I want to talk *with* you."

"I want to see you too," he said. "Can I?"

"Really?" I let out another stupid little laugh. "You don't hate me?"

"I so far from hate you." I could definitely hear the smile that time.

"But I got you in trouble. I got you into that stupid fight."

"Don't." His voice was light. "It was my choice. And I could tell what you were doing, you know. Trying to push me away. To save me from something." He paused for a second. "But I don't need to be saved. I don't *want* to be saved."

I laughed again, and almost inhaled a teardrop. I hadn't even realized I was crying. "Maybe you're crazy too."

"So . . ." One more pause. Teasing this time. "Can I see you?"

"Yes." The word flew out before I could think. "Wait. No." I paced across the room. "You can't come here. I can't go anywhere except school, and now you're not going to be there for a while."

"I don't know if I can wait a whole week."

"Me neither." My body was full of helium balloons. I could practically feel my toes rising off the carpet. "What if . . . what if I get out of rehearsal a little early?"

"When?"

"Tomorrow. I'll leave at four. I'll give Mr. Hall some kind of excuse, and get out before anybody else notices."

"I'll pick you up in the parking lot."

"No—someone might see you. Just meet me two blocks away. On the corner of Twenty-second."

"Impressively devious." I heard the smile in his voice again. "All right. I'll see you there."

"Yes. There."

We hung up.

I stood in the middle of the floor for several seconds, just beaming at the phone. If I'd dived out the window just then, I'm sure I would have soared.

CHAPTER 20

Places for Act Three!" Ayesha's voice sliced through the darkness. "Players! Fairies! Crew! Let's go!"

I crawled carefully onto the rolling platform. Anticipation made my whole body feel brittle and quivery, like one frozen strand of hair. I lay down on the green velvet. Half an hour. Just thirty minutes more.

I was trying to remember my first cue when a figure rippled into my peripheral vision.

"I need to talk to you," it said, in a hard voice.

My skin went cold. "I can't talk right now."

"I've been trying to find you all day," said Pierce, not quietly enough. A few nearby crew members backed uncomfortably away. "I looked for you before first hour. At lunch. Before rehearsal." Pierce's voice got sharper with each word. "Are you avoiding me?"

"No," I said, not looking at him. Onstage, the lights shifted to forest-night blue. "I just—I can't deal with this right now. I'm about to go on."

"Why didn't you answer my calls all weekend?" Pierce

demanded. "Quick. Before you can make up another excuse."

"Music cue," called Ayesha's voice.

Recorded harp notes fluttered through the dimness.

"We'll talk *later*," I whispered.

"When?"

"On the drive home today."

"So you're not just going to run away from me again?"

"No. I promise." The music faded out. The run crew inched closer, grabbing the corners of my platform. "We'll talk later."

"The platform should be on by now!" Ayesha shouted.

The crew shoved the set piece forward. I sank down into the wire-stemmed daisies, trying to look regal and unconscious. Blue light slid over my sealed eyelids.

"The throstle, with his note so true." Tom hopped closer to me, singing. "The wren, with little quill . . ."

That was it. My cue.

I sat up. The ache in my head flashed, sending a whip of fire down my spine. I fought not to flinch. "What angel wakes me from my flowery bed?"

Tom's head was hidden in the donkey mask. Its long gray nose and flapping ears enclosed his entire face. He spun clumsily around. "The finch, the sparrow, and the lark, the plain-song cuckoo gray . . ."

When he turned back to me, the donkey's head was gone.

Tom himself was gone. The person left standing there was taller, dressed in dark linen and high boots. Through his leather carnival mask, I could see a pair of pale blue eyes. He lifted one hand, pushing the mask up into his tangled black hair, and said—

"Your line, Jaye."

Mr. Hall watched me from the lip of the stage.

"Oh. Sorry." I turned back to Tom, whose baggy sweater and donkey's head waited beside me. "Can I have the cue one more time?"

"Who would give a bird the lie, though he cry 'cuckoo' never so?"

"I pray thee, gentle mortal, sing again," I recited. "Mine ear is much enamor'd of thy note; so is my eye enthralled to thy shape . . ."

The crew was setting up for the next scene when I crept down the steps and up to Mr. Hall's seat.

He was scribbling something on a legal pad, but he glanced up and smiled as I approached.

"Nice job today, Titania," he said. "It's really coming along."

"Really? I missed that line."

"One line. Out of hundreds." Mr. Hall tapped his pen on the back of my hand. "You shouldn't be so hard on yourself. Even though it makes my job a lot easier."

"Well . . . thanks." I smiled back at him. "I don't think I can help it anyway." I hesitated, the charm of the stage lights and Mr. Hall's words holding me in place. But it was already almost four. "Um—Mr. Hall? Are you going to need me any more today?"

"Hmm." He paged through his yellow legal pad. "I don't think so. We're going to work the Athenians' scene for a while after this. Why?"

I scanned the stage. Pierce was nowhere in sight. "It's just—I've still got so much schoolwork to catch up on. I was wondering if you'd mind if I left early, so I could spend some time in the library."

He nodded understandingly. "Sure. Go ahead. And, really, Jaye. Nice job."

"Thank you."

I gave him one more smile before darting up the aisle to the seat where I'd stashed my things. No one seemed to notice as I creaked out through the auditorium doors.

I stopped in the outer hall just long enough to throw on my coat and scarf. Through the glass doors to the parking lot, I could see that it was snowing again, but I didn't care. I was made of electricity. Cold couldn't even touch me.

As I grabbed the door handle, someone appeared beside me. He leaned against the entry wall, crossing his legs in their dark blue tights.

"These violent delights have violent ends . . ."

Against my will, I turned to face him. Shakespeare's hooded blue eyes held mine for a second. Then I turned and ran out into the chilly air.

A damp, rapid snow was falling. The packed ice on the pavement was already coated with slush, and the air whipped my face with tiny frozen kisses. I rushed across the parking lot, keeping my head down, ignoring the pressure building inside.

The school slid out of sight behind me. I passed rows of quiet houses, trees drooping with fresh mounds of snow.

What if he didn't show up? What if I'd imagined that whole phone call? What if I'd just wished for it so hard that my broken brain had created this too?

But there. On the corner of the next block. A tall, dark shape.

Rob turned toward me. Black hair fluttered around his face. His eyes were even more gorgeous than I'd remembered—even though a big purple bruise puffed up from his left cheekbone, and one side of his mouth was split with a jagged red scar. He saw me, and his face broke into a smile.

I wished I'd rehearsed something to say—something clever, or memorable, or not utterly moronic. I couldn't even remember how normal people acted. Should I have been smiling so widely? Should I have been running the way I was running now, not even looking both ways before charging across the street? Would Audrey Hepburn have lunged at him like this?

Probably not.

But it didn't matter. Because Rob stepped forward too, and we met in the middle of the street.

"Are you really here?" I asked him.

"Really here." Rob held out one hand. "Are you?"

I pressed my hand against his, palm to palm. "Really here," I said.

Then his fingers closed around my hand, and he raised it to his lips.

A sparkling hole in the snow. A hospital room. A masked ball. A thousand other times, and the very first time.

I felt the tightness in my head fissure into a cloud of fireflies. I was spinning. Glowing. Weightless.

"We should probably get out of the street," I said, in a voice that was breathier than usual.

Rob didn't let go of my hand as we headed up onto the sidewalk. His grip was warm and dry with just the right amount of tightness, like his hand had been formed to fit around mine.

He grinned down at me. "What a coincidence."

"What?"

"That I just happened to be standing on that corner when you walked by."

I smiled back. "And what a coincidence that I just happened to decide to leave rehearsal early on the same afternoon you decided to stand on that street corner."

"Where are you heading?"

"My house."

"Another coincidence! I was going that way myself."

I laughed. "You don't know which way my house is."

"Shh." Rob widened his eyes. *"Coincidence."*

Above us, the sky was turning an ashy violet. Bare twigs sank upward into its darkness.

"So, how was the first day of suspension?"

"Fine. You can get your schoolwork done amazingly fast when you're not actually at school."

His tone was light, but a droplet of guilt trickled down into my stomach. "I hate that I got you into this."

"Like I said—I made my choices." He shrugged. "And I wouldn't change any of them."

"Really?"

"Of course. I mean, everything that happened brought me here."

I tucked my chin into my collar, smiling like a goon. "That's a weird thought."

"What is?"

"All the little things that have to go right or wrong, and all the choices you have to make to get exactly where you are. Like—if this had never happened to my head, would I even have talked to you in anatomy class? I don't know. I definitely wouldn't have called you *Romeo.*"

"Yeah." He smiled down at me. "I've wanted to ask you. Why *did* you call me that?"

"I told you. Head injury. It's my excuse for everything."

"But why *Romeo?*"

"Oh." I could feel my face heating. "It's . . . God. I saw lots of characters from Shakespeare at first. Because of the concussion or the painkillers or the brain rest and crazy dreams or whatever. And a couple of times, Romeo showed up. And he looked like you."

"How did you know he was Romeo?"

"Because he just . . . *was*. He said Romeo things. He acted like Romeo. He called me Juliet. He sat next to me at night, when I was alone. He held my hand."

I glanced up at him. Rob looked back down at me. Then he gave my hand a gentle squeeze.

The fireflies zinged inside me. *You're awake*, I promised myself. *You're awake*.

"How far is it to your house?" he asked as we shuffled down the snowy sidewalk.

"About a mile and a half more. Pretty far."

"Good." He paused. "Unless you're cold. Should we walk faster?"

"I'm fine. I don't need to walk faster. Maybe *you* do, with your thin West Coast blood."

"No. I'm not cold at all." He grinned. "Hold on a second." He tugged off one glove. Then he reached out and gently touched the side of my face. "You've got snowflakes in your eyelashes."

I felt the world go still. For the space of a heartbeat, we were frozen, his fingers against my cheek, our faces inches apart, everything waiting for the kiss that's just about to come, like the tableau at the end of an act, when the lights fade out.

276

And that was when a glossy black car glided past.

It slowed as it reached the corner just ahead. Then it sped up again, barely braking at the stop sign before streaking into the next street.

I went stiff. "Was that a BMW?"

Rob glanced around. "Where?"

"That car. The one that just turned right."

"I didn't notice." He turned back to me. "Are you a big fan of German engineering?"

"I think it was Pierce." I hated my voice for wobbling. "I think he's looking for me."

"Why would he be looking for you?"

"Because I didn't tell him . . ." *I didn't tell him that I was meeting you. That he wouldn't be driving me home. That I don't think I want to be with him.* I stared at the spot where the car had disappeared. "I'm pretty sure it was him."

Rob followed my eyes. "Well, if he circles the block, we'll know."

We held still for a minute, both of us staring up the street.

"He's going to be so angry," I whispered.

"Well . . . maybe we should just let him find us."

I stared at Rob.

"I'm not afraid of him." Rob looked back down at me. His eyes were steady. Almost amused. "Seriously. If he wants to come and confront us, let him."

We waited for another minute.

"I don't think it was him," said Rob at last.

"Maybe," I murmured. "Let's take another street. Just in case."

We turned at the next block. The ache in my head had come raging back. I pulled my fingers out of Rob's grip, rubbing my temples with both hands.

"Are you okay?" Rob asked.

Twilight seemed suddenly too bright. I let my eyes slide halfway shut. Between my eyelashes, just around the next corner, I caught the glint of a glossy black car.

"There!" I pointed. "He just turned!"

Rob frowned. "I didn't see him."

"Look! He's heading up the next street. He just sped up. He saw us." I whirled around, breaking into a jog. "He saw us."

Rob hurried after me. "Jaye—I don't think it was him."

"It was him. It was him. He'll be so— Oh my god, he'll tell my mom. She'll pull me out of the show."

"Jaye—"

I lunged off the curb, across the street. "We have to run."

Rob kept up with me, his voice calling over my shoulder, "Should you really be running right now?"

"It doesn't matter. It doesn't matter." I raced onto the next stretch of sidewalk. The drifts here were deeper. My lungs burned. My legs ached. "We can't let him catch us."

The sky was getting darker. Headlights swept through the gray-and-white streets, making my vision smear.

Behind me, I could hear a soft, almost inaudible growl. I glanced back.

The black car. Just a block away.

"He's right behind us!" I begged my legs to move faster. Faster.

"Jaye?" Rob's voice seemed to dwindle with each word, like he was on a raft that was quickly drifting away. "Jaye, hang on! There's . . ."

No matter how hard I tried, I couldn't outrun it. The black car crawled up beside me. From the corner of my eye, I could see its crushed black hood, its shattered windshield, flecked with blood.

No. NO. I squeezed my eyes shut.

Blindly, I pounded over an icy patch. My feet skidded beneath me. For a heartbeat, I was sure I was going to fall. I threw out my arms. My vision speckled with dirty black flecks, then narrowed to the beam of one shaky spotlight.

He'd warned me. He had warned me.

"Jaye, wait!" Even farther now. "Stop!"

I couldn't answer. The ache had sealed my mouth shut.

My lungs screamed as I broke back into a run. The black car surged to keep pace. *Don't look. Don't look.*

Someone was still calling my name.

I didn't turn.

The sky was deep purple now, and the snow caught in my eyes, and my vision was a blurry pinprick. It could have been anyone. It could have been anything.

When my foot hit another patch of ice, everything went still.

Very slowly, I floated backward, and the slushy pavement reached up to catch me.

The ache that couldn't swell any bigger cracked open like an egg on the rim of a bowl, and the darkness inside it broke free.

CHAPTER 21

I could smell the roses.

The syrupy scent slid down my throat and into my lungs. Even without looking, I could tell they were red.

Sometimes I got roses after a play. Mom brought them now and then. Dad had given me roses just once, after coming to see me in the chorus of *A Christmas Carol* at the Guthrie. "Here you go, Drama Queen," he'd said, handing them over. He obviously hadn't known what else to say. To him, it looked like I'd just stood around at the back of a patch of floor, wearing a poofy dress and oily makeup, pretending to be a guest at a party where only one person talked out loud at a time.

Roses.

Red roses.

So the show must be over. I had the right kind of empty feeling, that sort of silvery sadness that comes after the curtain call. What play had we done? I dug for memories. Romeo had been there. Several fairies. And Juliet's nurse. And Hamlet.

Wait.

Wait.

When I opened my eyes, there was only fog. Everything was white and edgeless. No stage. No actors. Just one gigantic blank page.

I blinked again. Dimensions started to form.

A narrow white bed. My feet, under a thin cotton sheet, poking up like two tiny mountains in the distance. Plastic railings on either side. To my right, a little table. A box of tissues. A plastic cup with a bendy straw. A vase of red roses.

Against the white room, they stood out like wounds.

Red petals.

Blood on the snow.

Red droplets on a black stage.

Red.

Red—

I sucked in a breath.

"Jaye?" said a voice.

Someone was sitting in the chair to my left.

I turned my head. The motion set off a grumble of pain that traveled down my neck, out through my arms, into my legs.

The person in the chair stood up.

Square chin. Hazel eyes. Wavy gold hair.

My body jerked back.

My right arm was trapped, taped to a cluster of tubes. My legs refused to move at all.

Pierce stepped closer. He lifted my left hand from its spot on the blankets.

It took every scrap of strength I had, but I yanked my arm back out of his grip.

"Jaye," he said again. His empty hand hovered in midair. "It's me. Pierce."

"No." The voice that came out of me was weird and raspy and about an octave too low. "Not you."

Pierce's hand fell. He blinked down at me, confused.

The air behind him rippled.

Someone stood beside him, an arm around Pierce's shoulders.

"Having now provided a gentleman of noble parentage," said Shakespeare, patting Pierce's arm, "youthful, and nobly trained; stuffed, as they say, with honorable parts—"

"I know what you're trying to do," I growled in my weird new voice. "You think you're being so clever, but I see it. But maybe I don't want that. Maybe I don't want the right thing."

"And how can we know what is right?" asked Ophelia, sitting beside me on the mattress. She touched my arm. Her hand was like a dead eel. "We try to obey them . . ." She trailed off, her eyes sliding away. "I hope all will be well. We must be patient. And yet I cannot choose but weep, to think they should lay him in the cold ground . . ."

I yanked my arm away. "Don't," I whispered. "Don't say that."

"Say what?" asked Pierce.

Puck clambered onto my bed. The fairy crouched above me, squatting on my chest like a nightmare. When I looked close, I could see that his eyes had no pupils, only thousands of tiny, spinning, flickering lights. "Here she lies, curst and sad," he chanted. "Cupid is a knavish lad, thus to make poor females mad."

"I'm not crazy," I breathed. "Just go away. All of you."

Pierce moved tentatively toward me again. "Jaye . . ."

They were closing in. Shakespeare. Juliet's nurse, who was fawning over Pierce again. The fairies, the witches, Hamlet with that goddamned broken skull.

"Get away from me!" I screamed the words now. My entire body recoiled, trying to climb out of bed, up the wall, anywhere. "Get away!"

The door clanged open. People in blue uniforms rushed inside, cutting through the crowd. They surrounded me, coming closer and closer, until even Puck and Ophelia began to dissolve.

Behind them, a few steps from the bed, I could see my mother. She was standing very still, as if she was afraid to come any closer. Her eyes were sad. Sad and horrified.

Pierce moved toward her, putting one arm around her shoulders.

The room became an unglued collage. My arms and legs shredded into four separate fragments. My hands, shoving other hands away, tore into two more. I could barely feel the cold, stinging point that slid into my arm somewhere very far away from the rest of me.

With my last speck of energy, I lashed out, my knuckles connecting with the vase of roses. The vase smashed against the wall. Droplets of water showered me, melting holes in the snowy white blanket. Petals tumbled down. The walls dribbled toward the floor, dissolving like soap suds rinsed from a window.

And then there was nothing left.

Nothing but the bed, with me in it.

Empty stage, I thought. *Empty stage. Empty stage . . .*

Until at last even the bed dissolved, and then my body, and finally, what was left of the light.

CHAPTER 22

The smell of coffee burned through the fog.

I opened my eyes. The light behind the plastic blinds was bright, and the white walls and bed and floor looked solid.

I rolled my head to the right, following the smell. The ache rolled with it.

Sadie sat in one of the vinyl chairs.

She was wearing a dark green sweater and a silvery scarf, and her red-gold hair was wadded up into a loose knot. She looked up from her AP History textbook. "You're awake?"

". . . I'm awake."

"How are you feeling?"

"Not . . . I don't know." I tried to lift my right hand to my head, but it was bound to the railing with a Velcro strap. IV tubes trailed from a flap inside my elbow. "Just . . . fuzzy."

"You know where you are?"

"Hospital." My voice was still rough and strange.

Sadie set her cardboard coffee cup on the bedside table,

next to two red roses in a plastic vase. "Do you remember what happened?"

I stared at the roses. ". . . Skiing accident."

"After that," she said briskly. "After you went back to school."

"Oh." I tried to touch my head again. The restraints jerked, and I lifted my left arm instead. The scar on my forehead was right where I'd left it. "I thought maybe the dream was . . . just . . ." I dropped the arm again. "How long have I been here?"

"Two days. This time."

"When do I get to leave?"

Sadie's mouth tightened. She let out an angry breath through her nose. "They're doing some more tests tomorrow. If those look okay, then I guess you get to come home. Again." She crossed her arms, looking like the lawyer I was sure she'd be in a few years. "Do you remember what happened that put you back here?"

"Is this a test?"

"I'm supposed to help keep you oriented." She leaned back in her chair. Her voice was clipped. Sharp. "Plus, I'd just really like to hear it from you. So?"

I swallowed. The hospital smell was starting to crawl out from under the scents of the coffee and the roses. "I was walking home . . ."

"You were *walking* home?" There was no question in Sadie's question. "Even though you were supposed to get a ride with Pierce. Even though you promised you wouldn't do anything stupid."

"I know. But I was . . ." I followed the fragments. *Midsummer* rehearsal. Rob, on the other side of a snowy street, turning toward me. Starting to smile. I felt myself start to smile back. "I was meeting somebody."

"Somebody?"

". . . Rob Mason."

"Rob Mason," Sadie repeated. "That guy you're not supposed to see? The one who got expelled after less than a week of school?"

"Suspended," I mumbled.

Sadie's mouth looked pinched. Her nose looked pinched. Her whole face looked pinched. "So you snuck out of rehearsal to meet him instead of riding with Pierce, like you *promised* Mom you would do."

I looked down at my hand resting on the blankets. An ID bracelet was taped crookedly around my wrist. "Where *is* Mom?"

"I made her go to her office. She's missed too much work already. You know what her boss is like." Sadie met my eyes. "And it's better for her not to be here every single minute." She folded her hands on top of the textbook. "Back to Monday afternoon. What happened while you were walking to meet this guy?"

"Pierce . . . He drove up behind us. So we ran. I ran."

"You ran." Sadie's voice got even sharper.

"I know. It was stupid. But he kept chasing us. It was like—he was trying to run us down."

"Jaye." Sadie gave a weird little laugh. "Pierce *saved* you."

"What?"

"Pierce is the one who found you lying there. He's the one who got you to the hospital."

"Sadie. No." Fog started to seep out of the walls again. "He was chasing us. What he did on the stage—to Rob— and his car—and I guess he beat up some guy at a swim meet—"

Sadie frowned. "What are you talking about?"

"Some guy from another school. I—I heard he had to get surgery or something . . ."

"Wow. 'Some guy.' It sounds like you've got all the facts perfectly straight."

"No, this—I was *there*, Sadie." The crushed black car. The icy road. "I was—"

"Pierce noticed that you'd left rehearsal early," Sadie interrupted, in a loud, carefully paced voice. "He went looking for you, and he found you lying on the sidewalk on Twenty-third Street. He called for help. He called Mom. Then he drove here behind the ambulance and made sure you were safe."

"But . . . what . . ." My thoughts were boiling. "That's not what . . . No. I don't remember—"

"I'm sure you don't. You were only half-conscious, I guess. He said you were saying some strange things."

"What about . . ." Steam. Fog. Snow. "What about Rob? Where did he go?"

Sadie shook her head. "You were alone when Pierce found you."

"What?" My skull was going to shatter. "No. *No.* He was there. He was with me."

"Then I don't know." She gave a small, bitter shrug. "I guess he took off."

He took off. He took off?

He took off.

Gone.

If he'd ever really been there.

I was suddenly hollow. All the organs and blood and warmth removed. Nothing left but the bones holding up my skin, and the ache. The ache. That was all.

The room was quiet for a minute. More fog crept in, softening the silence that pressed around us.

"You do this, you know," Sadie finally said. "You take a situation, and you twist it around and build it up in your head until it's this huge, awful, dramatic thing."

Indignation brushed a little of the fog away. "When have I done that?"

She widened her eyes at me. "*Always.* How unfair your teachers are. How mean people are to your friends. How directors always play favorites. How Pierce is some horrible monster. How Dad was so mean and biased and angry with you—"

"He *was* angry with me. *All the time.* Maybe you never saw it, because you were the perfect daughter." The words came faster, slurring a little. "Or maybe you're the one who doesn't remember right, because you don't *want* to."

"Jaye——"

"*Sadie.* It happened. It got worse and worse. There was something going on at the end. Something big."

Sadie's eyebrows tugged together. "What do you mean?"

"Don't you remember how all his stuff disappeared? How he wasn't home anymore, even on weekends? He completely stopped speaking to me. He didn't even come to my very last show before . . ." A lump was growing in my throat. "He just—wasn't there. I think Pierce was right. I think Dad had moved out."

"That's insane," said Sadie sharply. "You think Mom and Dad would have split up? Why? They were perfect together. They never even had a fight."

"They did. They just hid it." I forced the words out. "And I think—I *know* it was because of me."

"Jaye." Sadie's face was a mask. "Why are you doing this?"

"I don't know." I swallowed. The lump was still there, heavy and dangerous. "Sometimes I feel like . . . like maybe he's still trying to tell me what to do. To make the right choice. And I *still* keep failing. I know it's too late. It's way too late. But someone's still trying to tell me . . ." I shook my head. "I don't know. Maybe I'm imagining that too." I gave a little laugh, and the lump almost choked me. "Would that be worse? God. I can't even keep track of who's right beside me. In the real world."

I reached out into the space beside the bed.

Sadie took my hand and squeezed it.

"I'm horrible," I whispered.

"You are not."

"Yes, I am."

"You are *not horrible,* Jaye." Sadie squeezed my hand again. "You're just an oversensitive, irresponsible weirdo. But we still like you."

I couldn't answer. I just held her hand tighter.

"You know what?" said Sadie, after a second. "You should talk to Pierce. If you want to be nicer to the people who are actually beside you . . ." She swung my hand gently back and forth. "Want me to bring him in?"

My body jolted. "What?"

"He's here." She nodded toward the door. "He's been here ever since rehearsal got out."

"He's outside?"

"In the waiting room. With how you reacted when you saw him yesterday, he wasn't sure he should come in."

Ophelia. Puck. Pierce. Red petals. The smashed black car.

"I've never seen him so upset," Sadie was going on. "Seriously. Even with the Dad stuff. I guess last night he sat with Mom and cried."

Pierce Caplan crying. I couldn't even picture it. My

brain sent up an image of the tragedy mask with Pierce's wavy hair. ". . . Why?"

"Because. He blames himself. For making you mad at him with that fight, for not keeping you safe in the first place . . ." Sadie's tone softened. "It's kind of sweet, actually."

I looked at the vase with its two red roses.

Pierce Caplan had cried over me. Pierce Caplan was bringing me flowers.

I should have felt something. The thoughts just brushed across me, whipping away like snowflakes. The only thing I wanted to hold on to was that moment on the snowy street, when Rob lifted my hand to his lips.

But the memory was smeared and blurry now, like someone had reached out and run their fingers through it.

Fog. Headache. *He took off. Pierce saved you.*

You were wrong. Wrong. Wrong.

Another thought, one that had been waiting in the background, teetered forward. Two more days. More tests. More time.

"Sadie . . ." I began. "Do you know what's happening with the play?"

Sadie hesitated. Her eyes flicked away from me. "You should talk to Mom about that."

An icicle started to drip in my stomach. "Am I out?"

"*Jaye.*"

"Fine. Okay. I'll wait."

"Good." Sadie got to her feet. "Should I let Pierce in?"

"Oh." I tried to sit up straighter. "Yes. I guess."

"Wait." Sadie leaned forward and fluffed my hair with her fingers. "There. That's better."

From the doorway, she turned back to me. "Be nice to him when he comes in, or he might fall apart again."

"I will."

I pulled the sheet up over my wrinkled GUTHRIE THEATER T-shirt. Fluffed my hair again. The scar, the shaved spot. Still ugly. Still there.

The door inched open.

Pierce leaned inside like he wasn't sure what would be waiting for him. Our eyes met.

"Hi," he said.

"Hi."

He edged into the room, keeping his distance. "I'm glad you're awake."

Even from several feet away, I could feel him, his presence making the whole room shift. The air shuddered like a low-frequency sound wave. Or maybe I was the one shuddering.

Pierce saved *you.*

"You can come closer." I swallowed, pressing the tremor out of my voice. "I promise not to karate chop you."

He stepped forward. He looked fidgety, his hands moving from his sides to his pockets and back out again. His eyes slid past me to the tabletop.

He was nervous too, I realized. Pierce Caplan was nervous.

I'd never seen him like this.

I followed his eyes to the vase of roses. "You're the one who brought those, aren't you?"

Pierce shrugged. "I just—needed to do something."

"Sadie told me . . ." I swallowed again. The fragments swam and scrambled in my brain. Why was I still afraid of him? "She told me about everything else you did. Finding me. Getting me here."

Pierce didn't meet my eyes. "That was nothing. I shouldn't have let it happen in the first place."

"No. It wasn't your fault. I shouldn't have lied." His fist. The sword. The glossy black car creeping up behind us. *Pierce saved you. Stop shivering.* "I'm sorry." *You should be sorry. At least* pretend *to be sorry.* "I'm sorry for all of that. And for how I yelled at you the other day."

Pierce shrugged. "It's okay. I get it. You're not yourself right now."

An argument almost shot out of me. *You don't even know who I am.* Who was I, anyway? I was the girl who had made all the choices that brought her to that spot on the icy sidewalk, lying to her family, hurting everyone who tried to keep her safe. I was the girl who'd do it all over again.

Oh my god. What an idiot. Here was my chance—one more chance to choose the wiser thing.

I molded my lips into a small, hopeful smile. "Can you . . . I mean, do you want to stay for a little while?"

"Um. Okay. Sure." Pierce strode around the end of the

bed and sat down in one of the vinyl chairs. His movements were graceful as ever, but now there was something self-conscious about them, like when an actor is playing to an audience.

"Sadie said you came here after rehearsal."

"Yeah." Pierce didn't go on.

I had to force the next words out. "So . . . Michaela did my part?"

"She's already got most of the lines memorized." Pierce bent one leg, heel over knee, and leaned back in the chair. "It's different from having you there. But she knows what she's doing."

"Yeah." *The auditorium. The fresh paint smell. The colored lights splitting the shadows of the trees.* I bit the inside of my cheek. "Would you tell everybody I miss them? And tell Mr. Hall that I'm really, really sorry."

"You don't need to do that. Everybody understands." He gave a little shrug. "You've been acting weird because of your head, and—"

"No. I knew what I was doing." *Most of the time.* "I made everybody worry, and I did things that hurt the show, and that hurt all of you . . ."

"Stop. It's just as much my fault as yours. I'm supposed to be looking out for you, and instead . . ." He gestured at the white room. "*This.*"

"Pierce . . . you don't have to look out for me."

"Yes, I do." He finally looked straight at me. "I promised I would."

"Just because my mom asked——"

"No. Not that." Pierce's voice got lower. "Your dad asked me to."

I felt a coolness on my skin, like someone had thrown open a window. "He did?" I glanced across the room at the closed blinds. Shakespeare sat in his usual chair below the windows, watching me. Watching us. "When?"

"Not too long before it happened. When he was"—he paused, looking flustered—"at our house."

"He asked you to watch out for me?"

"He was worried about you. He said you were failing a bunch of classes, and getting in trouble at school, and some of your friends were using drugs and were really messed up . . ." Pierce ran his fingers through his glinting hair. "He wasn't around you very much anymore. And he said you didn't listen to him anyway. He knew I'd see you at school, so I'd know if you were getting into anything serious. And I should try to stop it."

The chill was making it hard to breathe. "So . . . is *that* why you actually did the show? Why you've been talking to me again? Because you were watching me for him?"

"No." Pierce looked genuinely surprised. "Jaye—I *like* you. I think I always did. I just wasn't paying attention."

"Oh." I looked down at my hands.

"I know I screwed up. I shouldn't have hit that kid. I shouldn't have let my anger take over. But I was just thinking about *him*, and you, and how I would feel if you got into some bad situation . . . And then I got you into a bad situation."

"No, you didn't," I said. "Pierce."

I put out one hand, palm up, like I'd done with Sadie. Now I had to fight to keep it from shaking.

Pierce looked at my hand for a second. Then he reached out and clasped it. His skin was dry and warm.

"Can I ask you one more thing?" I said. My voice came out just above a whisper. "You already know why I . . ." *Why I lied to you. No—let him think it was the injury. Maybe it* was *the injury.* "Sadie said, when you found me, I was by myself." I took a deep breath. "Is that right?"

"Yeah." Pierce nodded firmly. "You were lying there in the dark, in the snow. I don't know how long you'd already been there when I found you."

"So Rob wasn't—" It was out now. I had to know. "Rob Mason wasn't there?"

Pierce stared straight into my eyes. I almost flinched. "No," he said. "I didn't see him."

"Oh." *Don't cry. Oh my god, you moron, don't cry.* I lifted my chin. "Thank you. Thanks for actually being there."

We were quiet. Even Shakespeare kept perfectly still, his dark blue eyes fixed on us.

I was that hollow thing again. Empty. Cold from the

inside out. Even the warmth of Pierce's hand, wrapped tight around mine, couldn't warm me up.

Eventually, I saw Pierce's eyes flick to the clock. "Damn. It's already after seven. I was supposed to be home by now." He got up, dropping my hand. "I can come back tomorrow, though."

"Okay," I said. "Good. Tomorrow."

"Oh. Before I forget." He reached into his jeans pocket and pulled out a folded square of notebook paper. He put it in my palm.

"What is it?"

"Get-well notes Nikki and Tom wrote at rehearsal. They knew you wouldn't have your phone, so . . ."

"Oh." I set the note next to the vase of roses. I gave him another smile. "Thanks for passing notes for us."

"Thank *you* for making me feel like I'm in third grade again." Pierce started to smile back. It was like a crack opening in a perfectly painted wall. "It probably says, 'Do you like me? Circle YES or NO.'"

Now I felt myself smile for real. "Probably."

What had I thought was so frightening about him? What had I actually seen?

He was *here*, this gorgeous, golden boy, bringing me roses, trying to make my life better. Actually here.

Juliet's nurse appeared at the end of the bed. "He's a lovely gentleman." She patted Pierce's arm, beaming at me. "I think you are happy in this second match . . ."

Pierce took a first step toward the door. Then he stopped, whirling back toward me. "I'm just going to say this," he said, speaking fast. "I know you're probably going to need some time. And maybe I screwed up too much already. But when you feel like yourself again, I'll be here. Because I don't give up, and I don't lose. Not when I care about what I'm trying to win."

"Okay," I whispered at last, because it was literally the only thing I could think of to say.

He shot me that heart-tripping half smile.

The door clicked shut behind him.

My sister didn't come back right away. Maybe she and Pierce were talking; maybe she was checking in with Mom. Poor Sadie. Poor Mom. Stupid me.

I stared up at the ceiling.

Suddenly, I was exhausted.

Someone's hand lifted the sheet, smoothing it over me. I was sure I'd been asleep, and Mom or Sadie had come back. But when I lifted my eyelids partway, there was Shakespeare, gently tucking me in.

"Get some sleep," he murmured. "Sleep that knits up the raveled sleeve of care . . ."

My eyelids slid down again.

I thought I heard him say "Good night, Drama Queen," very quietly, before they sealed themselves shut.

CHAPTER 23

I woke up on a tray.

Or maybe I had already been awake.

Maybe I just opened my eyes on a tray, and realized where I was for the first time.

The rest of the room was bare. Panes of glass ran along one wall, revealing a bank of screens and keyboards. A youngish man with white clothes and spiky blond hair stood above me, blocking the fluorescent light. I glanced down at my own body. Blue cotton robe. Matching socks.

"You know the drill," the technician was saying. "Just keep as still as you can. Breathe normally. You won't feel anything. But just in case . . ." He put a squishy gray bulb in my right hand. "This is the panic button, remember? If you need to, you can squeeze it, and I'll have you out in three seconds. Got it?"

"Got it," I answered.

I stared at the ceiling beyond his head, its square beige tiles arranged in perfect rows. It felt good to focus on something real. Ceilings were real. Squares were real.

"Remember that the machine makes some loud noises," the technician went on. "You'll hear some thumping or knocking sounds. It's all perfectly normal."

"Thumping," my mouth repeated, for some reason. I held back a giggle.

Beneath me, the tray started to buzz. I slid backward into the machine like something on a checkout counter.

The beige room dwindled into a shrinking gap above my toes. I could see the technician standing there, watching me disappear into the machine. His hair had turned a paler shade of blond. His white clothes were black. Hamlet raised one hand in a jaunty little wave before we both slid out of each other's sight.

The inside of the machine was one curving, pearly wall, like the interior of a seashell. It came uncomfortably close to my face. I couldn't have sat up if I'd tried. I probably couldn't even have turned over. This thought made my chest tighten. Immediately, my neck began to itch.

Don't scratch it, I told my arm. But my arm was too heavy to move anyway. Everything was too heavy. My fingers. My thighs. Even my hair. I could feel my spine sinking, as if the tray was made of snow.

I drifted downward, away from the sunlight or spotlight or whatever light it was that kept trying to peel back my eyelids. I sank through velvet curtains, through black-painted floorboards, down to someplace cool and dim.

There everything stopped.

The bed went still.

I took a slow, chilly breath.

There was something strange in the air. Something rotten.

I opened my eyes. Only more darkness.

Where had I been a minute ago? That smell made me sure that I'd been somewhere else. I couldn't have ignored that smell. I couldn't have forgotten it.

Very carefully, I sat up.

The darkness began to thin. In the distance, I could see a steady yellow light. It glimmered on the surfaces around me. Mossy stone floor. Stone walls. A low, curving ceiling. Pillars jutted up here and there, like a few teeth inside a sealed stone mouth.

The platform beneath me was made of stone too. I scooted to its edge and dropped down to the floor. My clothes had changed again. Now I was wearing a long, dark dress, one I thought I'd thrown away two years ago.

The air was damp and cool. Subterranean. Stone platforms, stone floor, little nooks and shelves carved into the walls.

Of course, I realized. This was the Capulet vault. The end of *Romeo and Juliet.*

It all made sense somehow. Sort of. At least that's what I told myself.

I headed toward the light. The smell grew stronger. Rancid sweetness filled my throat, my nose, my mouth, until finally I had to cup a hand over my face to keep from gagging.

Vinegar. Rot. Burned coffee. And something else. A thick, perfumey scent, like too many different flowers crammed into too small a space.

I knew that smell.

The voices dribbled around me, murmuring. Whispering. The air was getting thicker. I stepped into the pool of lamplight, and there it was.

It was positioned neatly between the silk-shaded lights. Two little tables with framed photos and bouquets of fresh flowers and big bowls of sickly-sweet potpourri stood at either end.

A coffin.

A gleaming, red-brown, satin-lined coffin.

Its lid was open. Even though I wasn't near enough to see over the edge, I knew what was inside.

I glanced around.

The room was crowded. Friends from marathons and camping trips, employees, all the runners he'd coached over the past ten years, kids from my school with their parents, hundreds of people I'd never even met. I saw the cousins and Uncle Paul in one corner, gathered around Sadie, whose fists were full of soggy tissues.

The Caplans were there too, of course. The three of them were dressed in tailored black suits, looking grieved and beautiful. Patrick's face still wore a few bandages over the deepest cuts. So many employees and friends and high-schoolers were gathered around them, you'd have thought *they* were the family. After kissing Mom and paying their respects, they'd kept their distance from her for the rest of the night.

Most people had.

I found her just where I knew she'd be, in her seat on that stiff floral couch.

I hadn't misremembered it: She looked like someone staring into another world. Her face was bloodless. Her hands were turned up, open, in her lap, like she was pleading for something. When people spoke to her, she stared straight through them. She usually didn't answer.

I turned my back.

The photos on the end tables glinted with gentle electric light. There was the shot of Dad on the finish line of the New York Marathon, the same one that hung on our hallway wall. There was a picture of the whole family when Sadie and I were small, me in a baby carrier on Mom's chest, Sadie a toddler in Dad's backpack, everyone but me beaming, the edge of a bluff revealing soft green hills, row after row, behind us. And there was the most recent picture of Dad, taken on their fall camping trip, when they'd left me at home: Dad and Sadie and Mom, their heads close together, smiling into the camera.

I'd been in my first professional play that fall—or at least, the first where I'd had a non-chorus role. I had two actual lines and a hundred-dollar stipend. I felt rich and very adult.

The play was *Peter Pan,* at the Blue Moon Theater. I was one of the Lost Boys.

Dad hadn't come to the show. He hadn't seen my very last performance.

I'd cried when the police brought the news to the house, but I didn't cry at the funeral home. I felt like I'd been sealed in plaster; like my entire body had been coated in something hard and cold that kept everything inside. I didn't have to think about my face, my expression, whether it was right or wrong or real enough.

I remembered that gleaming brown coffin perfectly. But I hadn't ever looked at what was inside it. It would have been wrong to see him lying so still.

This was my chance. I could take just one step closer, look inside, see that all of this was real.

But I turned away again instead.

I wound through the crowd of people, around a corner, to a small purple sofa. I sat down and put my face in my hands. My head was pounding almost hard enough to crack the plaster. I wished I were somewhere else. I thought of the lights at the Blue Moon Theater, the twinkling lights behind the blue scrim that made a magical nighttime sky, the way the lights shifted and grew warmer and brighter as the set changed from London to Neverland. I wanted to be there.

Someone sat down on the sofa beside me.

I felt an unfriendly flash. Why couldn't they sit somewhere else? I didn't want to talk to anyone. I didn't want anybody's sympathy. I kept my face down, my hands hiding my eyes.

The cushions shifted again.

A voice said, "Hey, Drama Queen."

My head whipped up.

Shakespeare sat beside me.

"Don't call me that," I said through my teeth.

"All right. How about *Juliet* instead?"

"My name's Jaye."

"I know your name." He tipped his head to one side, smiling slightly. "I'm just having fun with you."

"I'm not having fun."

"I know," he said, more softly. "I know."

Ahead of us, I could see the gate that led up to the crypt stairs. Moonlight coated the stone steps. From above, just loud enough to cut through the murmur, there was the clash of metal.

"What's going on up there?" I asked him.

Shakespeare looked surprised. "You know how the play ends," he said. "Romeo and Paris fight. Paris falls."

"And then Romeo comes down here and thinks Juliet's really dead, so he kills himself, and then she wakes up and sees that he's dead, so she kills herself too. Everybody's dead. The end."

"Right."

"Right." I snorted. "*Why?* Because somebody's just a few minutes too early, or too late, or because somebody missed a message by leaving at exactly the wrong time?"

"Because they all make choices. They act the way they have to act."

"But you could have *changed* it." I turned toward him. His blue eyes were steady. I could almost see myself reflected in them. "It didn't have to turn out that way. You could have written a different ending. Let them make the right choices for once."

"But that wouldn't be the truth." Shakespeare's voice sounded different than usual. Lower. A little softer. A little rougher. "Do you know how hard it is to just sit back and watch, when you already know what's coming? You created them. You care about them. You know they'll make mistakes. You know that they'll get hurt. The world will hurt them, they'll hurt themselves. There's nothing you can do. That's just the way the story goes."

"I'm going to change it."

I stood up and strode across the stone floor to the gate. It was locked, its heavy bars bolted in place.

"Romeo!" I called up the steps. "Paris! Stop fighting! She's not actually dead!"

Shakespeare hadn't moved. He watched me from the purple couch, his face calm. "They can't hear you."

I ignored him. "Hey!" I yelled. "Anybody! I'm down here!"

My voice rang up the staircase. The clanking from above got louder. Now there was another sound beneath it—a deep rumbling, like something huge and heavy beginning to collapse.

"Juliet . . ." Shakespeare said softly. "This is just how the story goes."

"Stop!" I was screaming now. "Stop! I'm awake!" I wrenched at the bars. "*I'm awake!*"

Behind me, a massive stone slipped from the ceiling and smashed against the floor. Two more stones fell against one of the pillars, which cracked, tumbling to the floor in an explosion of shards. The ceiling sagged inward. I pressed myself against the gate, shielding my face with both arms. Mortar and black dirt rained down. More stones fell, their crashes echoing. The light flickered out.

And then there was a new light.

Brighter. Paler. Everywhere at once.

A silhouette flickered over me. Behind its spiky head, I could see tubes of white light against a beige ceiling. Rows and rows of perfect square tiles.

I sucked in a breath. My heart still pounded like it had nearly been crushed. My head throbbed.

"All finished," said the technician. "Are you doing all right?"

I smoothed my face. Vivien Leigh in *A Streetcar Named Desire*. Katharine Hepburn stepping onto the set at the end of *Stage Door*. "Yeah," I said. *Don't let them know what you see.* "I'm fine."

CHAPTER 24

Yellow flowers were in bloom on the riverbank. They opened around me while I slept, and the fairies sang their lullaby in my dreams until all of their voices became just one voice, and I opened my eyes. Mom was sitting beside me.

"Are you warm enough?" she asked, rearranging the old yellow afghan around me.

"Yes. Thanks."

I blinked at my feet, stretched out to the other end of the living room couch. The air was misty. It was daylight, but Mom was dressed in yoga pants and a zippered sweatshirt, not in her work clothes.

"You don't need to stay home with me," I told her. "I'll be fine."

"I'm going to do half days for the rest of the week." Mom looked at me anxiously. "Maybe we should get somebody to come and stay with you."

"Mom, really." Two yellow flowers sprouted up from

the blanket between my fingers. I blinked and they vanished again. "I'm fine."

Mom rose to her feet. "Would you like some sparkling water? I was going to get some."

The rest of the week. More days—how many? Three? Four?—on top of the days I had already missed.

"Mom?" I tried to sound cool, accepting, in case I'd asked this before. "I'm out of the play. Aren't I?"

Mom stopped, halfway out of the room. "Once you've recovered and you're feeling back to normal, Mr. Hall says there's no reason you shouldn't be able to do the next show."

Don't crack now. "The *next* show? In fall?"

"I know it sounds like a long way off. But you'll be . . ." Mom stopped again. She looked at me for a long moment. "I'm sorry."

"No." I swallowed. A screw twisted behind my right eye. "Mom—*I'm* sorry."

Mom nodded. "I know you are." Her voice was papery.

"Not just for this. For everything." I was at the crest of the hill. Time to plunge down. Fly. Fall. "For being stupid. Not listening. For being bad at skiing. For making you go through this all over again . . . the hospital and the doctors and the tests . . ." Deep breath. "For everything with Dad. How I was. At the end." I stared at a knot in the blanket. "I know he left us."

There was a short, awful silence. Mom's legs moved

into my field of vision. She stood beside the couch, looking down at me. "What are you talking about? You think he left?"

"Pierce told me. He said Dad stayed with them for months. Like . . . he'd moved out." I wormed three fingers through the holes of the afghan. "I remember you two fighting. All the time. Usually after I did something. I'd hear you in your room, with the door shut, trying not to let us notice."

"Jaye. All couples argue sometimes."

"I know. I *know* that. But then he -sort of faded away. He was never home. He stopped speaking to me. He didn't come to my very last play before—"

"*Peter Pan?*" Mom interrupted. "The show you auditioned for without even asking permission?"

I groped backward. "I—"

"You knew we'd say no, because it was during the school year, and you'd have to get downtown for rehearsals, and we already had that trip to Colorado planned, remember? And you snuck out and did it anyway."

"But . . ." My thoughts bumped off of their path. "I guess I didn't think it would be a big deal."

"Your dad wanted to make you quit that show. You got so upset when he threatened to call the director and tell him you were out that you started hyperventilating. So I said we should let you choose. Remember? I really thought you'd do the right thing, go to Colorado with your family, make up for lying to us. But you picked the play." Mom's voice was gentle. Cool. "*That's* why he didn't come to the show."

"But . . . No. That wasn't all." I looked up into her face now. Her lake-water eyes. "He was gone. He *left*. I hadn't even seen him for weeks when . . . when everything happened."

Now Mom's tone had a hint of exasperation in it. "Like I told you, he was traveling for work a lot that winter." She shook her head. "Jaye . . . I know things have been confusing for you lately. I'm not sure what your brain is—"

"No. Please." I almost put my hands over my ears. "Please don't tell me I don't remember."

Mom let out a long breath. "Okay," she murmured. "Fine. Think what you want."

She turned and walked slowly away, into the kitchen.

I slumped back on the couch. My head was pounding. My stomach felt like a wrung towel. I could hear Mom in the kitchen, cabinets opening, cups clinking. After a minute, I swung my legs over the side of the couch and shuffled toward the stairs.

As I climbed, another memory floated to the surface. That winter, two years ago, lying in bed each night with my door open. Listening for the sound of Dad's car in the driveway, his feet creaking up the staircase. Falling asleep before the sounds came. Every morning, before heading into the bathroom, I'd peek through Mom and Dad's bedroom door. The bed was always empty by then, the blankets smoothed and pillows rearranged, so it was impossible to tell if only one side had been used. But I always looked anyway.

I knelt down beside my own bed. At first, when I reached underneath, my fingers found only empty space. My stomach twisted harder. Then I remembered that I'd moved the bundle closer to the side. And there it was: the soft, dusty cotton of Dad's old T-shirt.

I pulled the bundle out into the daylight.

I unfolded the T-shirt. Dad's running shoes were still tied with loose bows. I wondered if he had tied them, or if Michelle Caplan had done it, or if it had been Pierce himself, neatening them up before putting them away. Saving them for me. There were little scuffs on the toe of each shoe.

"It wasn't because of you."

I turned around.

Mom stood in the doorway. Her eyes moved over Dad's shirt, the worn running shoes in my lap, almost like she'd expected to see them there. "I need you to know that."

I held on to one shoe, afraid to move. "It wasn't?"

Mom leaned lightly against the doorframe. Her eyes lingered on the print on the T-shirt. COACH. "Things had been getting rough for a while. Your dad was on edge all the time. Work problems, the track team's performance, family stuff . . . He'd blow up about every little thing."

Mom chafed her hands together. "But the big issue was the business expansion. Such a huge investment, all at once . . . I didn't think we should take the risk. He thought we should. For once, I put my foot down." She gave a little shrug. A tiny smile. "And it turned out that I was wrong. The new locations were a huge success, and it paid off for the Caplans in a way that it didn't for us, which made your dad crazy. And then I found out that he'd actually invested more than we'd agreed to, just not as much as he originally wanted, which he saw as a compromise, and I saw as a lie." She rubbed her hands again. Chapped knuckles. Ragged fingernails. "We just needed a little time apart. But he didn't *leave* us. That's not what it was."

"Were you going to . . ."

"It was temporary," Mom said, when I couldn't finish. "It was supposed to be temporary."

I ran my fingers over the shoelaces. "Why didn't you tell us?"

"We promised each other that we'd protect you and Sadie from all of it. We didn't want you worrying about something that was really between the two of us. Something that we thought would pass." She paused. "It feels kind of like I'm breaking that promise to tell you even now. But I suppose that's better than letting you think it was because of you."

I twisted the shoelace around my finger. Tight. Tighter.

Dad's angry voice on the other side of the closed door.

Dad driving me home from another meeting with the counselor, his hands rigid on the wheel. Dad racing away up our dark street, disappearing through the circles of lamplight.

"I know it was partly me," I said. The ache in my head was a constant, screaming pitch. "I know I made things worse."

"Jaye . . ."

"You even said 'family stuff.' I know that's code for *me*."

Mom stepped into the room. She sat down on the edge of my bed, facing me, so that my eyes were on a level with her knees. The chapped hands folded in her lap.

"He was worried about you," she said. "That's all. You know how many times we got called by your school office during that last year?" She reached out and swept a strand of hair out of my eyes. "He just wanted you to do better."

There was too much inside of me. The swollen ache in my head, the lump in my throat. It forced the tears out of my eyes. I looked down, tilting my face so Mom couldn't see.

"I wish . . ." I began. "God. I don't know. I wish I had made him proud."

I heard Mom take a yoga breath. In and out, very slow. "You still can."

We sat together for a while. Cold wind blew outside the house. Mom tucked the afghan tighter around me.

The yellow flowers bobbed and nodded.

I blinked. I was back on the living room couch, with Mom sitting beside me, rubbing my feet through the blankets.

I glanced toward the stairs. Were Dad's running shoes and worn T-shirt still lying on the floor beside my bed? Had one of us—or both of us—gently rewrapped them and tucked them away again?

Had I pulled them out at all?

I looked back at Mom. A few strands of soft brown hair were slipping out of her ponytail. A cup of tea steamed on the table behind her. She caught me watching her and gave me a little smile, her hands still rubbing, the look in her eyes soft and fragile, like something that's just started to thaw.

I wasn't going to ask.

The memory was good enough.

I woke up shivering.

The air was gray. Crushed red roses stuck to my skin. When I moved, I felt snow crumble around me.

I looked around. I was still on the living room couch. There were my own black drawstring pants, stretching away into the distance; my *Arsenic and Old Lace* T-shirt. The blanket was gone. The yellow flowers. Was that why I was so cold?

I rolled onto my side. A vase of red roses stood on the

coffee table. My phone sat beside it, within easy reach. Under the phone was a note from Mom.

Call if you need ANYTHING. Then her work number, even though she knew I already had it, and the number of the nurses' station at the hospital. *Remember, the phone is for emergencies only. Get some rest. Take care of yourself. XOXO.*

I picked up the phone and flicked it on.

A text from Pierce was waiting.

Thinking about you, it said. *See you soon.*

Another shiver raced over my skin.

Pierce saved you, I reminded myself.

Rob wasn't even there.

He wasn't there.

I stared straight at the phone for a while, like that could make another message appear.

Maybe I should send one instead.

Tom, could you find out . . . Find out what? How?

Nikki, would you ask Rob to . . .

No. No, you idiot. You're going to choose right for once.

Thinking about you.

What should I write back?

Hamlet sat on the corner of the coffee table, leaning his head on one hand, watching me. He sighed. "Words, words, words . . ."

I typed *Thinking about you too.* Then I turned the phone off.

The couch creaked as I rocked to my feet. The room was empty. Hamlet had vanished again. The sounds of the furnace and the refrigerator rumbled in the background. I was alone.

I started up the staircase.

"My Oberon! What visions have I seen!" My voice rang through the empty house. No one there to hear me playing Titania. No one would ever hear me. "Methought I was enamored of an ass. How came these things to pass?"

I sounded strong. Clear. Queenly. Not crazy.

"Silence awhile," murmured Oberon's voice beside me. He stood halfway up the steps, fireflies dancing around his long, pale face. "Titania, music call, and strike more dead than common sleep of all these five the sense."

I climbed past him. "Music! Music such as charmeth sleep!"

Below me, fairies twirled through the living room, singing their lullaby.

I threw myself down on my bed. I felt freezing and feverish at the same time. Heat swelled inside my skull and cold climbed up from my fingers and toes, the two fronts clashing until my whole body shook.

I wrapped myself in the rumpled purple quilt. Something crinkled under my head, and I reached up, fumbling for it.

It was a folded square of notebook paper. That's right—

the notes from Nikki and Tom that Pierce had brought to the hospital. I'd forgotten all about them. Mom or Sadie must have put them on my pillow.

The notebook paper had been tucked into a tight little packet. As I unfolded the flaps, a second, smaller square tumbled out. I looked at the outer page first.

At the top, in Nikki's blocky handwriting, it read THE STATE OF THINGS IN THE FAIRY COURT. Below that was a mean but pretty accurate caricature of Michaela Dorfmann, complete with snooty nose and heavy makeup, being stabbed by a swarm of fairies with pitchforks. Under the drawing were the words: *When you get better, I'll kill you.*

I smiled.

I picked up the note from Tom.

Instead, what I unfolded was a letter. A long letter. In handwriting I didn't recognize.

> *Jaye—*
>
> *The EMTs wouldn't let me ride with you to the hospital. At least they told me which one they were taking you to. I ran home for my car and drove there, but the staff told me I couldn't see you because I wasn't family. And they wouldn't tell me how you were, or if you were going to be okay, and that's been making me crazy ever since.*

I called your house over and over, and I left a lot of idiotic messages on the machine, and finally your sister picked up and told me never to call again.

So now I'm writing you a note. Nikki agreed to help me get it to you, and if you're reading this right now, then she figured out a way to do it. I hope you are.

This isn't just an apology, although I need you to know how sorry I am. I'm sorry that you were hurt, and I'm sorry that I was part of it, and I'm sorry if I've made things worse for you in any way, and I'm sorry that I can't tell you all of this in person. Although maybe you want to never see me again. I would understand. Even though I'd be sorry about that too.

I've been losing my mind since Monday afternoon. Not knowing if you're all right. Thinking about how you looked, lying there on the sidewalk, because I was too late to catch you. Putting this on paper helps a little bit. But it's not the same as getting to talk to you. Getting to sit across a coffee shop table from you. Getting to walk down the street beside you.

Last week, I didn't even know you. Now

not knowing you or seeing you or thinking about you feels totally impossible. Sorry if that's weird.

There. That's my last apology.

If you don't want to answer, that's all right.

I get it. I'll stay out of your way.

But if you do, I'll be here.

R.M.

His phone number was written at the very bottom.

I read the note again. Then I read it one more time.

My teeth were chattering. The ache pounded with each pulse of my heart.

You're awake. I dug my fingernails into the palm of my free hand as hard as I could. *You're awake.*

Everything they'd told me. Everything Pierce said. Everything Sadie said.

It was all wrong.

Or *this* was.

My nails left pink splotches on my skin. I shivered harder. I pulled the quilt tight around me.

When had Pierce brought me the note? How many days had already gone by?

Rob had been waiting for an answer all that time. I hadn't given one.

And that was good. That was *good*. Because I would have had to make the choice anyway.

The right choice.

Keep Rob safe. Keep yourself safe. Keep your promises. Make your family ... make them all proud.

Try.

"You must be cruel only to be kind," said Hamlet, lounging at the bottom of my bed.

I looked away.

Deep breath. Empty stage.

I ripped the letter into pieces. I tore up his phone number. I tore up my name. I read the words as they fractured—*hospital*—*crazy*—*sorry*—*beside you*—thinking about him thinking them, writing them down. Then I tore them into smaller and smaller bits, until they were as fine as a handful of snow, and my chest was full of lead.

It took three tries to rock myself out of bed. My body was too heavy, and my head was like a broken compass, the needle waggling everywhere. Finally, dizzily, I slid off the mattress and onto my feet. I shuffled across the room with the quilt wrapped around me.

The sky was a thick, sunless gray. Afternoon. Maybe already evening. The window frame was chilly, partly frozen in place. With one shoulder, I started to heave it open, getting ready to scatter the paper bits into the wind. I hadn't moved it an inch when there was a soft *thud* right beside me.

A snowball had hit the edge of the window. A clot of snow still clung to the sill.

I looked down into our snowy backyard.

Standing there, his long black coat fluttering against the whiteness, packing another snowball, was Romeo.

CHAPTER 25

I laughed out loud.

I unlatched the storm window and shoved my pounding head out into the cold.

Romeo did a quick double take. The snowball dropped from his hand, leaving a fresh divot in the snow. "Hey," he said.

I leaned my elbows on the sill. "Aren't you supposed to say 'What light through yonder window breaks?'"

"Sorry." His smile widened. "I haven't really learned my lines."

"Then you'll have to improvise."

"All right. Um . . ." He ran his fingers through his wind-tangled hair. "He says something like, 'It is the east, and Juliet is the sun,' right?"

"Exactly."

He raised his voice. "It is the east, and—" He stopped, pointing in my direction. "*Is* that the east?"

"I think so. Kind of."

"Okay. This might be the east, and Jaye is . . ." He stopped again. "You're not like the sun."

"I'm not?"

"Like a giant yellow ball of burning gas? Not really. You're more like a constellation."

"Just so you know, we're *way* off the script here," I told him. "And 'a constellation'? Which one? The scales? That mer-goat thing?"

He gazed up at me for a second, considering. "I'm not sure. I see something new in it every time I look."

That made me shut up for a minute. I just beamed down at him, and he smiled up at me, and I thought how nice it was that my imagination had decided to adapt the scene this way. Then a fresh blast of wind made me pull back, shivering. The ache swirled.

"I'm freezing," I called down to him. "Aren't you freezing?"

"Kind of."

"Come to the back door."

"Are you sure you don't want me to climb up to your window? I think that's what's in the script."

I waved a hand. "We're changing the blocking. Back door."

I slammed the storm window and yanked the inner frame down.

The bedroom swam around me as I rushed toward the

hall. I nearly fell twice on the staircase. The pain had built a wall between my thoughts and my feelings, and nothing could get through to make me worry anymore. It didn't matter if I fell. None of this was real anyway. This was just a dream. Just a much better dream.

I skidded across the dining room, through the French doors, and pulled open the sticky sunroom door.

Romeo stepped inside.

Snowflakes clung to his hair and shoulders. Between the lapels of his coat, I could see a sliver of black cotton T-shirt. Cold radiated off of his body. Snow from his boots crumbled onto the carpet. When I stepped closer, I could feel it seeping between my bare toes.

Too cold. Too real.

"Wait a second," I heard myself say. "You're—you're actually here."

"I'll leave if you want me to." He took a rapid step backward. "I just needed to know you were all right. I'll go."

"No." I lunged past him, slamming the door shut. "I don't want you to leave. I just . . ."

I placed my palms on his chest. His wool coat was scratchy and damp with melting snow. Beneath it, his body was solid. Alive. I didn't even care that I was wearing drawstring sweatpants and a faded T-shirt. I could feel his breath against my face as I rose up onto my toes.

I kissed him.

The lips parting mine were warm, waiting. I breathed

in soap and cloves and winter. His hands pulled me closer, and something began to glimmer through the ache. Sparks. Stage lights. Snowflakes. The shimmer filled my rib cage, my body, my head—

Swaying slightly, I pulled away.

Rob blinked down at me. "I'm sorry."

"Why are you sorry?"

He started to smile. "I don't know."

"I'm the one who kissed *you*. If there's anyone who should be sorry, it's me."

"*If* there's anyone who should be sorry."

He moved toward me again, and I moved toward him at the same second. His hands cupped my face. My fingers laced through his hair. We kissed until I could feel my heartbeat in my earlobes. He smelled like snow.

"I just found your note this afternoon," I finally whispered into the crook of his neck.

Rob's whole body relaxed against me. "Oh," he said with a giant sigh. "God. Good. When I didn't hear from you, I thought maybe the injury was really serious. Or maybe Pierce had—I don't know—maybe he'd told you something—"

"He said you'd left. That he found me just lying on the sidewalk. Alone."

Rob's body tensed again. "I'd already called 911 when Pierce drove up." His lips were tight. "I'm not sure how long it had been. You'd blacked out. I couldn't wake you, and I didn't want to move you, so I just—I just sat there. Holding your hand."

I slid my fingers into his. "I'm all right," I whispered. "I'm fine."

Rob squeezed my hand back.

"Then—why did you leave?" I pulled back so I could look up into his face. "Did he—like—threaten you or something?"

"He was pretty upset," he said dryly. "He said you'd gotten hurt again because of me. And he wasn't wrong. He said if your family found out about you sneaking out to meet me, things would be a lot worse for you. I'm sure he wasn't wrong about that either." Rob shook his head, aggravated. "But I couldn't just leave. I had to know you were okay. I've been waiting, and wondering . . ."

"And I'm *fine*." I smiled up at him. "I'm better than fine."

Rob glanced around. "Wait. Am I going to get you in more trouble by being here?"

"I don't care." I grabbed his arms before he could back away. "Besides, no one's here."

"How long do we have?"

I shook my head. "It doesn't matter. I've changed my mind. I'm not—I can't be something just because—"

His lips were distracting. I leaned toward him again.

His mouth found mine. The soft rasp of his skin against my cheek, his breath, the velvet of his lower lip . . .

I broke away again, dizzy.

"Stop looking worried." I wove my fingers more tightly through his. *I am going to hold on to this, no matter what tries to pull it away. I'm going to hold on even if it breaks my fingers.*

The dining room clock chimed the quarter hour. Rob's eyes flicked to the wall behind me. "Does your sister come straight home after school?"

"Usually. Why? Is it that late already?"

"Close. We've got five minutes. Maybe ten."

"That's not enough."

"I know." He let out a breath. "Maybe you can call me tomorrow. Or text me, at least."

"I don't want to text you. Or call you. I don't want to sneak around, stealing tiny little bits of time." I dropped his hand. "So. Let's go."

"Go?" Rob's eyebrows went up. "Go where?"

"You've got your car, right? Let's go somewhere. Anywhere that isn't here."

He started to grin again. "Are you sure?"

"Positive. I'll leave a note. Just let me grab my jacket."

When I turned away, I realized how strong the ache had grown. I just made it out of the room without stumbling. Once I was sure I was out of his sight, I sagged against the wall, fumbling over the end tables for a pen and paper.

With Rob, I scribbled, in handwriting that didn't look like mine. *I'll be home soon. Don't worry.*

As I headed toward the coat closet, I caught sight of my phone, lying where I'd left it in the clutter of the coffee table. If I brought it along, I'd just be confronted by its constant buzzing, Mom's number glowing on the screen. Even its weight in my pocket would be a reminder.

I set the phone beside my handwritten note. At least Mom would know not to bother calling.

"I'm parked on the corner," said Rob as we slipped out the back door and crossed the snow-deep yard. "I thought I shouldn't park right in front of your house, just in case."

"Good thinking."

The rusty blue car still held a hint of warmth. When Rob started the engine, a breath of hot air whooshed out around my ankles.

"Thanks, Merle." I patted the dashboard.

Rob smiled.

I glanced over my shoulder. The backseat was wonderfully Shakespeare-free. Just a few empty paper coffee cups, a sliding stack of notebooks, a hooded sweatshirt with WASHINGTON printed on its chest. Relief blew over me like the warm air.

But as I started to turn back around, I spotted it. The glossy black car gliding up the street.

"Oh my god," I whispered. "It's him."

Rob looked back, frowning. "Who? Pierce?"

The car was distant enough that I couldn't get a glimpse

of the driver, but I didn't need one to feel sure. "Yes." The ache swelled. "You see him this time, right?"

"He should be at rehearsal right now."

Midway down the block, a turn signal flicked on. The black car coasted toward the end of our driveway.

"It's him," I said again. "Right there. The black car. You see it too, right?"

Rob squinted through the back window. "Yeah," he said slowly. "I see it."

My heart hammered against my ribs. "Just drive, please. Go."

"All right." Rob swung the wheel sharply to the left. The engine roared. We shot out into the snowy street.

"He's going to my house." I sank down into the seat, trying to compress myself below the window line. "Do you think he saw us?"

"I don't know." Rob kept his eyes on the road. I could hear the hint of doubt in his voice. "I didn't see his face."

I inched up just enough to check the side mirror. A red minivan had pulled into the street behind us. If the BMW had veered back into the road, I couldn't tell.

"Which way?" Rob asked when we reached the next corner.

"Left, I guess. Let's just . . . let's just drive around for a while." The ache was swelling again. It seemed even larger and sharper-edged than before. "Just in case."

Rob glanced over, his eyes worried. "Are you okay?"

"Yes," I managed. "Just a little carsick."

"Tell me if you want me to pull over. Or if you need to turn around."

"No." My eyelids sagged. "Don't stop."

Gently, Rob angled the car to the left, and then left again, steering us toward the highway. When I took another glance into the mirror, the red minivan was gone. A white truck had taken its place. I could see it looming impatiently over our back bumper, even though the mirror—or my eyes—made it bleary.

"Keep going," I mumbled into my coat collar. "I want to make sure . . . that we lost him."

I heard the click of the turn signal. A moment later, we accelerated down an on-ramp into the stream of highway traffic.

Snow had begun to fall again. Tiny crystals skidded across the windshield, tumbling away into the dimming air. Twilight was coming fast.

"Would you—talk to me?" I asked. Both my thoughts and my voice were choppy. "I don't want to think about—any of this anymore. I want to think about something new."

"What do you want me to talk about?"

"Talk about your past. I want to know all the important stuff about you."

Rob touched the brake as a car in front of us skidded

slightly, its taillights casting bloody streaks over the road. "Important stuff? Like my medical history? My financial situation?"

"I know. Tell me about your very first kiss."

Rob laughed. "My first kiss. Let me think." One eyebrow went up. "Oh—I remember. Cal Pearson. I was seven."

"Was Cal Pearson a boy or a girl?"

"A girl. But it *was* during a wrestling match."

"Really?"

"Cal and her brothers were really into professional wrestling. They lived next door to us, and when we'd play together, no matter what we started out with—LEGOs, PlayStation, Chutes and Ladders, whatever—it eventually morphed into a wrestling match. They all had personas with pro wrestling names, so I had to have one too—"

"What was it?" I interrupted.

"I was the Grave Robber."

"Grave Robber," I echoed, my head rolling against the seat. "Rob, Robber. I get it."

"Nick was the Billion Dollar Man. He wasn't very inventive. I can't remember what Ethan's name was. And Cal was the Warrior Mermaid."

"You'd think that tail situation would make wrestling difficult."

"Well, her tail turned into legs whenever she was on land. She'd be pulled into the ring in her aquarium, which was actually an old humidifier box covered in blue marker, and then she'd flop out and wait for her tail to transform, and then she'd headlock somebody."

"What a showman," I said. "Or showgirl, I guess. But not the Vegas type."

"And she was good. For a second grader, anyway. I mean, I wasn't much competition; I was so scrawny and awkward and afraid to touch her anywhere but the shoulders. But one day she threw me down flat on my back—the floor was carpeted, but I still landed so hard it knocked the air out of me—and I literally saw stars. Exploding stars. Supernovas. And then she knelt on top of me, pinned my arms to the floor, and kissed me."

"Wow. Body slams and supernovas? Every subsequent kiss must have seemed pretty tame by comparison."

"For a while." He smiled at me. "What about you? Was it Pierce?"

A sliver of cold wormed through my warm dizziness. "No. My very first was a boy named Cy. It was kindergarten gym class. We were doing this 'Dances from Around the World' unit, and after the hula, he just walked over and kissed me." I paused. "Or maybe it was the polka."

"The polka is a pretty seductive dance."

I smiled. Then I took another glance in the side mirror. It was growing so dark, and there were so many cars around us, it was impossible to tell if any of them was a black BMW.

"Pierce was my second kiss." I rubbed my forehead lightly, remembering. "It was this big all-school field trip.

I was in fourth grade. Pierce was in fifth. A bunch of girls had been clustered around him all day, trying to sit next to him on the bus, fighting over who got to be his partner on whatever stupid confidence-building activities we were supposed to be doing, asking who he liked best out of all of them. And he told them that he liked me." I paused again. "They all laughed. One girl pretended to laugh so hard, she couldn't breathe."

"Why would they laugh?"

"Because there was no good reason that somebody like Pierce would have liked somebody like me. And then, to shut them all up, he came over and gave me a quick kiss on the lips."

"Hmm," said Rob. "So, do you think he's been thinking of you that way all this time?"

I snorted. "As the girl he can kiss when other girls annoy him?"

"As the girl he always thought he would end up with eventually."

Headlights flashed over the mirrors as a car whooshed past us. I winced in the slashes of light.

"I was just his friend," I said, after a minute. "And I wasn't even *that* for a long time." I shoved the hair off my burning forehead. "I don't want to talk about him any more. What's something far away from this?"

Rob narrowed his eyes, thinking. "Rodeos. Fashion design. Tropical fruit."

"I have very little to say on any of those subjects."

"Okay. How about . . . the most embarrassing song that you love. Or the stupidest thing you've ever spent money on. The worst food you've ever eaten."

"Tell me about your future," I said. The ache widened sharply, and the words came out almost like a sigh. "Where will you be in two years?"

"Two years," Rob repeated. ". . . I think I'll be in a city." The words were slow but even. "I'm not sure which one yet. I'll have an apartment. Maybe I'll be in college part-time, maybe I'll be working." He paused for a second, his eyes on the windshield. "There's this girl I hang out with. She has these crazy dark green eyes, and her hair changes color depending on the play she's doing at the moment. And she has this tiny scar on her forehead that you can only see in bright light."

I held my breath.

"We go to concerts. Movies. Coffee shops. On week-ends, we explore weird parts of the city." Rob paused for a second, like he was realizing something new. "I never get tired of talking with her. I feel like I'm still making up for the time when I didn't know her. But I'll probably always feel that way." He turned away from the wind-shield and looked at me. "There. At least, that's where I hope I'll be."

I was scared to speak. There was a lump in my throat, and if I opened my mouth, it would splurt out in a laugh or a sob or some weird mixture of the two. I reached out and took his hand instead.

For a minute, we just held on to each other. The ache wasn't lessening. Thoughts came more and more slowly, gathering darkness around the edges.

Rob's eyes flicked up to the rearview mirror. "I think if Pierce were still behind us, we would know for sure by now."

"You're probably right."

"So. Now that we're free . . . where should we go?"

I stared out the side window. The sky had darkened to the color of dirty wool. Streetlamps sent down beams of light that seemed to capture the falling snowflakes, trapping them in temporary slow motion. "I think there's a park up here. Near the river."

"At this exit?"

"The next one."

Rob veered right. We tilted up the off-ramp, snow bursting across the windshield like fireworks.

"You've been to this place before?" he asked.

It took a second for his question to seep through the ache. "Oh. Yeah. A long time ago." I swallowed, trying to steady myself. "My dad took us to every park in a thousand-mile radius. At least, when I wasn't being punished or left at home or something. We'd go hiking, or fishing, or biking . . ."

Rob waited for a moment before speaking again. "Does it bother you to talk about him? We can talk about something else, if—"

"No," I cut him off. "It usually does. But not with you."

"Do I turn left or right here?"

"Right."

We followed the road's tight curve. Rob drove slowly—but not quite slowly enough. The tires met a patch of ice, and for a sickening instant, we shushed sideways over the snowy center line. My body went tight. Rob jerked the wheel. My head snapped back, the ache streaking after it. My mind winked out like a flipped switch.

Then the darkness scattered, and the world was still there, and Rob was still beside me, steering the car back into its lane.

"God, I'm sorry," he said. "I'm not used to roads like this."

"It's fine. I'm fine." My lips struggled with the words. "We're almost there."

"I'm going to drive embarrassingly slow for the rest of the way."

"That's fine," I breathed, closing my eyes. "I'm fine."

I kept my eyelids sealed until the ground beneath the tires changed, and the car bumped off onto a rougher road, and from there into a graveled parking lot.

"Are we there?"

"I think so," Rob's voice answered. "I just followed the signs."

I blinked out through the windshield.

The park was unlit by artificial light. Even the glow of the surrounding city couldn't reach all the way through the thick trees. Pines towered around us, their limbs heavy with fresh snow. Somewhere in the cloud-covered sky, the moon gave off a weak, pearly light. Snowflakes settled gently on the windows.

"Yes. We're there."

"Do you want to get out and take a walk?"

"No." Clumsily, I rearranged myself in the seat, angling my face toward him. The ache lurched. "I just want to sit here with you."

"That's good too." Rob lifted my hand and brought it up to his lips. It made me laugh. He gave me a little smile in return before pressing a soft kiss to the back of my wrist.

I let my skull flop back against the headrest. "You did that the very first time I saw you."

"I did?" Rob still wore a smile, but there was a note of playful skepticism in it now. "I don't remember trying this in anatomy class."

"No. Not then. Maybe . . ." I pulled my hand away and rubbed my face. "No. It's just—that feeling. You know. Like you've been somewhere before, even though you know you actually haven't."

I wasn't making sense, even to myself. But Rob reached over and ran his fingers down the side of my face. "Yeah. I know."

I leaned forward slightly, hoping he would kiss me, that it would push away some of the ache.

The sharp beam of headlights sliced through the car.

Both Rob and I turned as a car zoomed by, its tires squealing around the curve, passing the park entrance. Its taillights vanished into the dark.

The park went quiet again. Snow cushioned the world. Everything felt soft, and muffled, and held gently in place, and Rob and I were two figures in a snow globe—except that the snow was falling outside the car, and we were sealed here together, warm and safe and dry.

"You didn't tell me about *your* future," said Rob, after a second. "Your turn."

I leaned back in the seat. "It's weird. I used to think about it all the time. I'd imagine the shows I might be in. The cities where I'd live. Places I'd get to see, characters I'd play. Half the time, if a teacher called on me, that's where my head would be. I've given some pretty stupid answers in algebra class."

He laughed. God, that voice. My spine rippled. That voice.

"But now, it's just—I don't know. Ever since all of this started . . . trying to stay in *this* time is enough." I ran my fingers over the scar. "Maybe that's because my brain's running at about ten percent capacity."

I could see him grin back at me, his face silver in the snowy moonlight.

"Or maybe it's because right now is . . . I don't know. Right now, there's nothing else I'm wishing for."

I heard the latch of Rob's seat belt click against the door. I unbuckled myself next. We both lurched forward, me awkwardly, Rob quickly, and somehow managed to knot our arms around each other while leaving just enough space for me to tilt my face up to his.

He kissed me, or I kissed him, for a very long time. His mouth was so warm. So much more real than anything I could have imagined. I could feel my body starting to dissolve, little bits of me zinging around the interior of the car, glittering, weightless.

"Any supernovas?" I whispered. "I feel like I need to compete with the Warrior Mermaid."

Rob's fingertips were cool against my neck. "I'm so glad I finally met you."

"Finally?"

"You know. All those places, all those people. And now you."

He pulled me toward him again. On the windshield, snow collected in thick white waves. We might have been there for minutes. We might have been there for hours.

Rob finally leaned back slightly, his breathing fast. "I don't want to stop here. Believe me." He brushed away a strand of hair that had tangled in my eyelashes. "But I'm starting to picture what your sister will do to me when I bring you home."

"Yeah." I was out of breath too. "She can be pretty brutal with a hairbrush. I speak from experience."

"In that case . . ." Rob reached for the gearshift. "God, I really don't want to leave. But I'd also really like to survive until next time." He turned back to me. "There will be a next time, right?"

I smiled. "Yes. There will absolutely be a next time."

"Okay then." Rob let out a long breath. Then he grinned at me, put the car in gear, and eased gently into the turn-around.

"Whoa," he said as we crunched to the edge of the lot. "Where did the road go?"

"See that sort of smoother snowy part? That's the road."

"So I just have to trust that it's there?" He pulled out onto the main road. The snow was deep and clean, the ruts of tire tracks already filling. "This requires some serious object permanence."

"Yeah, it's a good thing we don't let infants drive."

I heard Rob laugh. And then I heard the roar.

This time, the headlights came from the opposite direction. They smashed through the windshield like a battering ram.

There was a flash—headlights, or something else, something brighter. And then a sudden, crystalline explosion, thousands of glass diamonds and tumbling snowflakes decorating the frigid air. I heard the crunch of metal, the snap and grind of steel against steel against ice against wood. I was floating upward into the darkness. My fingers lost their grip on Rob's hand, and whatever it was that had seemed so real was gone.

CHAPTER 26

There was blood on the snow.

White, with a smattering of red. Like petals.

Two suns burned my eyes. Their beams poked through a net of my own tangled hair. The longer I squinted up at them, the surer I felt that they couldn't be suns; they were too close and too small to be suns.

No. They were headlights. Behind them, I could make out a glossy black car crumpled against a tree trunk, and another car—a smallish, bluish car—smashed to the side, its roof pressed against a wall of trees, its front end folded into the black car's hood like two pieces of wrinkled laundry.

Of course, I thought. *Of course.*

Somewhere, a motor ran pointlessly.

I inched backward on my elbows. The ground beneath me was cold and sharp.

Outside the pool of light, I stopped, breathing hard. There was a shrieking in my head, and a new ache in my side that twinged each time I inhaled.

The headlights sparkled on the snow. On bits of broken glass. On the dark spatter fanning over the snowbanks.

Wind hissed gently through the pines.

By rolling onto my side—the side without the twinge—I managed to get to my knees, and from there to my feet. The ground beneath me tilted with the trees.

Standing upright, I could see a dark shape hunched in the black car, mounded up against the dashboard. A few steps to my right, another shape lay in the snow.

I stood still. Sensation dwindled. The shriek in my head died down. I was suddenly disconnected from all of this: the crunched cars, the unmoving black shapes, the whirring engine. It was like a set once the stage lights had been switched off.

I turned toward the trees behind me. The headlights carved a path through the frosted trunks. I set off down the trail, dragging my feet. When I stumbled and plunged my bare hands into the snow, I couldn't feel a thing.

Of course you can't. This is all just pretend.

I got up again.

The beams of light began to dim, and the ground underneath me sloped downward, angling like a theater aisle. The surrounding tree trunks smoothed into pillars. Under the snowy branches, folding seats curved in rows, moss-soft and empty.

Just ahead of me, a little farther down the aisle, I caught

the flicker of a fairy's wing. Hamlet's outline shivered in the shadows.

"Whither wilt thou lead me?" he whispered as I wandered past.

I followed his eyes to the end of the aisle. An empty stage was waiting.

Empty stage. Empty stage.

My feet thumped up the wooden steps.

Trunks of trees, faint and misty, formed a backdrop. Dusty red curtains hung open to either side. I crossed slowly to center stage. The beams of twin spotlights found me. For a second, I was blinded, everything around me washed away in a flood of bleary white.

I blinked out into the rows of seats.

Hamlet had disappeared. At first I thought the rest of the house was empty too. But as my eyes adjusted, I could make out a single silhouette seated in the center of the theater.

The lights set off little flares in my eyelashes. I squinted harder. I couldn't see who it was, only that it was a man, by himself, his head tilted to gaze up at me. I shielded my eyes with one hand, and still, I wasn't sure if I could make out the waves of brown hair above a high forehead, the twinkle of a gold earring, or if that was just a trick of lights on the snow.

"So . . . is that it?" I asked. My voice sounded strangely clear. "What happens now?"

There was no answer. The silhouette was still.

"Am I dreaming this? I must be dreaming this. Right?" I looked around at the ripple of velvety seat backs, the moon-white stage floor. My own scraped hands. "Or am I . . . with you?" My voice lost its steadiness. "Am I dead?"

I waited again, holding my breath.

Still no answer.

"Can I have one more chance?" I pleaded. "Just one more. Please. I know I screwed up again. This time, I'll—I won't—" Even now, I couldn't say it. Not even in pretend. "Please. Just let me have another chance."

The seats swam. The light seemed to swell and soften around me. The silhouette didn't speak, but it stirred slightly, tilting its head. There was no gold hoop earring on its ear. There was no wide velvet collar.

"It's you, isn't it?" I whispered, my voice carrying through the stillness.

I took a step forward, staggering slightly. "Was this a test? Were you trying to save me, and I still wouldn't listen?" I paused. No answer. "Or were you just . . . I don't know. Were you trying to prove that I'd make the same stupid choices over and over, no matter how many warnings I got? Or are you just watching me? Are you just . . ."

My knees buckled suddenly. I sagged down onto the chilly stage floor. "Is that what you meant about 'how the story goes'? Just . . . all of us, being us? Ophelia *has* to fall into the river. Juliet *has* to pick up the knife." I let out a little laugh. "I would have thought you'd hate that idea. That we just are who we are, so why try to change it? Midnight Plum. Sad Spice and Scary Spice. Me and Rob." I laughed again, rubbing my head. "Maybe." The lights shimmered. "I just . . ." My feet were going numb. ". . . I'm not sure I can change anything. I'm not sure I *would* change anything."

The silhouette moved again, listening. Around us, the light glinted on a few drifting flakes. Something dripped onto the back of my hand; something warm and dark that trailed over the edge of my jaw.

"I still want to make you happy." My voice was starting to slur. "I always *want* to make you happy. Even though I know you're not really here." Words floated out of reach like a puff of blown snow. "But I don't know . . . I can't . . ."

The spotlights were dying. The glittering snow sank into gray. The pale columns of the trees began to soften, dwindling backward, the scene fading gradually into black.

"I know how the story goes," I mumbled. "But what if . . . what if we just changed the ending. Just once. Like— what if the spell didn't work. Or there was no duel. What if Juliet woke up just in time . . ."

My eyelids were starting to close.

"I'm so tired, Dad," I breathed. "I'm just . . ."

The light died.

Blackness.

Silence.

The light touch of snowflakes on the backs of my hands.

Someone lifted my elbow.

My fingers were numb. I couldn't hold on as my arm was wrapped through another arm. I felt my body being dragged upward with it.

He braced me against his side.

Our feet moved across the dark stage and down the steps, mine shuffling and stumbly, his steady and slow. What had been the aisle was now just a winding strip between the pine trees. I tripped on a snow-buried root. He held me up.

His arm was firm and ropy, just like I remembered it. His hand, holding my elbow, was solid. I could almost feel the warmth of breath coming from him. Almost.

We reached the break in the trees. The two crumpled cars—the broken glass and black flecks in the snow—pulled me to a stop again. I stumbled.

"You've got this, kiddo," murmured a voice in my ear. "One foot in front of the other."

I stepped forward.

The hand holding my arm let go.

Then I was staggering closer, through the clinking glass, to the side of the crushed black car.

The shape inside of it hadn't moved. I eased open the driver's-side door.

Pierce was slumped against the steering wheel. The airbag had opened. His face rested against the deflating gray pillow, looking almost asleep. Blood trickled from a gash over his left eye.

I held my fingers under his nose.

Breath. Shallow, but steady.

"Hold on, Pierce," I said out loud, reaching into his coat pockets as gently as I could. "I'm calling for help. Just hold on."

The 911 operator's voice sounded very far away, but calm and clear. I answered questions. Gave directions. Made my own voice as steady as I could. *Katharine Hepburn. Meryl Streep.*

"Police and EMTs are on their way," the voice told me. "Just hang on. How many were injured?"

"Three. Three of us." The ground trembled under my feet. "One is still in his car. He's unconscious, but he's breathing. The other one is . . ."

I turned to find the dark shape in the snow again.

The tinny voice in the phone asked something else, but I couldn't follow it anymore. I'm not sure where the phone went—if I put it into my pocket, if I dropped it into the snow, if it dissolved into the swirling air. There was nothing left in the world except the dark body half-sunk in the sparkling white.

I got down on my knees beside him.

Rob wasn't moving. Fresh snowflakes collected on his hair. Only half of his face was visible, crushed against the dull white drift. Gently, I wound my fingers inside his collar. I was pretty sure I could feel a pulse. I tried to remember the CPR unit we'd had in sophomore health class.

You weren't supposed to move someone in this situation, I was pretty sure. You were supposed to see if they were breathing. Check for immediate danger. Keep them warm.

With my bare hands, I scraped away the snow that had heaped around Rob's face. His skin felt so cold.

I picked up his hand. I raised it to my lips and kissed the back of his wrist. "Hey, Romeo," I told him. "Stay with me."

I unbuttoned my coat. Then I lay down beside him, wrapping half of the open coat over his side.

"Hey," I whispered into his ear. Cold strands of black hair brushed my lips. "Hey, you. Romeo."

He didn't move.

"Help is coming. They're on their way." I tightened my arms around him. "Just hold on."

The snow softened around us, enclosing us, folding us in. Above us, the night sky was a purple scrim painted with wisps of pine. A few windblown flakes touched my face, coming to rest as lightly as petals.

Petals.

I closed my eyes.

When I opened them again, light surrounded me.

It wasn't a spotlight or sunlight this time. It was a million tiny fragments of light shimmering on every side, raining down on me like the sparks of a firework.

Fairies, I thought.

Some were red. Some were blue. Some were steady and silver, and I knew that those must be stars.

My cheek hurt. Everything hurt.

I turned my head to the left, and found that I was looking into another face. A familiar face. Arching eyebrows. Messy black hair. His eyes were closed, but I knew that if they opened and stared back at me, they would be a pale, clear blue.

My coat was spread over both of us. I wriggled closer, pulling my body against his.

His lips twitched. "Hey," he whispered, like someone just waking from a nap.

"Hey," I whispered back. "You're still really here."

"Yeah." One side of his mouth went up. "Still really here."

There was a thump of metal doors. Rattling stretchers. Lots of voices, all speaking at once.

My eyelids lowered themselves again, and the snowy world disappeared like a stage behind a curtain. I felt myself being lifted, and heard him being lifted beside me, both of us rolling toward the shimmering lights as snowflakes fell over our faces, over our bodies, covering us as lightly as petals.

I could smell the roses.

ACKNOWLEDGMENTS

Thanks to all the teachers and directors who opened the door to Shakespeare for me, and to all of my own former high school English students—I hope I held the door for them.

Thanks to Chris Richman for getting the ball rolling, and to Danielle Chiotti and everyone else at Upstart Crow for keeping it in motion.

Thanks to my marvelous editor, Jessica Dandino Garrison, for her patience, her faith, and her extraordinary insight. Additional thanks to the eagle-eyed Regina Castillo, the magic-maker Lindsay Boggs, the magnificent designers Maggie Olson and Jenny Kelly, and the rest of the team at Dial. It's a privilege.

Finally, thanks to my big, supportive, wildly varied family. Special nods to Dan and Katy for medical and running input, to Alex for early reading and encouragement, and to Grandpa Jack, who gave thirteen-year-old me an old family copy of the Collected Works of Shakespeare.

Mom and Dad—thank you for reading, commenting, and emergency-babysitting while I worked feverishly on final drafts.

And thanks most of all to Ryan and Beren, who make life beautifully complicated and full of joy.

JACQUELINE WEST is the author of the beloved *New York Times* bestselling middle-grade series The Books of Elsewhere, and is a two-time Pushcart nominee for poetry. She lives amid the bluffs of Red Wing, Minnesota, with her husband, son, and the family dog, Brom Bones. This is her sixth novel, her first for teens.